Lara Temple was three years old when she begged her mother to take the dictation of her first adventure story. Since then she has led a double life—by day she is a high-tech investment professional, who has lived and worked on three continents, but when darkness falls she loses herself in history and romance…at least on the page. Luckily her husband and two beautiful and very energetic children help her weave it all together.

UNLACED BY THE HIGHLAND DUKE

Lara Temple

MILLS & BOON

First published in Great Britain 2019
by Mills & Boon, an imprint of HarperCollins*Publishers*
1 London Bridge Street, London, SE1 9GF

Large Print edition 2019

© 2019 Harlequin Books S.A.

Special thanks and acknowledgement
are given to Ilana Treston for her contribution to
The Lochmore Legacy series.

ISBN: 978-0-263-08174-9

MIX
Paper from
responsible sources
FSC **FSC® C007454**

To my Highland co-conspirators—
Janice, Elisabeth and Nicole.

I always wanted to be one of the
Four Musketeers—thanks for
making that a joyful reality.

Chapter One

London—1815

'Lady Theale is here, Your Grace.'

Benneit didn't know what was worse—those words or the explosion of light that struck him as Angus hauled back the curtains. He groaned on both counts.

'Aye,' Angus replied and positioned himself at the bottom of the bed. With his scarred face he looked like one of the gargoyles carved on to the embattlements at Lochmore Castle come to perch by Benneit's bed to remind him of his duty. Benneit shoved his head into his pillow.

'What the devil does she want?'

'Jamie.'

Benneit tossed the covers aside and scraped himself off the bed.

'Over my dead, drawn, quartered and pickled body.'

Angus grunted. 'Aye, lad. Shall I shave you?'

It was more a suggestion than a question and, instinctively, Benneit dragged his hand over his jaw, wincing at the rasp.

'No. She shall have to accept me in all my glory. What time is it?'

'It is gone nine in the morning.'

'Nine? *Nine?* I've barely slept three hours. What the devil is wrong with that woman?'

Angus's scarred face twisted into a momentary and awful grin.

'You can sleep when you're dead, Your Grace.'

It was Benneit's turn to grunt as he dragged off his nightshirt and went to the basin. There was a brutality to Angus sometimes and whether he meant to allude to Bella or not, it struck up her image, interred in the Lochmore family crypt. Eventually Benneit would be there, too. A fate worse than death... He breathed in to calm the reflexive queasiness at the thought, reminding himself that when that day came he would at least know nothing of it.

'Send Jamie to her until I'm ready—if he's awake. After half an hour of his undiluted company she might think twice about this campaign to take him to Uxmore.'

'He's down there now, lad.'

Benneit wiped the water from his face and glanced at Angus, meeting the twinkle in the giant's blue eyes.

'Great minds thing alike, eh, Angus?'

'When they think at all, Your Grace.'

Benneit sighed and returned to the freezing water.

'Good morning, Lady Theale.'

'You need a shave, Lochmore.'

Benneit stopped, gathered himself and the comment hovering at the tip of his tongue, and proceeded.

'Had I been given more warning of your arrival I would have obliged.'

'Had you been given more warning of our arrival you would have been halfway to the border by now.'

Benneit advanced on the elderly lady seated in his favourite armchair, plucked her weathered hand from where it rested on her cane and raised it to his lips.

'No, only as far as Potter's Bar. Not even for you would I set off before dawn.'

She sniggered and gave his face a small slap before he straightened.

He turned to search the room for his son and stopped. The word 'our' hadn't registered at first, but now it did. Jamie was seated on the sofa, his stockinged feet drawn up under him, and on the other side of his favourite book of maps was a woman.

'Papa, she's helped me find Muck!' Jamie announced, bouncing a little on his knees.

'Did she? That is indeed impressive. But can she help you find Foula? Good morning, Mrs Langdale.'

'Your Grace.'

Her voice was deep, but as bland as her grey wool dress—flat and without inflection. During Bella's Season six years ago Mrs Langdale, then Miss Watkins, wore Bella's cast-offs and, being shorter and less endowed, she always looked like a scrawny hen rolled in a bed of shredded peacock feathers—those ostentatious clothes coupled with her unremarkable looks had not been a good combination. She was unremarkable except for her deep grey eyes that Bella had laughingly called the 'orbs of truth'.

'No one can lie to Joane if she puts her mind to their speaking the truth. She only has to look at you and before you realise it, the words are out there. Papa said she would have been useful to Wellington during the war.'

He remembered Bella's assessment of her poor cousin because it struck him as very apt and one of Bella's rare flashes of insight.

'And how is Mr Langdale?' he asked politely.

'He isn't,' she replied.

'Died two years ago,' Lady Theale hissed. 'Really, Lochmore!'

He felt his face heat with unaccustomed embarrassment and he bowed.

'I am sorry for your loss.'

Mrs Langdale nodded without a word and the sting of heat on his cheeks spread. It was absurd that without any visible effort this mousy woman made him feel ten years younger in the worst possible way. He turned to Jamie.

'Feet off the sofa, Jamie.'

Jamie blinked at him and smiled, as if well aware this sudden interdiction was merely for his great-aunt's sake.

He stuck his feet out.

'But I took off my shoes!'

'Very proper,' Mrs Langdale said.

'It won't do,' Lady Theale announced.

Benneit turned back to her. And so it began again. Since Bella's death two years earlier, the Uxmores had made several valiant attempts to convince him Jamie would be better off in the care of their large and rambling family rather than alone with Benneit in Scotland, and every time Benneit sent them scurrying. Since his father's death a year ago, their insistence lessened as they respected the period of mourning, but clearly they were only marshalling their troops.

And their field marshal was Lady Theale, Lord Uxmore's sister and the matriarch of that ambitious clan.

'It is very kind of you to come all the way to town to see Jamie, Lady Theale, but we are departing for Lochmore tomorrow. There are matters I must attend to there and we cannot stay.'

'Really? Is the entertainment in town running thin?'

'Not at all, but it has been sufficient for my needs at the moment. Until next time.'

Lady Theale bared her teeth. 'Joane, I would like a private word with Lochmore. Take Jamie into the adjoining room.'

Mrs Langdale stood.

'Where is the wall map you mentioned, Jamie?' she asked and Jamie hopped down.

'It is *enormous*. But not as big as at home. Grandmama painted it for Papa when he was littler than me. And there are darts!'

'Darts! Then I must definitely see it. Come.'

'In his stockings, Lochmore!' Lady Theale snapped as the door closed behind them.

'What do you want, Abigail?'

'You know what I want, Benneit. I want Bella's boy to grow up like the son of a Duke he is and not like a wild animal.'

Her voice faltered a little at his look.

'At the very least he should have female guidance.'

'He has his nursemaid.'

'Nursemaid! She must be seventy if she's a day. That boy needs someone young and with the energy to see him through the next couple of years until he is sent to school. Or better yet, send him to school at St Stephen's as you were and, as it is a mere ten miles from Uxmore, we will be at hand to visit when necessary. It is still an excellent institution and will prepare him well for his role. Your father and mother approved of it, so I see no reason to cavil at their choice. I am sure had Bella lived she would have advised you the same. She always meant to maintain close ties with the family, as you are well aware. This would fulfil all their wishes.'

Benneit turned away, locking his jaw against the fury her words evoked. *Better yet...* What the devil did she know about sending a child hundreds of miles away from everything he cared for simply so he could become her idea of a proper Duke?

'My father and mother did not send me to St Stephens at five years old to prepare me for my role, but to get me out from underfoot so they could concentrate on making each other miserable without any assistance on my part. As far as I am concerned, the same does not apply to Jamie. He will learn to be Duke of Lochmore by understanding Lochmore down to its last acre and tenant, not by being caned by a brutish headmaster and bullied by upper-form boys.'

Lady Theale inspected the head of her cane and sighed.

'Your mother was one of my closest friends, Benneit, and since it was through me that she met your father, I confess to a sense of responsibility. I am the first to admit that, though she was a brilliant woman, she had a volatile temper and was not…warm. Unfortunately your father was much the same which made for a tumultuous union. However, despite their failings, they cared deeply for each other and cared for you as well, though I dare say they were not adept at showing it.'

'I am not asking for sympathy, Abigail. For the very last time, I will not, ever, cede Jamie to be taken to Bella's family. He is my son, my family, and I am his. No one will ever love him as I do. Do you understand what that means?'

'It may surprise you, but I do. You always were the closest to him. Made Bella jealous, the two of you, even as young as he was. Said you loved him more than you did her and that, believe me, was a cardinal sin to someone like Bella. But that is *not* the point. I admit when she died I thought it would be best to have the boy with us. A babe is not an easy endeavour for a man alone and in that great big draughty monster of a castle... Well, it stood to reason. But I've come to see that however surly you may be, it is not too much to his detriment to be raised by you. Therefore I have decided to leave him with you.'

'Generous!'

'On one condition...'

'There are no conditions, Abigail. You have no authority to impose conditions and neither does Lord Uxmore. I want Jamie to know and love Bella's family and they are more than welcome to visit us in Lochmore or in London, but that is as far as your power extends. I am tired of this brangling.'

'You look tired of more than brangling, Benneit. Do you still miss her so that you can find no better way to pass your time than hiding up in the freezing hills or burning the candle at both ends here in town?'

'I am perfectly well and so is Jamie. And, aside from his dislike of carriages, he comes to no harm being in town with me. If I bring a female to Lochmore, whether it be as mother or companion, I will be the one to choose.'

'I would have hoped so, but thus far for the past two years all you have done is indulge yourself with your high flyers. Who is it now? Lady Atkinson? Or was that your last visit to town? And if you must indulge, need you drag the poor boy all that long way? Surely your aunt can see to him at the castle?'

'Good God, I wouldn't leave a rabid dog in Morag's care. Besides, she doesn't want anything to do with Jamie—she stays in her corner of the castle and only raises her nose sufficiently from her glass of whisky to complain her stock of spirits is running low.'

'That bad? All the more reason to have a stable female presence—'

'Lady Theale,' Benneit interrupted. 'You are the uncontested general of the Uxmores, but Bella is gone and you have not and never will have any authority over Jamie. If you push me much further on this you will find out precisely what Bella meant when she called me unbearably stubborn.'

Lady Theale surprised him by smiling.

'I think I have a fair assessment. Bella never did really have your measure, you know. She thought you were what she and everyone saw on the surface—the handsome, charming and wealthy future heir to a dukedom. That is the way with people who are so accustomed to receiving whatever they want from birth.'

He laughed, a little bitterly, and she shook her head.

'I was referring to Bella, not to you. But whether you wish to hear it or not, I am right about Jamie. Keeping him with no companionship but your own in that great echoing monstrosity of a castle is no more a wise solution than the path your parents chose for you, Benneit.'

He sat, rubbing at his stubble. Lady Theale might be a busybody, but she was not a fool and she genuinely cared for Jamie. He sighed.

'If it soothes your nerves, I agree he needs female companionship and, more importantly, he needs siblings. Therefore I have decided to wed again.'

'You have? Who?'

'This time someone who won't mind the freezing hills or sacrificing her figure for her offspring.'

Lady Theale sighed.

'Bella meant to like your castle, boy. But Lochmore is a long way from London.'

'Precisely.'

'So. Do you have someone in mind?'

'It might reassure you that I have Jamie's welfare so much in mind that I am considering in one fell swoop to find him a mother and repair the rift between the Lochmores and McCrieffs.'

'And they agree? I understood that there was always bad blood between the families.'

'That is an understatement. We have a long and inglorious history of real and imagined causes for mutual resentment. Even the fact that my grandfather convinced old King George to grant him a dukedom and compounded that insult by keeping the clan name as title was another stick in that fire. I think the balance was partially redressed once my father's rejection of a McCrieff bride was met with their rejection of my Aunt Morag as a suitable bride for Lord Aberwyld. But unlike his forebearers, McCrieff realises the contention between us affects the sheep and kelp trades in the area and, being substantially poorer, he can afford that far less than Lochmore. It is also interfering with other plans of mine and I cannot allow that, so now my father is dead I am testing the waters.'

'One doesn't test the waters with a man like McCrieff. If this is the case, no doubt he has already engaged lawyers to draw up the settlement papers.'

Benneit shrugged. It was close enough to the truth.

'So I see this trip is in the nature of a last escape, Lochmore. Still, even if you've marked your bride, it will take time, this wooing and wedding business. Why not allow Joane to go with Jamie until you make other arrangements, either for Jamie or for yourself. If at any time you find her presence *de trop*, send her back to me.'

'You talk about her as if she was a book or a piece of furniture. Take her up to the Highlands, send her down when you are through with her.'

'Well, it will do her good, too. My niece Celia has become a tad too dependent on Joane. The poor girl barely had time to mourn.'

'What happened to him? To Langdale?'

'He broke his neck in a fall from a horse. Most unfortunate. Died in debt and the house and everything was entailed. She has a competence, but no more.'

'Langdale fell from a horse? I thought the man was born on one.'

'We are at our most arrogant where we are most comfortable. I dare say he appreciated finding his end in such a manner since he cared more for his horses than anything else, possibly even more than for poor Joane. In a year or so I shall find her another husband, but for the moment it could suit both our purposes for her to see to Jamie until you wed again. She is very good with children.'

'I don't care if she is the St Francis of children,

I… Oh, never mind. But this is the very last time you interfere with me or with Jamie. Am I clear?'

'I could hardly misunderstand. Really, Benneit, you used to be so much more polished—these years in the freezing north have stripped you of your charming veneer. Go fetch Joane and your little boy. And do have him put on his shoes. A future Duke running about barefoot is most improper.'

Chapter Two

'Look!' Jamie bounced up and down in front of the wall.

Jo had to admit the map was magnificent. It was not a framed painting of a map, but painted directly on the wall, and it was, as Jamie had said, enormous.

'My goodness! It is as big as the world itself!' she concurred and Jamie laughed. He had his father's laugh and it was strange to hear that deep rumble from the little child, but like his father's it was infectious and she smiled. It was strange what one remembered, even after so long. Though the man in the drawing room hadn't looked capable of laughter. Was he still in such pain over Bella's death?

'No, it isn't, silly,' Jamie replied, reaching up as high as he could. 'It can't be or there wouldn't be room for everything that is, would there?'

'That is most true! You are clever!'

'I know. Papa says I'm cleverest of all the Lochmores, even him!'

'Does he now? Though I suppose you have to

be very clever to know someone is even cleverer than you.'

He frowned.

'So is Papa cleverer than me or me than him?'

'Well, you are both cleverer than I, so I certainly won't be able to answer that question.'

Jamie stared up at her, his eyes surprisingly warm despite their dark colour. He had Bella's eyes, thick lashed and slightly uptilted at the corner, but she could not tell yet if the rest of his face favoured his father's sharper-cut lines and rough male appeal or Bella's delicate beauty. Whatever the case, with two such impressive parents he would probably be a handsome young man.

'I think *you* are very clever,' he said seriously, as if still working through her answer. 'You found Muck and I have been searching for days. I shall be an explorer, you know.'

'You look like an explorer. You certainly have the feet of an explorer.'

He glanced at his feet in wonder.

'I do?'

'Oh, yes. I am good at seeing what people really are. Will you explore Muck?'

The wonder became a grin.

'Papa says I explore muck too much. Mud muck, not this Muck.' He pointed to the map. 'You said we will find Foula.'

'And so we shall. Shall we sail from Muck?'

'No, from home. Do you know where my home is?'

She turned to search the map, tracing the road from Inveraray.

'Here?'

'A little more, no...' He was straining to reach upwards and she picked him up. He stiffened for a moment and then adjusted to settle on her hip and poked one still-plump finger to the tip of a tiny spit of green surrounded by blue. The colour was a little faded there, as if it had been touched often. By Jamie or by a younger Benneit Lochmore?

'Here.'

He was not very heavy, though he was taller than her four-year-old cousin, Philip. His arm curved around her neck as he leaned forward to show her the point of the map and his body was snug against hers. She often held her cousins' children. It was part of what she did—Aunt Joane picked up and put down and fetched and fixed and...

And this was different.

She did not pick this boy up because he expected it of her, but because he didn't expect it at all. She saw it the moment he was brought into the drawing room that morning by his elderly nurse and the scarred, red-haired giant. He was, like his father, an island, self-sufficient and inward-looking despite his cheerfulness. Six years ago she'd noticed the same quality in Benneit Lochmore—behind the smiling charm was something still and watchful and unreachable. It had made her uncomfortable around him, as if he could see past her own armour and read her secret, resentful thoughts.

'You have pretty hair,' Jamie said, his voice dreamy.

She almost dropped him, but his legs tightened around her waist.

'I do?'

'It is like the colour of the desert in my new book. Papa bought it in the great big book store and it is my favourite book and Papa reads it to me, but I can find words, too. I will explore the desert when I am big. There are camels! Do you know what a camel is?'

'Tell me.'

'It is like a horse because you ride it, but it has a hill on its back and it has a sad face like Flops. Flops is my dog.'

'I like his name.'

'His real name is Molach, which means hairy, but I call him Flops because he does—he comes into a room and flops. Like a rug. A hairy rug.'

'This I must see.' She laughed.

'Apparently, you shall,' a much deeper voice said behind them.

Jo stiffened, but did not let go of Jamie as she turned to face the Duke.

He stood in the doorway and there was such animosity in his eyes she had to resist hugging Jamie's body to her like a shield. The moment he entered the drawing room she noted how much he had changed in the years since she had last seen him, but the difference between this man, with the grey beginning to show at his temples, with his jaw tense and unshaven and his eyes narrowed with resentment, and the younger man she remembered was even more pronounced, as if he had aged again in the short moments that passed. He looked like the Duke of Lochmore might have looked two hundred years ago as he prepared to enter battle to defend his domain. Which was perhaps an accurate depiction of the state of affairs as he saw it.

She lowered Jamie.

'Am I? I admit to being surprised. I wagered my aunt you would dismiss her offer.'

'Had it been an *offer*, believe me, I would have dismissed it. Jamie, come here.'

'Are you angry, Papa?'

She met the Duke's dark green eyes, watching

as fury was called back like troops from a failed attack. This expression of cold blankness was also new to her. She thought she had taken Lochmore's measure six years ago in London when he had fallen under Bella's prodigious spell, but perhaps not.

'Yes, Jamie. But not with you,' he answered, smiling at his son. There was nothing feigned about the smile and it surprised her. It was also new to her, despite having seen him smile often at Bella.

'With Auntie Theale? Or Cousin Joane?' Jamie asked, half-anxious, half-curious.

'Mostly with myself, Jamie. Never mind. Come say your goodbyes to Lady Theale.'

'But Auntie Theale does not like feet, Papa. Shall I fetch my shoes first?'

Lochmore inspected Jamie's stockinged feet before looking at Jo, his long eyelashes only half-veiling the mocking challenge in his eyes.

'No. I think not.'

Chapter Three

'My pudding box hurts,' Jamie moaned, shifting on the carriage seat.

'Close your eyes and try to sleep, Jamie,' Benneit replied without any real conviction even as he nudged the small basin out from under the carriage seat with his boot in readiness for the inevitable.

He hated leaving Jamie alone in Scotland when he came to London, but the journey itself was purgatorial. After Jamie's first excitement, bouncing around the carriage and watching the sights of London, he became steadily more ill and miserable, which made Benneit cantankerous and miserable, which made Nurse Moody morose and miserable.

Adding Joane Langdale to the mix had so far not achieved his aunt's desired effect. The past few miles had passed in silence, Jamie leafing through the little book of maps Benneit had bought him at Hatchard's, Nurse Moody dozing and snorting occasionally, and Joane Langdale gazing absently out the window. Now that disaster was nigh, Benneit contemplated taking the coward's way out and switching with Angus who rode a hired hack alongside the carriage.

'It hurts, Papa...' Jamie moaned again and Benneit straightened, but before he reached for the basin Joane Langdale took Jamie on to her lap, turning his face towards the window with a light sweep of her hand down his ashen cheek.

'That's because you have forgotten to feed it,' she murmured.

'I don't want food,' Jamie cried.

'Not food, silly. Stories. Your poor belly knows there are dozens and dozens passing us by outside and you haven't offered it even one. No wonder it is upset.'

Jamie glanced out the window. They were cresting a rise and overlooking fields and a few houses tucked against a copse of old oaks. There was nothing but bland English countryside and as a distraction it was woefully inadequate. Benneit frowned at Joane, but she either didn't notice or ignored him.

'I don't see any stories.' Jamie said suspiciously and Joane's brows rose, making her eyes look even larger.

'Really? What about Farmer Scrumpett's performing pig over there?'

Jamie leaned towards the window, his small hand catching the frame.

'Where?'

'Well, you just missed it, but there are other stories everywhere. See that little house over there, the white one?'

Jamie leaned his forehead against the window, both hands splayed on the frame now.

'That one?'

'Exactly. That is where Mrs Minerva Understone resides with her magical mice. That is why the house is painted white, you see. Because of the cats.'

'Cats don't like white?'

'Oh, no, they love it. It makes them think of milk and they come by the score.'

'But cats eat mice!'

'Well, that is true, but not magical mice. You see, cats chase mice because they are each trying to find their one magical mouse and they become very cross when they don't, which is why they eat them. Did you know that cats and mice were once best of friends? And that mice were once as big as cats and twice as clever? But then an evil sorcerer cast a spell over them and made them small and meek. Well, for one day each year, the spell is lifted and all the cats remember their friends and come to Mrs Minerva Understone's cottage and they dance and play as they once did before the spell.'

'I don't see any cats.'

'That is because they only come once a year, on Summer's Solstice.'

Jamie frowned.

'That is a sad story.'

'It is both sad and isn't. It would be sadder still if they did not have that special day when they remembered they liked each other.'

'But why does this happen at this Minderda's cottage? Is she a wizard, too?'

'Oh, yes. A very powerful one. Minerva taught me a spell once, would you like to hear it?'

'A real spell?'

'Well, no, it is more a song about a spell. This is how it goes.' Joane Langdale cleared her throat, lowered her chin. 'Boil and bubble, toil and trouble, you'd best put on your shoes or I'll shave all your stubble.'

Jamie burst into laughter.

'That wasn't Minerva, that was Auntie Theale!'

'Goodness, was it? Well, perhaps they're secret sisters.'

'Minerva sounds far too benevolent to be related to Lady Theale,' Benneit interjected and Joane Langdale looked over at him, her eyes warm with his son's laughter, but Jamie tugged at her sleeve.

'Tell me more stories, Cousin Joane.'

'Very well, but you must call me Jo. Cousin Joane doesn't tell stories, she finds shawls and hems handkerchiefs. It is Jo who tells stories.'

'Which one are you?' Jamie asked seriously.

'Some days I am one and some days I am the other. Just like some days you are an explorer and some days you are Jamie who cannot find his shoes.'

He grinned.

'I always know where they are, but some days I don't *wish* to find them.'

'Exactly. So today I do not wish to find Cousin Joane and so I am Jo.'

'Tell me another story, Jo. If you please,' he amended, and she shifted him on her lap so that he was once again looking out the window.

'Very well, tell me what you see and I shall tell you a story about it.'

Jamie's hand traced up and down the window frame as he searched the landscape.

'That,' he said finally, his voice hushed. 'That big tree near the stream.'

'Oh, *that* tree. You are a true explorer, Jamie. Not many would have seen how wondrous that tree is…'

Benneit leaned back, half-listening to the story that unfolded, with foxes and rabbits and a goat who sounded amazingly like Godfrey, Bella's brother, and a weasel who sounded even more impressively like Celia, Bella's sister. There was also a little girl who had been taken captive by a blind but kindly old mole so she could help him search for a quizzing glass lost in one of a myriad of tunnels. It was both absurd and touching and, most importantly, it held Jamie captive, his eyes searching the landscape for the places she mentioned—a little hut, a grizzled old man walking a pig, a shape in the clouds.

Finally, Jamie's fascinated questions began to flag. He yawned and leaned back against Mrs Langdale's shoulder, his eyelids slipping. Her voice continued, sinking into dusk, but it was only when Jamie's body gave the distinctive little shudder that spoke of deep sleep that she stopped, her breath shifting the dark curls by his temple.

'Thank you.' Benneit's whisper sounded rough even to him, certainly not grateful, but she smiled. Against his son's dark hair, her profile was a carved cameo, a gentle sweep of a line that accentuated the pucker of her lower lip and the sharp curve of her chin. Stubborn. Joane Langdale might be the Uxmores' drudge, but Jo was another thing entirely, he thought.

Perhaps it would not be so terrible for her to stay with them until he finalised his affairs with the McCrieffs. He would be busy with his own matters and the preparations for the feud ball and she could make herself useful; anyone who could talk his son out of a bout of illness in a carriage was worth keeping around.

Chapter Four

'England is now behind us, Mrs Langdale,' Lochmore said, his voice low. 'Welcome to the land of the green and grey, sheep, cows, swift weddings and whisky, of which I wish I had a flask about now.'

Jo glanced out the window, but there was not much to see. The rain was alternately pouring and spattering on the window and, despite the hot bricks at their feet, it was chilly. The cloak Celia had given her after hers was ruined dragging one of the children out of the muddy millpond was of poor material and unlined and it was not much help against the cold penetrating the carriage in gusts as they lurched over a rutted stretch of road. She leaned her hand on the pane, its surface cold and slippery. Blurry cottages slunk by, tucked low into the green. Scotland.

She untied and pulled down the curtain, blocking the view.

'Don't.'

She jumped at the sharp word, turning.

'Tie it back. The curtain.'

She was too surprised to obey immediately. 'It is cold.'

Lochmore shifted Jamie's sleeping form and reached under the seat to pull out a colourful afghan.

'Here. Put that around you. Leave the curtain open.'

She retied the sash and unfolded the blanket. The wool was fine and warm and she wrapped it about her, grateful but confused. Then annoyance struck her, a little late but welcome. She was not here to stay. She need not be compliant as she was at Uxmore.

'Please,' she said and he frowned.

'Please, what?'

'Please, Mrs Langdale, would you mind leaving the curtains open? I find it easier to brood while viewing the rain and gloom in all its glory.'

His chest expanded, then his breath came out in a long hiss.

'I used to consider Lady Theale an astute woman, but now I am doubtful—she assured me you would give me no cause for complaint, Mrs Langdale.'

'I apologise for giving you cause for complaint, Your Grace.'

He sighed and shook his head.

'You should apologise for making me feel like a churlish fool.'

'I only assume responsibility for *my* mistakes, Your Grace. Not for a state of affairs beyond my control.'

It was a risk, but it paid off. The tension evident in the grooves in his cheeks eased into the glimmer of a smile.

'Kicking a man while he is down is not sportsmanlike, Mrs Langdale.'

'It may not be, but he is much easier to reach when he is, Your Grace.'

He laughed and turned to inspect the passing scenery and, after a moment, Jo did the same.

The silence fell again but for the patter of rain and the sounds of the sleepers. Benneit watched the slide of green and grey beyond the rain, caught between amusement at Mrs Langdale's impertinence and frustration at himself. How the devil did he always manage to come out the worst from their exchanges?

She had a point, though. His reaction had been instinctive, but far too harsh. He usually controlled the outer manifestations of his condition, but sometimes when he was weary that control slipped. And when it did, it left this foul ache in his arms and chest, as if he had gone a dozen rounds sparring with Angus at his best. He shifted his shoulders, cursing his weakness. Thirty years had passed and he was still as cracked a vessel as ever.

He glanced at Joane Langdale but she did not turn. She looked like an urchin, tucked into Mrs Merry's blanket. His housekeeper had used every colour of wool she could find and the result bordered on disaster and yet was charming, like an English spring garden chopped up and woven together. Against its riot of colour Mrs Langdale's delicate colouring was more ethereal than pixyish. Soft.

She raised the shawl, brushing her cheek with it furtively, the way Jamie did when he was sneaking a tart from Mrs Merry. Even through the clop of the horses' hooves and the creaking of the carriage, he thought he could hear the faint burr of fabric on flesh and his own cheek warmed, his fingers tingling as if making contact with the shawl, or her cheek. A snake of a shudder made him shift his legs in surprise and discomfort and he shoved his hands into his pockets and turned again to the blurry greyness outside.

Boredom and a wayward mind were dangerous things. Especially after an exhausting week of travelling, his mind caught between Jamie's ills and the daunting challenges awaiting him back home. He should keep his thoughts on those challenges, but the image lingered like a painting in a gallery one kept returning to inspect—the curve of her cheek just brushed with colour and the surprising lushness of her lower lip nestled against the blanket. His mind fixed on it like an eagle on prey—circling, honing in on every angle and aspect, trying to understand what on earth was so appealing and why his hands were hot and buzzing with discomfort that had nothing to do with his ancient weakness.

He looked resolutely at Jamie, recalling his visit to McCrieff Castle the day before his departure for London. McCrieff preening like a prize cock, Lady Tessa calm and sweet, her generous figure presented in a slightly garish pink that spoke more of her mother's tastes and ambitions than her own. She was intelligent, too—thoroughly aware of the political and financial import of such a union and clearly willing to undertake it. She was the perfect bride for the Duke of Lochmore.

If only he were not that Duke.

Chapter Five

It was early evening by the time they stopped. It wasn't raining, but the courtyard was deep in puddles. Jamie ran ahead in Angus's wake, heedless of the wet, but Jo—weary and stiff after the interminable week of travelling, but mindful of her one pair of inadequate boots—took the circuitous route around the collection of small lakes in the courtyard. It was only when sunlight crashed through the clouds on the horizon with the suddenness of a charging bull that she looked up from her careful manoeuvring.

What she saw stopped her short. From within the fogbound confines of the carriage she had given up trying to make out the landscape and she was utterly unprepared. The inn stood between the road and a wide rushing stream and beyond it were mountains. Not hills. Mountains. Steep uncompromising eruptions that reached into the sky, the setting sun turning green into emerald and grey rock into gleaming obsidian. The peaks ruffled the clouds, turning the sky into something alive. She could well imagine that beyond those clouds in this strange land there would be another world, some place the valiant and brave could reach if they scaled these verdant monsters.

She didn't even notice Lochmore come to stand beside her.

'Is something wrong?' he asked, frowning up at the hills.

'What? Oh, no. It is merely that I have never seen anything so magnificent. Ever.'

He smiled and, though he looked as weary as she felt, this sudden softening of his features, and the flush of sunlight raising the green to prominence in his shadowed eyes and emphasising the raven silk of his hair, made her feel that her words would be as true for him as well. Otherworldly. Unreachable.

'You like it.'

It was such a mild reflection of the passion the sights aroused in her, but said with such uncharacteristic satisfaction that she laughed, warmed from within.

'Yes, Your Grace. I like it very well indeed.'

'That is good, most people find it…daunting. Too stark for their tastes. They miss the rolling English pastures.'

They. She had heard as much from Bella when she visited Uxmore. Along with a host of other complaints. She looked away from him and back at the peaks. The clouds were tearing free of them, revealing more and more grey and green to the sun. They looked miles high, but also just within reach. It was dizzying.

'It is stark, but that is precisely what is so magnificent. I love the English countryside, but it is a mild, warm kind of love. This is…different. Overwhelming. I don't want to stop looking.'

They stood for a moment in the quiet of the courtyard, looking. The water gurgled and rushed past, filling the silence with life. Then he sighed and took her elbow gently.

'There will be plenty more mountains to see, I promise. But now we should feed Jamie and put him to bed. By the tone of his grumbling those last miles, we will be lucky to avoid a scene and I, for one, do not feel equal to it. It has been a very long day and even longer week.'

She nodded, absurdly warmed by his casual hold on her arm and the assumption of intimacy in the way he shared his thoughts about Jamie. Perhaps if Alfred had lived, if they had had a family, she might one day have found herself at a similar moment. If… If… If…

The Duke's prediction, unfortunately, proved accurate. Jamie's grumbling and grizzling in the carriage were not calmed by the food. He kicked off his shoes, complained about the chair, the food, the fire and hovered precipitously on the verge of a full-blown tantrum.

Jo wished it was her right to sweep the over-tired boy into her arms, yet all she could do was distract him and entertain him, but to no avail. A chance comment towards the end of the meal reminded him of his dog and his eyes, already red from weariness, glazed with tears.

'I want to be home! Why didn't we bring Flops? I wouldn't be sad if I had Flops.'

'We cannot bring a dog on such a trip, Jamie...' the Duke replied. He, too, was losing the battle to remain calm and his voice sounded like gravel crunched underfoot.

'Yes, we can,' Jamie shot back. 'I would care for him and he would sleep with me and I would hold him on my lap in the carriage.'

'There is hardly any point to discussing it now, Jamie. In a few days we will be home.'

'No, I want to be home *now*! I hate going to London.'

'That isn't what you said when we visited Astley's and Gunter's, the Menagerie at the Exeter Exchange and...'

Jamie surged to his feet, sweeping his plate from the table. It cracked into two half-moons and a flash of fear flickered through the storm on his face.

Jo instinctively bent to retrieve the piece closest to her, but Benneit's hand shot out and grabbed her arm, stopping her.

'Pick up those pieces, Jamie.'

She felt the rumble of his voice through the hand that held her arm. He was not exerting any force on her, but somehow she was incapable of extracting her arm so she sat there, watching the two Lochmores.

Jamie breathed deeply and then the word came out like a puff of smoke. 'Shan't!'

'James Hamish Lochmore. Pick them up *now*.'

Jamie proceeded to kick the piece closest to him. As he was only in stockings this was not a wise move. The cut was not deep, but he stared at the tiny stain of red at the tip of his toe and ran into the small adjoining room where his cot was laid out, slamming the door behind him.

She waited for the wails of crying, but though she heard the creaking of the cot as Jamie flung himself into it, there was no other sound, just the Duke's breathing, harsh against his clenched teeth as he glared at the door. He had not let go of her arm and she was not about to draw attention to herself. So she watched his fingers on the grey wool of her pelisse. The lines across each knuckle, sharply drawn. She wished she could put her other hand on his, soothe the tension, tell him not to worry.

His grip softened and though his gaze was fixed on the door as if engaged in a staring contest with it, his hand smoothed the fabric of her sleeve twice. Then he caught himself, looked down and drew his hand away. If she had not felt peculiarly bereft at his withdrawal, she might have smiled at the flush of embarrassment that marked his high cheekbones.

'I apologise, Mrs Langdale. I did not want you to pick it up for him. He must learn to master these tantrums of his.'

'Must he?'

'Of course. He will one day have to assume serious responsibilities and there will be no room for such outbursts.'

The silence fell again as she weighed her words.

'What a pity one cannot hire children.'

'What?'

'I think two or three would do. Once we arrive we could send them back.'

'What the devil are you talking about?'

'I am talking about a four-year-old boy trapped for days on end in a carriage with three adults, all in various states of ill humour. Jamie's only sin is that, unlike some of us, he has not yet learnt to mask his ill humour. Having often travelled with a herd of ill-behaved children in carriages, I can assure you Jamie's brand of tantrums would have gone utterly unnoticed in the Uxmore carriage over a mere hour's journey. So perhaps if we filled the carriage with other children, Jamie's behaviour might not appear so offensive to you. Goodnight, Your Grace.'

She didn't wait for him to respond, but left the parlour. Running away before he could counter-attack was cowardly, but she, too, was tired and blue-devilled, and her arm was still pulsing from the warmth of his hand.

Benneit remained at the table, his mind searching for an appropriate response to Mrs Langdale's lecture. He should at least have told her that it was inconceivably annoying how people who had no children always held such firm opinions about how to raise them.

Devil take the woman.

The silence from Jamie's room was deafening and for a moment Benneit was struck with the horrid thought that Jamie had climbed out the window and disappeared. His heart squeezed and kicked as he stood and went to the door. It was ridiculous. Jamie was only four years old and, though he did sometimes wander off, he had never done anything truly dangerous.

Four years old. Almost five now.

Still only a whisper away from a babe, but already with a mind as sharp as a boy's. He could see sometimes how confused that made Jamie, that internal struggle to place himself on either side. He thought himself a little man, ready to explore the world.

Jamie did need children about him to remind him he was only a boy.

Not *hired* children, blast and double-blast Joane Langdale. She had the uncanny ability to confound, embarrass and surprise him, all within the passing of an hour. She had surprised and touched him with that show of childlike passion about the mountains and he had felt quite in charity with her despite the difficult dinner. Perhaps that was why he had forgotten himself and… What had he been thinking to grab her arm like that? Certainly he should not have sat there holding her as if it was quite normal. It had been far too…intimate. Strangely, it had felt right. As if they truly were facing the conundrum of Jamie together.

It was not smart to depend on her on that front. Jamie was his to raise and soon Tessa McCrieff would be standing by his side, to help and to support.

Benneit tried to impose Tessa McCrieff's image

over that of Joane Langdale's slim pixie figure but his mind was probably tired because the image remained stubbornly elusive. He shoved those empty thoughts away and entered the small room, sitting cautiously on the bed next to the mound under the blanket.

'I didn't mean to break it.' The words were hardly audible through the wool.

'I know, Jamie.'

'Will they be cross with us?'

'Maybe a little, but if we tell them we are sorry, I think they will forgive us. Do you know, I read somewhere that in Ancient Greece breaking plates was a good thing?'

The blanket eased back a little.

'It is?'

'That was how people showed they were wealthy—by breaking plates after a banquet.'

Jamie looked around the small room with its low roof.

'I don't think the people here are wealthy like those Greeks.'

'Probably not. Which is why we will pay for that plate.'

Jamie turned over towards Benneit.

'I have the coin I found on the beach. I can give them that.'

'I think you should keep that. You might need it for when you break something really large.'

Jamie giggled, but then the smile dimmed again.

'I wish we were home already, Papa.'

'I know, Jamie. Just a few more days. You've been a brave lad.'

'You're not angry?'

'No, Son. We're all tired and we do foolish things when we are.'

'You growl when you're tired.'

'So I do. I'm sorry I growled at you.'

'I'm sorry, too, Papa. I promise I won't throw things again. Or growl.'

'Don't promise, Jamie. We might need you to growl at a monster to send him running. If you promise, then where will we be?'

'In a monster's belly.' Jamie's chuckle became a yawn and he turned over with a sigh. Benneit looked at the soft rise of his son's cheek, the dark feathering of his eyelashes. He looked more like a grown boy with each day. He could hardly remember the baby Jamie. Would this image, too, fade in a few years? It was hard to believe that possible, but it probably would. He didn't want that to happen. Peculiarly enough, he wanted to remain precisely at this moment. There was a clarity to it. His father was gone, Bella was gone.

It was only Jamie and him now. He could live with that.

'Sleep well, Son.'

Nurse Moody was waiting in the parlour and he stood aside to allow her entry to Jamie's room. The door leading to the other small bedroom where Mrs Langdale was to stay was still open and the room empty.

'Where is Mrs Langdale?' he asked Moody as she passed and she stopped.

'Outside. Said something about putting the mountains to bed.'

'To what?'

'To bed. Angus went after her. Goodnight, Your Grace.'

She closed the door and Benneit remained immobile for a moment. One door away there was a lovely fire crackling in his bedroom and a well-aired bed.

Blast the woman.

It was dark outside and he frowned, trying to make out the shapes across the courtyard. The distinctive scent of Angus's pipe guided him towards a row of trees that lined the stream and Angus turned at his approach, removed his pipe and raised his finger to his lips before pointing it in the direction of the water. On a large boulder by the water's edge, Benneit made out the line of a hooded figure, the sliver of a moon giving its contours a faint glow.

'I'll see she comes inside safe and all,' Angus murmured, his voice a low grumble beneath the sound of the water.

'What the devil is she doing?'

'Come to see the mountains, she said.'

Benneit shook his head and followed the path down to the stream. With all due respect to Angus, he was not comfortable with a woman under his protection standing outside in the pitch black. It was not precisely the proper behaviour of a dowdy widow or even the temporary companion to a future Duke. He stopped at the foot of the boulder.

'What are you doing? Come inside.'

She shook her head, but he was not certain she had heard him.

'The mountains are even more amazing at night. No wonder people imagine they are populated by all manner of beasts.'

'Not just imagine. Now come down from there before you go headlong into the water. It is freezing and I am da—dashed if I'm going to fish you out.'

'I wouldn't expect you to.'

The reply was calm and matter of fact and devastating. It was not an accusation, but a statement of fact.

I wouldn't expect you to.

He suppressed the spurt of sympathy and held out his hand.

'Come down, Mrs Langdale.'

She looked down at him, a slim column, the moon catching her eyes. She looked like something out of the tales she conjured for Jamie.

'Please,' he added.

She untucked her hand from her cloak and he clasped it. It was almost as freezing as the water rushing by and without thought he closed his other hand around it.

'Little fool. You're frozen through.'

She gave a little tug, but he held her hand and raised it to blow on it as he did on Jamie's hands when he returned from his explorations with his cheeks red and the rest of him a block of ice. The warmth of his breath carried back her scent, the same elusive rose that lingered in the carriage. It did not suit her; it was too lush a scent for someone so slight, unfurling and warming the air as he breathed it in. He turned her hand over without thought, seeking the source of that anomaly, but she stepped forward and nimbly jumped down from her rock.

He followed her up the narrow path towards the

inn. Angus and his pipe were gone, but inside the landlord hovered in the hallway and Benneit sent him to prepare tea and punch. Inside the empty parlour he looked at the drab brown cloak she was untying.

'Have you nothing warmer to wear?'

She shook her head and walked to the fire, holding out her hands.

'I honestly did not think Lady Theale would succeed in convincing you to take me along.'

'I see. Well, we shall have to find you something more suitable. You won't be much use if you fall ill.'

'Or drown.'

'Lady Theale would definitely hold that against me. She appears quite fond of you.'

'Most peculiar, I know.'

'Do you take me for a fool, Mrs Langdale?'

She looked up from the fire, her eyes wide and a little worried.

'No. Why?'

'Why? Because you insist on speaking to me as if I were several steps below Jamie on the scale of human understanding. These snide little darts might have worked well with the marvellously thick-skinned Uxmores, but the only effect they have on me is to make me wish I had shown more fortitude in the face of Lady Theale's demands.

If you wish to say something to me, then say it and be done with it.'

Blast, he had gone too far. Her eyes widened even further, showing a ring of dark blue around the grey and her mouth wavered out of its prim line. What the devil was wrong with him? First Jamie and now her. Now she would cry and he would have to comfort her. He had sunk low indeed to be taking out his ill humour on children and widows.

A sudden spurt of laughter escaped her.

'You are quite right, Your Grace. I have developed some dreadful habits over the years. I am not accustomed to people showing concern for my well-being. I know that sounds dreadfully self-pitying, but it is merely to explain that I was not quite certain how to react and so, to use Alfred's description, I prickled.'

'I see.'

The door opened and the landlord entered with a tray. Benneit hesitated, but poured her a glass of the steaming punch.

'To help with the prickles,' he explained and she smiled—a full, wide and wholly surprising smile.

'It had best be strong then,' she answered and sipped. He watched her face, the dip of her eyelashes, as long and thick as Jamie's and a shade lighter, which was strange with hair her colour.

She was strange. A magical mouse who some-times looked distinctly like a cat. As she did now, her eyelids a smiling curve as she savoured the hot punch. No, neither a mouse nor a cat but a pixie—it was there in the slight slant of the large eyes, the finely drawn brows and the little inden-tations at the corners of her mouth. It was a much more generous mouth when she smiled than when she wore her prim and proper expression.

The Uxmore women were renowned for their perfect mouths—lush and of a deep coral pink that drew the eye. Bella had made good use of her mouth, drawing attention to it with every trick in the book—a gentle tap of her fan, a little pout-ing sigh… No doubt in an earlier time she would have delighted in wearing a patch beside it. Mrs Langdale hadn't inherited the Uxmore mouth, or height, or beauty, but now that he looked he re-alised how perfectly drawn her own mouth was. It reminded him of the petals of one of his moth-er's favourite pink Centifolias, the petals in the centre curving in on themselves, the pale pink ending in a shade of warmer blush and their tex-ture was softer than silk, warm to the touch…

She sighed and opened her eyes. 'Perfect.'

He went to sit on the far side of the table and turned his eyes to the fire.

'Jamie tells me I growl when I am tired. I apologise for growling at you.'

'I think anyone would be growling after a week cooped up in a carriage.'

'You aren't.'

'You just told me I did precisely that. You growl, I become snide. I do hate that word. The image it conjures is very weaselly.'

'Like Celia the weasel in your wondrous tree tale?'

'Oh, dear, was it that obvious? I do hope Jamie did not make the connection, I would not wish for him to repeat that in her presence.'

'I do not think he did. He is not accustomed to deciphering *romans à clef*. I gathered you were the little girl taken captive by the kindly mole. I could not tell if Uxmore was the mole or the bear until you mentioned the quizzing glass and remembered Uxmore was forever misplacing his. Was that one of your tasks at the Hall?'

'It was my chief task as far as he was concerned and I think the main reason he was not happy with Lady Theale's plans.'

'So who was the bear? He received a very kindly treatment, but I could not place him. It was certainly not Celia's husband, George. There was too much strength of character.'

'No, George was the owl. The bear was Alfred, my husband.'

'I see. I am sorry.'

She shrugged and sipped her punch.

'I was lucky to have had him in my life, however briefly.'

He concentrated on his punch. He should really go to his room; it would be another long and tiring day on the morrow.

'Out of curiosity, what animal would I be?' He kept his voice light, feeling rather foolish that he was even asking. She frowned, her eyes meeting his. His skin tingled and he had to actively resist the urge to look away.

'You and Jamie. A wolf and cub.'

'That sounds ominous. And lonely.'

'Not at all. I read once that wolves are pack animals and very loyal and intelligent. Unlike many other animals, the cubs remain for many years with their pack before striking out on their own.'

Her voice was pedantic and impersonal, but he felt her words keenly, like a verdict. He thought of Jamie curled up in the small trestle bed in the adjoining room, his arms tucked around the blanket, probably wishing it was Flops. A wave of mixed fear and love surged through him. His cub.

The chair scraped as she stood.

'Goodnight, Your Grace.'

Once again she was gone before he could even gather himself to answer her.

Chapter Six

'Do you think it will be a huge ship like last time, Papa?' Jamie asked enthusiastically as he devoured a third scone in the luxurious parlour at the Tontine Hotel. Jo considered hiding the rest of the scones before they suffered the same fate. The less that went down, the less that would come up in the carriage as they covered the last leg from Glasgow to Lochmore. She wished they could spend more time in this fascinating city. They had not seen much as they drove in last night, but enough to wake her curiosity.

The Tontine Hotel itself was as fine as any London house she had ever visited, with lush carpets and furniture, and her bed, in one of the four rooms leading off the palatial private parlour they dined in, was enormous and as soft as a cloud. She would happily spend a week here, exploring. She remembered reading that there were lovely gardens and theatres in Glasgow. What would it be like to explore—not in London where everything was overlaid with memories of that agonising Season and her life with the Uxmores—but in a whole new city, where she could invent herself anew…?

Joane Langdale, independent widow…

'I don't know, Jamie,' the Duke answered absently, turning the pages of a newspaper. 'Angus made the arrangements. We will ask him when we depart for the port.'

'For the port?' Jo asked, finally registering the import of their discussion.

'Did I not tell you? We will proceed by water from here. It is faster than going overland and Jamie enjoys it. The carriage will join us a day or so later at Lochmore. Next time we travel to London I think we will sail the whole way, what do you say, Jamie?'

'Oh, yes, please, sir! Do you like ships, Jo?' Jamie asked, his whole body quivering with excitement.

'I don't know, Jamie. I have never been on one.'

Jamie stared at her, aghast.

'Never? Not ever?'

'It is a dreadful fault in me, I know. I have been on a rowboat once, if that helps.'

Jamie looked disgusted.

'*Everyone* has been on a rowboat. This is a ship! A real ship with sails and rigging and funny smells and funny people who speak funny and gulls and waves and…things.'

'Well, there is a first time for everything.'

'I was on a ship before I was even me,' Jamie insisted. 'Papa told me I tried to crawl to the crow's nest when I was not even a year old.'

'That is impressive. Why are there crows on a ship?'

Jamie rolled his eyes.

'There aren't crows. It is where you climb so you can see far, far away before anyone else on board and then you yell *"land ho"* so everyone knows you are close just like in the stories.'

'Then why are they called crow's nests?'

Jamie frowned and turned to his father.

'I don't know. Why are they called that, Papa?'

'I'm afraid I don't know either, Jamie.'

Jamie's face fell and Jo watched with a little amusement the shift of expressions on the Duke's face. It was touchingly obvious he did not like disappointing Jamie. Before he could concoct some answer merely to counter his son's disappointment at his ignorance she folded her napkin and spoke.

'I shall add that to the Great Big List, Jamie.'

'The what?'

'The Great Big List of Things I Did Not Know I Did Not Know, But Now I Know I Don't. I think everyone has such a list, don't they?'

Jamie's frown deepened as he followed her nonsense, making him look even more like the Duke.

'What else don't you know?'

'A great many things. One of them is where you ride on a camel. From the illustrations of camels I have seen, I can't imagine riding on the hump is very comfortable, but there does not seem to be much room elsewhere, unless you are left clinging to his neck which strikes me as rather awkward.'

'In the *Desert Boy* book Papa bought he rides on a saddle on the hump,' Jamie announced categorically.

'On it. Well, now I know. That is one less item on my list. Thank you, Lord Glenarris.'

Jamie's eyes widened at her use of his title and then crinkled in laughter and he gave a little bow, glancing at his father.

'I like this game. Tell me something on your list, Papa.'

'I do not know what it will take for you to make a pair of shoes survive longer than a fortnight, Lord Glenarris.'

Jamie laughed.

'That's not a real thing you don't know.'

'It feels real enough in the morning when we are late to get underway.'

Jamie raised his feet.

'I found them, didn't I, sir?

'Mrs Langdale found them, despite your best efforts, boy.'

Jamie turned his grin on her.

'You're like the mole girl, Jo.'

'Mrs Langdale, Jamie,' the Duke corrected.

'I gave him leave to call me Jo, Your Grace.'

He finally looked at her, his grey-green eyes reflecting a mixture of annoyance and resignation. Despite the significantly more comfortable accommodations of the past night, he still looked tired and she realised it was not merely the long trip that was taking its toll on him. The closer they came to their destination, the stonier he became, as if gathering himself against an incoming blow. She waited for him to insist on formality, but he merely shrugged and stood.

'I must speak to Angus. I will send him to find you when we are ready to depart.'

The silence that followed his departure was disturbed only by the thud-thud of Jamie's foot kicking the table leg. She breathed in to calm herself.

'Why doesn't Papa like you?'

Jo straightened, surprise and hurt pinching at her insides. It was one thing to know it; it was quite another to hear the truth from the mouth of babes.

'I think perhaps he likes having you to himself, Jamie.'

Jamie's kicking stopped.

'Will he like you better if I call you Mrs Langdale?'

'I don't know, Jamie. I do not think that is the problem. Come, we should find your coat if we are to be ready to leave. Will you show me the crow's nest when we arrive at the boat?'

Jamie nodded, but half-heartedly, and jumped off his chair.

It was not quite the great ship she had been imagining. It had only two sails and, according to Jamie, no crow's nest.

'Why can't we sail on that ship, Papa?' Jamie pointed to a much larger three-masted ship anchored further out on the swelling waves.

'Because that ship is not sailing close to our home, Jamie.'

Jamie's eyes lit.

'Where is it going, Papa?'

The Duke looked down at his son and the stern look gentled a little.

'I'm afraid that is on my Great Big List of Things I Don't Know. Where would you like it to sail?'

'Zanzibar!'

'Why Zanzibar?'

'It has a pretty name. There are dragons there, too.'

'Dragons?'

'Yes, remember? You showed me Zanzibar in the Map Room and there was a green and yellow dragon sitting on the waves, poking it with its tail.'

Whatever answer the Duke was contemplating was interrupted as Angus beckoned them towards the ship. Jo approached the vessel with a little trepidation. The wind had picked up and the clouds were moving along the horizon, shifting as they went like rising smoke. The ship itself was rocking and she wished she could cling to something or someone as they made their way across the damp deck towards a doorway set into a raised platform in the rear of the ship.

'Jamie and I will stay above deck, Mrs Langdale, but Angus will take you to a cabin where you may rest. It will not be a long voyage to Crinan, but it might be a little rough with the north wind so stay close to something you can hang on to.'

'Wouldn't you prefer to leave Jamie with me?'

'Jamie fares better in the fresh air.' The answer was curt and he turned away, holding Jamie's hand.

Jo had no choice but to follow Angus down what was more ladder than steps into the dark and narrow passageway and into an equally narrow cabin. It had no window, a narrow cot and a small table and chair with a chamber pot attached to the wall with a chain. She nearly told Angus she, too, preferred to face the elements above decks than in the coffin-like space, but years of practice made her keep her peace and she smiled and thanked him and went to sit on the chair and took off her bonnet and prepared herself for a very boring few hours.

Chapter Seven

Benneit braced his leg against the coil of rope and wrapped his boat cloak more securely around Jamie's body so that only his dark hair and eyes were visible above the thick fabric.

'Here comes another!' Jamie's words were muffled, but the excitement was evident in the tension of his quivering body.

The wave rose, the water pulling out from under them, causing the ship to pitch to the side a moment before the wall of water struck, sending a fine cold mist over them, pearling on Jamie's curls. Jamie bounced and crowed with pleasure, almost cracking Benneit's chin as he bent to press a kiss to his son's damp head.

'Did you see that, Papa? Did you? It was *enormous*!'

Benneit laughed. He was stiff, cold, wet, tired and every mile they closed on Lochmore added what felt like a year to his life, but Jamie's joy was winning against all the rest. It was so pure and simple. Just joy.

Had he been like this as a boy? He must have been, at least a little, but for the life of him he could not remember. He certainly had no memory of his father holding him. His mother, yes. In the garden of The House as she read to him, or on the sofa in the Map Room as she showed him her latest addition to the wall. He hoped Jamie would remember this. He should do more to give him moments such as these to balance against all he could not give him.

'Jo! Jo! Did you see that?' Jamie struggled to snake a hand out from Benneit's grasp and Benneit turned his head to see Mrs Langdale, cloaked but bareheaded, holding the railing as she made her way in their direction. A shaft of alarm coursed through him. She should be below decks where it was safe. He tightened his hold on Jamie, afraid he would try to run to her.

The ship pitched again and she stopped, turning to watch the surge of the wave as it closed on them. For one panicked moment Benneit thought she would let go of the railing and retreat, which would be the worst possible thing to do. But she held firm, silhouetted by the rise of spray, a grey-on-grey figure except for the flash of her flaxen hair about the elfin face raised to the elements. As the wave fell away she turned to them, but instead of the fear he expected he saw a mirror of the exultation he felt in every muscle of Jamie's body. Her eyes were laughing and her lips parted.

She looked nothing like Bella's drab and silent cousin or the prim and proper Widow Langdale.

She managed the final yards to their more sheltered hideaway, lowering herself to sit on the deck beside the coil of rope. Her face was wet with spray, her eyelashes spearing drops of mist.

'Do you like it, Jo?' Jamie's question was so loaded with yearning she laughed.

'It is *amazing*. I thought the whole ship would turn over like a tortoise on its back!'

'You should have stayed below,' Benneit said above the roar of the wind.

'I could not bear it any longer.' Her hand tightened on the rope as the ship began to tip again, but her eyes were bright and laughing still. 'It was like being inside a barrel rolling down a hill. I would rather have to run atop it than be bounced about inside.'

Jamie laughed as well and swiped the damp from his face. Benneit tucked his son's arm back inside the cover of his cloak.

'Here comes another, hold on.'

At some point in the hour that followed, as they were buffeted by waves coming around the sound, he began laughing with them. The sailors, hurrying about their business, gave them a wide berth. The sensible passengers were where they ought to be—cowering below decks. The weak-minded and the young and the foolish could do as they wished and be washed overboard if that was what God and Neptune willed.

The waves calmed as they approached Crinan, and Jamie snuggled deeper into the cavern of Benneit's cloak, resting his cheek against his chest, his eyelids drooping. Benneit stroked the damp from his cheek and Jamie sighed. The clouds, too, lost their vigour, thinning and showing blue at their edges, and even the sun struck through occasionally, raising chestnut lights in Jamie's dark hair. Benneit was so tempted to kiss his son's head, but held back. What he did in private was different from what he showed in public. Instead he turned to Mrs Langdale.

'Your clothes must be soaked through. You can ask Angus to bring your portmanteau so you can change before we proceed.'

It was a perfectly practical statement, but somehow it felt far too intimate. The thought of her plain grey dress soaked with sea water all the way to her skin, the spray she wiped from her pink cheeks mirrored elsewhere, soft and curved and moist… He shifted his leg and turned away, shocked by the surge of heat that struck through him at the image, the sensation of his hands joining hers in peeling back the damp fabric from her shivering skin. She made it worse by laughing, the same warm tumbling laugh like the fall of surf on the beach. He moved Jamie away slightly as if to remove him from the contamination of his thoughts.

'It is mostly my cloak. I had no idea sailing could be so marvellous. When I return to England I would like to do so by sea if I may?'

'If you wish.'

She struggled on to her knees and, as the ship gave a gentle roll on a swell, she pitched against his shoulder, her hand steadying herself by grasping his arm as she sank back down.

'I'm so sorry. My leg buckled; it is all tingling.'

'You sat too long in one position. Stretch it out,' he advised, tightening his arms around Jamie.

She did as she was told, stretching out her legs, the damp hems of her skirts catching at her calves. She did not even notice as a sailor walking by slipped and skimmed into the railing at the sight, barely catching himself before hurrying on. Benneit looked away as well. Whatever those horrid grey gowns advertised, they were clearly not a good representation of at least part of this woman's anatomy. Her ankles and calves were as fine and shapely as a Roman sculpture—slim, delicate lines that promised a mixture of fragility and strength. It was impossible not to wonder if the rest of her continued that promise.

'Try to walk a little. That might help.' It might help him at least.

She stood, thankfully leaning on the railing rather than on him. She gave a childlike little grunt, but proceeded towards the gangway to the cabins. He did not turn to watch her go, but from his line of sight he could see the sailors who had been working aft were watching her all too readily. He glared at them and they went back to their tasks.

Chapter Eight

'Survived it fairly this time, didn't we, lad?'

Benneit turned from the window overlooking the bay. It was a corner of comfort in the monstrosity that was Lochmore Castle—that view over the inlet and the steel and indigo sea beyond it, the fall of the cliffs towards the wide sandy shore that stretched until the rock fall crowned by the Devil's Seat. In the afternoon there was a moment of stillness to the sight, between the winds of the morning and the excitement that always struck the water before nightfall. At this moment the elements rested, even the waves looked languid and half-hearted and he could see beyond them to the distance, to the point where his domain ended and the world began.

'We did, Angus. I told you it would become easier as he grew older.'

''Tweren't only that and you know it.' Angus grunted as he threw back the cover of the trunk and began taking out linen.

Benneit ignored his comment and focused on Angus's methodical actions. For such a large man his movements were graceful, but then a man who had dealt in gunpowder for many years during the war would have to be dexterous. Angus never spoke of it, but Benneit knew from another soldier from Lochmore land that the explosion that had marked Angus's body was not his fault. Somehow, unlike so many others who returned from the war, Angus had kept his calm centre, but his very contentedness to remain at Lochmore and not stretch his horizons as he had when he joined the army was telling. Benneit never pried or pushed, but sometimes he wondered if he should.

Angus and he had always been fast friends despite the difference in their age and stations. There had been few boys his age near Lochmore and, until he was sent away to school in England, Angus had been his closest friend. And despite his parents' concerns, every time they returned to Lochmore they picked up the threads of their friendship, disregarding time passed and social barriers.

'You shouldn't be doing that, Angus. That is Ewan's duty.'

'Clears my mind. Simple things.'

Benneit nodded and looked back out the window. Downstairs a stack of not-so-simple matters was awaiting in the estate room, alongside his long-suffering steward, McCreary.

'You should go to The House in the morning before McDreary snares you in his net. Clear your mind,' Angus continued behind him.

'I might.'

'She'll keep an eye on Jamie.'

'No doubt.'

'You'll be eating up here or downstairs?'

Benneit hesitated and Angus shut the trunk.

'There won't be nought to bother ye downstairs, Mrs Merry said, as Jamie asked Mrs Langdale to share his tea in the nursery. And Lady Morag won't venture out until you're settled and she accepts there's a new face in the castle. If then. She's getting on and her bitterness is firming her in the tower like a barnacle on its rock.'

'I'm tired, Angus. I will eat in the study. Tomorrow I will sort out the details. Has Mrs Merry been civil to Mrs Langdale?'

Angus straightened with a grin.

'Tried not to, then came under the great wide-eyed stare and crumbled like week-old kelp in summer. There'll be a fire in her parlour, don't you worry.'

Benneit nodded.

'Keep an eye on her.'

'With pleasure, Your Grace.'

'On Mrs Merry, Angus. Not Mrs Langdale.'

Angus's grin widened and Benneit resisted the

urge to curse. He had stepped right on to that cowpat with his eyes open.

'She won't be staying, Angus.'

'Aye, I know. Best plough ahead on your plans to bring someone that will, then. Jamie's growing.'

Benneit grunted and turned back to the view—already it had changed, the afternoon wind ruffling the sea's surface and clouds gathering on the horizon like sheep around a trough.

He held out another hour before he headed down the corridor towards the nursery. There was nothing wrong with wanting to see if Jamie was settled after the journey. But it was wrong to have to make excuses to himself.

The nursery parlour was empty, the empty plates still on the table. He frowned and went to the bedroom. That, too, was empty.

'In the schoolroom,' Nurse Moody murmured behind him and he turned.

'At this hour?'

She shrugged and shuffled out.

The first thing he noticed as he entered was her hair. It was not in her usual tidy bun, but in a queue held back by a single blue ribbon, falling down her back in a lush tangle. It was still damp from bathing, but beginning to dry into waves warmed by the firelight into the colour of sunny wheat. If not for the horrible grey dress he might not have recognised her.

Flops was lying with his paws splayed wide by the fire, looking more than ever like a skinned fur pelt set out to dry. He raised his cream and tan head with a panting grin and tapped the floor with his tail before subsiding again into a shape-less mop, clearly too exhausted from Jamie's joy-ous homecoming to even come to Benneit for his usual ear-scratching.

Benneit remained in the shadowed doorway, watching them as their heads drew even closer over some object Jamie placed in her hand.

'See? This is special,' Jamie said and Jo nod-ded, her voice as hushed as his as she answered.

'I've never seen anything like it. It looks like it has been struck by lightning. Do you think that is what happened?'

Jamie took it back, inspecting the coloured stone with the slash of white through its centre.

'The mermaids left it for me.'

'You are very lucky then,' she replied. 'They never left anything for me.'

'Do you live near the sea, too?'

'No. But there is a pond. With frogs.'

Jamie giggled.

'Mermaids don't live in ponds.'

'I imagine they don't. They would be pond-maids, wouldn't they? What is this?' she raised a smooth disc of glass to catch the glint of firelight.

'Papa said this is from Jules Keezers's quizzing glass. Grandfather Uxmore has a quizzing glass and it makes his eye look like a beetle.'

'I did not know Julius Caesar had a quizzing glass, but I like that it is blue. Do you think he had one in every colour? Perhaps when it was cloudy he used a yellow one to brighten up the world.'

'And then he could put the yellow with the blue to make the world green. Papa showed me that. I could take it to the desert with me because Papa says there is no green there. Not much anyway.'

'No, I dare say there isn't. But there are oases, aren't there?'

'O-a-sees?' Jamie enunciated.

'Yes, springs of water in the middle of the desert. Imagine—you are riding on your camel's hump for days and days, all thirsty and hot, and suddenly at the edge of the world you see green and then you come closer and there are trees and a spring of cool water. It must seem like magic, too.'

Jamie stared up at the ceiling, as if the world was opening up above them and the image descended from the heavens, then he turned and finally noticed Benneit standing in the doorway.

'Papa! I am showing Jo my treasures.'

'Not "Jo", but Mrs Langdale, Jamie. We should observe the proprieties now we are at Lochmore.'

Benneit moved forward, nodding to Mrs Langdale as she shifted on to her knees unhurriedly and stood.

'It is my fault, Your Grace. I forgot and asked him again to call me Jo.'

'I see. Bedtime, Jamie. It has been a very, very long week.'

Mrs Langdale nodded, as if well aware the admonition was for her.

'Goodnight, Jamie. Thank you for showing me your treasures.'

Jamie shrugged sulkily, but as she reached the door he spoke: 'Tomorrow will you come see where I find them, J—Mrs Langdale?'

'Of course, Jamie,' she answered. 'Goodnight. I will dream of deserts tonight, I think.'

Benneit stopped her by her room down the hall from the nursery.

'A word, Mrs Langdale.'

She drew back her shoulders, but her face remained a complete blank, standing with her back to her door as if guarding dangerous prisoners inside, or protecting them.

'I am grateful you accompanied us to Lochmore and I admit your presence made the trip a great deal more bearable for Jamie. But as you are not planning to remain here more than a few days I think it is best not to establish too great a degree of intimacy with my son. He does not attach easily, but for some reason he has decided to be more open with you than is his nature.'

His carefully measured oration began to flag under the absolute blankness in her eyes. Once again he had the sensation that somewhere far behind the still grey gaze she was dissecting him just as he had once seen the men of the Royal Academy dissect a dog's cadaver—efficiently and utterly without mercy.

'Am I clear?' he persisted.

'As clear as the Scottish wind, Your Grace, and just as brutal. Shall I confine myself to my room until my departure? Perhaps give him the cold shoulder when he addresses me? If that is what you expect from me, I suggest you make arrangement to send me back to England at first light tomorrow.' She breathed in, visibly reining in the flow of words, then continued in a more conciliating tone. 'I do not believe Jamie will be harmed by a show of interest on my part, even if it makes our parting more difficult. Your son is a lovely boy with a thirst for company and while I am here I intend to be as I am. If that is not what you wish of me, you have the power to send me on my way. You may inform me of your decision in the morning. Goodnight, Your Grace.'

He stared at the door that shut in his face. Whatever response he had expected from her, he had not anticipated such long-winded insolence. His foot twitched with a long-forgotten urge to give her door...*his* door...a savage kick. However, that might draw her back out and he was damned if he knew what to say to her after that tongue-lashing.

Chapter Nine

Jo could not remember the last time she had lost her temper anywhere but in the confines of her own mind.

Yes, she could, actually. After her mother told her they must leave their home to live with Lady Theale, she had thrown a fine tantrum, blaming her mother for everything—her father's death and the loss of their home and freedom and pride. Her mother held her through the weeping that followed her outburst, but later that night Jo heard her crying and felt like a worm and apologised the next day. She had not openly lost her temper again since.

Until last night.

Her usual defences were failing her too often recently. Perhaps it was the exhaustion of the trip, the daunting bleakness and imposing size of the castle as they approached it last night, huddled on the rainy promontory like a glum grey giant. Or perhaps it was that the Duke's stern lecture brought back unpleasant memories of that dreadful Season six years ago when he had regarded her with the same critical exasperation as the rest of the Uxmores, making her feel irredeemably wrong-footed. During the trip north that sensation faded, at least until last night as she stood backed against her door, the light of the single candle in the sconce accentuating the harsh lines of his handsome face. He was too big, too sure of himself, too disapproving and far too oppressively male…

And the worst, the absolute worst, was that he turned her pleasure in Jamie's company, the one bright spot in her confusion, into something objectionable. Part of her understood his concern, but another part—already tender and afraid of the future—wanted to curl into a ball and cry. That or lash out and do as much damage to him. So she had.

It was not the first time her tongue had slipped its leash in this impossible man's presence, but this time she had truly gone too far. She was a beast to have spoken to him so and rebuked him, too, merely because he was worried about Jamie being hurt. Whatever she thought of the Duke of Lochmore, she did not doubt he loved his son deeply, or that Jamie utterly adored him.

Perhaps she was jealous. Of both of them.

She was a worm. And a sanctimonious one at that.

She stopped as she saw Angus exit a room to her right.

'Angus, where is His Grace?'

'Here in the estate room, Mrs Langdale. He and Mr McCreary are battling the dragons of debits and credits.'

'Oh, dear. Do you think it would be a bad idea if I asked for a moment of his time?'

'I think he would be happy for any excuse to escape, Mrs Langdale.'

She rather doubted that, but she nodded and when he opened the door and announced her, she stepped in with her chin up and her heart somewhere below her knees.

'Your Grace, may I have a moment of your time?'

He glanced up from a ledger and stood, his face glacial, and her heart sank to ankle level. But at a glance from him his bespectacled steward left the room and she rushed into speech before the door even closed.

'I wish to apologise for what I said last night. I had no right and I know you only spoke out of concern for Jamie. But I do not think I can be indifferent so perhaps it is best I leave now. I shan't be returning to Uxmore so we needn't even tell Lady Theale. By the time she discovers I am not here you will no doubt have wed, thus obviating the need for her to plot against you again.'

He appeared to gather himself as he followed her tumbled speech. 'What do you mean you shan't be returning to Uxmore?'

'Just that. I have been saving my annuity and all my settlement and I think I have enough to lease some place small in town and not worry for at least a year or so and by then I shall no doubt find employment so I do not eat into my settlement. I will try seeking employment at one of the schools for young women. I have all the skills. It cannot be too hard.'

He came towards her.

'Sit down.'

She glanced around and sat on the nearest chair. It was hard and slightly warped and she wished she had chosen a more comfortable seat on which to receive her dismissal.

He pulled over a chair and sat as well, crossing his arms over his chest.

'I have another suggestion. Rather, a choice. After our…discussion last night I considered your words and I wish to amend our arrangement. I will be very busy for the foreseeable future. Besides the usual estate business, we are holding a ball on Summer's Solstice after which we will finalise an agreement with the McCrieffs. I presume once that occurs the wedding will take place promptly. And before you toss an accusation of vanity at me, I should say that this does not reflect in the least on my personal qualities, but on the Lochmore title and wealth and the unsettled nature of Scottish clan politics.'

'I was not...'

'You were thinking it and you said as much to me during the trip here.'

'I did not...'

'Did, too, as Jamie might say. But that is hardly the point. The point is that you have a point— Jamie is isolated here. Hopefully once I am married there will be siblings and eventually he can attend a school nearby. But while this is all in the making, he needs, as Lady Theale stated in her usual bludgeoning way, a companion. If there is one thing you have proven this week, Mrs Langdale, it is that you can appeal to children. Therefore I would be grateful if you would stay until the betrothal. I will of course compensate you. I doubt Lady Theale has been as generous with the Uxmore funds as she has been with your time, but should you remain here you will accept my terms.'

'I could not...'

'My terms, Mrs Langdale. Or not at all.'

Her relief held her silent and worried her. She

should finally be brave and strike out on her own, not fall into another position of cushy servitude, no matter how appealing her charge.

'Well, Mrs Langdale?' he prompted. 'This is your cue to say "I will", or, more consistently with your latest responses, "I will not..."'

In the silence the wind whistled in the casement and the clouds cast shifting shadows on the stone floor. The great fireplace was crackling and she was not cold, but she shivered a little. Perhaps it was merely cowardice now that she was determined to strike out on her own, but it would not be so very terrible to stay for a month, would it? She could not deny that she felt drawn to Jamie far more than she had to any of Celia's children. Both Lochmore men needed her in their own way and, even if she was only a temporary bridge, the thought of turning her back on Lochmore's offer felt...wrong.

'I will.'

He shook his head, but it was not a negation. Then he looked around the room, as if surprised to find them there.

'The castle is impossible to heat. I will have Mrs Merry find you a decent cloak for when you go outside. There are a few rules. Do not go to the north bay under any circumstances—the tide and currents there are brutal. Jamie knows never to go there without either myself or Angus. However, you may go to the bay to the south of the castle which is protected and quite calm. The shortest route is through the Sea Gate which is reached through a tunnel from the great staircase, but you mustn't enter any of the other tunnels or the cellars. They are dank and unwholesome and no longer in use—the kitchens and storerooms are in the keep and the servants are on the top floor. Jamie knows he is never to venture there. Is that absolutely clear?'

She nodded vigorously.

'Good. We rarely dine formally here as I often return late. So you will most often dine with Jamie or in your parlour. Occasionally, though hopefully rarely, we may be required to dine with my aunt, Lady Morag. Luckily she is highly unsociable and mostly remains in the north tower with her choice of comforts. I suggest you not invade her privacy—she is a...cantankerous person. Other than that you are to remember that you are an Uxmore and my guest and I have made that clear to Mrs Merry and the servants. I won't have you slinking around here like a governess or a drudge. Understood?'

Some of her relief was beginning to evaporate at his imperiousness, but she nodded again, a little less vigorously.

'Good. Now go find Jamie and have him show you the castle and the grounds. I have work to do.'

He stood, casting a look of such blatant loathing at the ledgers she almost laughed.

'If you hate it so, why not have your steward see to the numbers? Is he not trustworthy?'

'Very, but he is getting on and though he doesn't admit it his eyesight is failing. I must find someone to replace him eventually, poor fellow. Meanwhile I do my best to review his tallies. We are sadly behind because of my trip south.'

'I can help with that, if you wish. I saw to the housekeeping accounts at Uxmore.'

'What else did you do at Uxmore? Did you tend to their gardens as well? Air the sheets?'

Strangely she wasn't offended. Perhaps because *he* sounded offended.

'I did not mind it, truly. It was my quiet time. I had the library to myself then.'

He hesitated, clearly tempted, but she clasped her hands and carefully refrained from pressing. Finally he gave another of his peculiarly Latin shrugs.

'Perhaps later. But only if you prove you can actually tally and were not secretly siphoning off the Uxmore funds to the local butcher and baker and candlestick maker.'

'If I was, you will never know, I was very discreet.'

'Mrs Langdale…'

She waited for another list of prohibitions, but after a moment of hesitation he continued.

'I have not been very gracious. Thank you for staying. Jamie will be very happy. If there is anything you need to make your time here more… agreeable, please don't hesitate to speak.' He grimaced, as if aware of how stilted he sounded, and she did her best not to smile.

'Thank you, Your Grace. That is very kind.'

'Yes. Well. Where are you headed now?'

'Jamie wants to take me treasure hunting in the bay. With luck I will meet his mermaids.'

He smiled just as the sun cleaved through the clouds outside the window and the combination made her look down.

'You are being honoured indeed. I have yet to be introduced to them.'

'Jamie did not sound very hopeful. He says I might be lucky because I know Minerva, but usually mermaids think adults are too boring.'

He laughed and came to open the door for her. 'I tend to agree with them. I hope your connections with the magical Minerva serve you well. I will tell Angus to keep well back when he accompanies you so he doesn't ruin your chances with the dwellers of the deep.'

'Surely Angus need not be bothered to accompany us?' she asked as she stepped into the corridor.

'I do not want you going by the Sea Gate tunnel with only Jamie as guide on your first descent to the bay. The tunnel is… I do not want you wandering around and becoming lost.'

The shift from laughter to tension was so sudden it jarred her, but she did not wish to upset him again so she nodded.

'If you do not think Angus will mind.'

'I do not think he will mind in the least, Mrs Langdale.' This time his smile was sardonic and before she could respond he disappeared back into the study.

Chapter Ten

First impressions were often deceptive, Jo thought as she paused halfway along the beach and glanced back at the castle. Yesterday they arrived in near darkness, though it was only late afternoon, with clouds hanging low and submerging everything in sheets of unrelenting rain. Faraway lightning had sketched out the contours of the castle, marking towers and the remnants of walls. Through the watery grey the castle had appeared a gloomy monstrosity clawing at the sky.

In sunlight the castle was another beast entirely. It sat atop a promontory whose cliffs fell into the water like an anthracite skirt. It was still imposing and not terribly inviting, but as the sun gleamed off the deep grey stone of the castle and the remains of the walls around it, at least it no longer looked like the lair of an ogre.

From the south she could not see the tower where the Duke said his aunt lived. She wondered if the woman was truly as unpleasant as he warned. She tried to remember what Bella had said about her, but the previous Duke had still been alive then and most of Bella's commentary had been a barrage of complaints about her living conditions, her renovation of the castle, her plans to ensure they spent more time in London and her thinly veiled jealousy about how much time Benneit spent with the baby rather than her.

If Jo was doubtful about the castle, she had no qualms about the beach—it was beautiful. With the skies scrubbed clean of clouds and the scent of the sea and the soft sand beneath her boots, the world was a marvellous place. The bay was sheltered by a finger of the cliffs that extended into the water and further to the south by a tumble of rocks with a large boulder atop it that looked like a pillow just waiting for a large cat to curl on and lap up the sun's warmth. Beyond the finger of rocks, the waves were lashing at the cliffs, heavy with foam, but inside the bay they merely surged and hissed in retreat, more teasing than threatening.

Jamie soon abandoned his shoes on a rock and began inculcating Jo into the secret of finding treasures as he rooted about a clump of slimy brownish growth. The best finds, he informed her, were often tangled in gatherings of kelp the sea tossed up, especially after a storm. They found a lovely shell with a pearly inside, and a curved stick that looked like a pig's tail and which Jamie decided once belonged to a druid.

When Jamie grew hungry they gathered his treasures and turned towards the castle, Jamie running ahead in his stockings while Angus picked up his shoes and addressed Jo with a sigh and a smile.

'You needn't hurry after him, Mrs Langdale. He'll be gone in a cloud of dust before you reach the steps. I'll see Nurse Moody takes him in hand before nuncheon. Take your time and when you're ready to come in, take the stairs at the end of the corridor and you will find yourself by the great staircase and from there up two flights to the nursery. You'll be all right, lass?'

Jo nodded and smiled, happy to have a few moments to herself. She contemplated the tumble of rocks. Perhaps one day she would take a book up there. After all, she had a month. And then...

There was no point in thinking of that now.

She followed the edge of the sea where the waves licked the sand into firmness, stopping to pick up a shell sure to appeal to Jamie. Outside it was gnarled and a rather dull dun colour scored with what looked like the passage of worms in the sand, but inside it was perfection—a creamy pink sheen that would defy the finest artist. She brushed her finger along the sweep of its curve— as soft as silk, it almost felt alive. If she were a princess from one of the exotic dream lands Jamie was convinced these treasures arrived from she would have a dress of just this colour.

And she would be beautiful and wealthy and would depend upon no one but herself.

Strangely, her usual daydream felt rather grey and she trudged up the stone steps and through the Sea Gate and into the tunnel leading to the great stairs. It took her a while to realise she was lost. She finally stopped walking and raised her eyes from the flagstones. There was just enough light coming in from the narrow open slits on either end of the corridor, and she could hear the surf outside, so she did not feel particularly alarmed, just hungry and weary. Had she turned left or right at the Sea Gate? She retraced her steps, but the silence only deepened and so did the gloom.

She could not have come this way because at the end of the ill-lit tunnel with its vaulted ceiling there was nothing but a spiralling staircase heading downwards, which made little sense to her unless she had reached an entrance to the cellars? The Duke's words came back to her—the cellars were closed off so surely there was no point in going down. Unless by coming in from the side door on the cliff side they had entered higher than the main entrance and by going down she would find herself some place familiar?

Utterly confused, she considered calling out, but stubbornness or pride held her back. At least now she was paying attention. She would go down and if it led merely to the cellars she would come directly back and try something else.

A dozen steps down she paused and, as she watched the darkness below her, it began to shift, moving closer, carrying with it a whisper of sound, like a great beast sighing in its sleep. She took an involuntary step back up the steps, her body gathering and her breathing quickening.

'It is only a trick of the light and the wind.' The strange sensation subsided as if chased away by the sound of her voice. Still, she hurried up the stairs, laughing a little at herself. Finally, she found herself at the familiar staircase inside the castle and sighed with relief.

'Just like a child,' she said aloud as she reached the ground floor.

'What is?'

Her heart skittered at the Duke's deep voice and she turned to see him descending the main staircase.

'I am. I thought I was lost.'

He frowned and stopped two stairs short of the bottom.

'Were you frightened?'

'A little,' she admitted. 'Just for a moment. Angus and Jamie went ahead and I wasn't paying attention and took a wrong turn.'

His frown went from cloudy to thunderous.

'This is precisely why I told you to take Angus with you. He and Jamie should not have left you.'

'Nothing happened, Your Grace. It was only a moment's confusion.' She certainly would not tell him about the stairs. That would probably convince him to lock her in her rooms for her own safety.

'Nevertheless, I shall have a word with them.'

'Oh, please don't,' she said impetuously. 'We had such a lovely time finding treasures on the shore and Jamie was hungry and ran ahead and Angus told me to take my time... Please do not be upset with them. I do not require mollycoddling.'

He descended the two remaining stairs and she wished he had remained where he was. It brought him far too close, and with his superior height and breadth of shoulders, she felt frail which was a sensation she was not in the least accustomed to. He had made her ill at ease six years ago and there were still times she felt as tense as a filly being rushed down a cliff path. Perhaps it was his own tension communicating itself to her—the closer they came to his home the more evident it became, and she felt it vividly, like wasps in jar—humming, angry. She doubted she was its cause, but she did feel she was adding to his burdens instead of alleviating them. She wished Jamie was with her so the Duke could see how happy his son was after their visit to the beach, but perhaps that would make it worse.

She searched for a distraction and her eyes alighted on a portrait just beyond his left shoulder of a smiling young woman with dark hair and a lovely face that radiated curiosity and light. On the frame there was a worn inscription of a name: Marguerite. She had glimpsed it last night as they climbed to the nursery and even then it had struck her tired mind.

'Who was Marguerite?'

'Marguerite?'

'The lady in that portrait.'

His stern look vanished in a smile as he turned to the painting and her heart flopped like a landed fish.

'Oh, Daisy. She was an ancestor of mine.'

'Daisy is an unusual name for someone of that period, isn't it?'

'Her name was Marguerite but I couldn't pronounce that as a child, so my mother told me it meant *daisy* in French and that is what we called her.'

'Is that why the lovely botanical plate of a daisy is hung by it?'

'My mother painted that.'

'Truly? It is so very beautiful! I remember now Jamie said she painted the map rooms for you. She must have been very talented.'

He shrugged, smile faltering, and she wondered what she had said to make him withdraw.

'She looks like Jamie,' she said.

His eyes met hers again and there was a peculiar intensity there.

'Most people say he takes after Bella.'

She frowned, wondering why she no longer shared that same assessment. Perhaps her memory of Bella had faded or was overlaid with her image of the Duke and her knowledge of Jamie's character.

'I dare say he does. Or perhaps it is that Bella and your Daisy are rather alike as well.'

It was his turn to frown.

'How on earth hadn't I noticed that before?' The question did not appear to be addressed to her in particular, so she didn't bother answering, just watched his profile as his gaze moved over the painting. 'Perhaps it is not that surprising;

they were related, after all. Bella's maternal ancestors were from the same French branch long ago and they remained in sporadic contact when it served their political purposes. In fact, my father met my mother while visiting the Uxmores as a young man when he came to court. I can see the similarities now, but they are still quite different.'

'The colouring and the eyes and the mouth are similar, but the expression is different. Still, one cannot tell if that is the truth or the painter's choice.'

'By all accounts she was a very lovely woman, both in looks and spirit,' he replied absently and Jo felt herself shrivel a little, only too aware of her shortcomings. 'But then history has a way of reshaping the past to meet the needs of the present, so for all we know she might have been a shrew.'

'She looks kind.' She resisted the to urge to add—unlike Bella. She knew she was being unfair. Bella might have been spoilt, but she was not a bad person and she had charm in abundance. In her own way she had tried to be kind to Jo, and it was probably Jo's own fault they had not succeeded in becoming more comfortable with one another.

'My mother told me she planned to call me

Marguerite,' he said, a spark of laughter in his green eyes that dropped years from his face.

'That would have been…unusual.'

'She wanted a girl and she liked plant names. Unfortunately for her there were not many possibilities for boys, not to mention my father invoked his rights as clan chief and chose Benneit after his grandfather.'

'What a pity. Think of the possibilities—Bluebell, perhaps. Or if you prefer something less feminine she could have chosen chervil or clove.'

'Very amusing. She told me she suggested Rowan or Ash. I always thought if I had a daughter I would like to call her Marguerite.'

The smile faded again and he moved away from the portrait and she leapt to the next conversational gambit.

'You mentioned earlier I might be of some use with the accounts, Your Grace. I would be happy to try once I change.'

His gaze swept over her dress and she wished she had not called attention to it. Her hems were damp and stained with sand and the less pleasant smears from where she had brushed against the kelp or mossy rocks. As she followed his gaze she wondered if the stains could even be removed. She ought to be more careful with her few dresses. Not that there was any need for her to be presentable. She would be seeing no one but Jamie and the servants. And the Duke.

She sighed again and he stepped back as if from an unpredictable beast.

'Perhaps some other day. I will send for you if there is a need. Now I suggest you join Jamie before he eats all your nuncheon. He is voracious after his trips to the beach.'

He turned in the direction of his rooms without another word, leaving her to wonder again if she would ever quite understand the workings of Benneit Lochmore's mind.

Chapter Eleven

'Where are they, Angus?'

Angus poked his head out of Benneit's dressing room, a stack of starched cravats over his arm.

'They?'

'Where is Jamie? I just went by the nursery. He's not there.'

'I don't know for certain, lad. They've been all around. Took her to the stream this morning right after you left for The House. They sent leaf and stick boats over the waterfall to the Amazon in the north bay.'

Benneit tugged at his cravat and tossed it on the bed. He was exhausted and worried and the carefree image Angus's words evoked didn't have the expected uplifting effect on his spirits.

'It is afternoon now and it's raining. I presume they returned safely from Brazil?'

'Of course, Your Grace. They went to mark where those boats are likely to sail in the Map Room. Then they had nuncheon and went to the schoolroom to read and then the sun came out and they went to the copse to see how the bird-house we finished building yesterday is faring and then they came back for Mrs Merry's scones and then...'

'Are you annoyed at me, Angus? Have I ruined too many cravats? Evicted too many tenants? Sold your unborn child to a lowlander?'

Again Angus's face poked out of the dressing room, this time scars first.

'Ye sound a tad annoyed yerself, Your Grace.'

'Since you only call me "Your Grace" when we're in public or when you wish to goad me, you shouldn't be surprised.'

'Mayhap that's because this is the umpteenth time in the past three days you've asked me where they are. She's a grown woman and responsible; she'll not let Jamie stray. If ye dinna trust her, tell her to stay within the walls and be done with it. Or better yet, spend some time with them so you can see for yourself if she is trustworthy. Your Grace.'

Benneit counted to ten. Then to twenty. Then he gave up and left the room.

It was perhaps not provident that the first person he saw as he stalked downstairs was Mrs Langdale with Flops trailing in her wake.

'Mrs Langdale!'

She turned and Flops obediently flattened himself at her feet like a dropped muff, only his pink tongue visible through the mop of hair. In her grey frock and her hands clasped in front of her she looked even more like a demure nun. Two weeks ago he would likely have accepted that meekness at face value. Now he no longer was certain what she was. Misleading, certainly. A sham, most definitely.

Perhaps he had miscalculated asking her to stay a whole month. She was taking up entirely too much space in the castle. Even though he had been absent most of the last three days, from the moment he returned in the afternoons it was evident she had infiltrated the workings of the castle as effectively as weevils burrowed into hardtack.

'Yes, Your Grace?' she prompted as he stood and seethed.

'Where is Jamie?'

'In the nursery, Your Grace.' Her brows rose, fixing him with her Great Grey-Eyed Stare. Instead of disconcerting him this time, it added to his aggravation and he latched on to the only grievance he could reasonably find.

'I hear you have been to the north bay.'

'Did you, Your Grace?'

'I believe I told you that was one place you were not to take Jamie, did I not?'

'You did, Your Grace.'

He clawed together the scraps of his control.

'Then why, pray tell, did you take him there?'

'I did not, Your Grace.'

'Stop calling me...' He dragged in an audible breath. 'You just said you did take him there.'

'No, Your Grace. You said you heard I took him there.'

'Are you saying you did not take him there?'

'I am saying as little as humanly possible at the moment, Your Grace.'

Benneit pressed his hand to his brow. He felt physically hot with frustration and fury. He had been utterly right about this woman. She was a menace, a bane, one of those Highland curses that clung as stubbornly as a good Scottish feud. Centuries ago he could have sent her to plague the McCrieffs and they probably would have settled their feud just for the price of taking her back, saving the two clans generations of grief.

'Come with me, Mrs Langdale.' He moved towards the stairs and stopped. She had not moved. 'Pray accompany me to the library, Mrs Langdale.'

'Of course, Your Grace.'

'Benneit.' The name exploded from him and she blinked and something, a fugitive glimmer of laughter, narrowed her eyes for a moment and softened the prim mouth. Not a Highland curse, but an English garden pixie sent north to work away at the Scottish fortitude from within.

'You are a menace, Mrs Langdale.'

'And you are jealous, Your Grace.'

'Jealous!'

'As green as the glen. And it serves you right.'

She walked past him down the stairs and after a moment of stunned shock he followed her.

'Jealous of what?'

'Jealous that Jamie and I are outside enjoying ourselves while you are either cooped up like the saddest of counting-house clerks or off on errands from dawn till dusk simply because you don't trust anyone. Well, hardly anyone. You trust Angus, but there is a limit to the amount of responsibility that poor man can shoulder. I think you trust Ewan and Mrs Merry, but I am not quite certain of that.'

They reached the library and she stopped in the middle of the room. He remained standing by the door, his mind searching for a reasonable response to this barrage. He fell back on pettiness, regretting the words even as he spoke them.

'You are correct, I trust Angus and he told me you were sailing stick boats in the north bay.'

'No, he didn't.'

'Yes, he…' He pulled himself short. How the devil did she make herself sound so reasonable while he felt reduced to the level of Jamie?

He wasn't jealous. He was tired, worried, on edge. Ever since they returned to the castle, it was worse than ever and building. It should be quite the opposite—he was coming closer and closer to solving Lochmore's woes. He should be delighted with himself. In a year or two all his concerns for Jamie's future might be put to rest. But he didn't feel delight. Just growing gloom, a sense of something slipping out of his grasp— the future solidifying into stone—hard, grey, un- yielding. Just like the castle.

She took a step forward, unclasping her hands and raising them slightly in a peculiar show of concession.

'We sailed them down the small waterfall into the north bay. We never went down the cliff path and Angus was with us so I am quite certain he reported accurately, though he, too, might have wished to goad you a little. He worries about you, too.'

He worries about you, too.

The words flicked at him, but he shook them off.

She might have wished to goad him, but it cer- tainly was not out of worry, unless she was begin- ning to consider him one of her charges to prod into correct behaviour. He did not need people worrying about him.

'Angus is a natural worrier. I apologise for… accusing you.'

'Apology accepted, Your Grace. Is there anything else you wished to say to me?'

He searched his mind for something. She had reclasped her hands, now like a pupil patiently but hopefully awaiting dismissal. Contrarily he decided to thwart that unflatteringly obvious wish to escape his presence.

'Sit down for a moment. Please.'

He indicated the armchair by the fire and she sat. Against the warm burgundy brocade her grey dress looked glummer than ever. It was a pity she did not wear livelier colours; something that would not contrast unfavourably with her soft complexion and grey eyes. It might help, too, if she stopped dragging her hair back into that uncompromising bun. It had looked far more appealing that first night when they arrived, tied back with a ribbon and still damp from her bath. Jamie was right, her hair was a pretty colour— not wheat but barley just after harvest, no longer brittle, softening as it passed its prime.

'Yes, Your Grace?'

He started at the prompt.

'I hate when you call me that. How the devil do you succeed in injecting so much contempt into a title?'

Her eyes widened in surprise.

'Contempt?'

'You hardly even realise it, do you? Is this another of your tools of quiet insurrection? Like the great grey-eyed stare?'

Her cheeks turned gently pink. Even her blushes were restrained. What would it take to unravel her? Force that blush into real heat?

She unclasped her hands and ran them down her thighs, an unconscious gesture of discomfort that relaxed him. It was ridiculous to take her so seriously and unkind to challenge what few weapons she had in this hostile world.

'I apologise, Mrs Langdale. I have no right to berate you. In truth, I am very grateful you are here with Jamie. As you can see I am very busy and likely to remain so for the upcoming weeks and the fact that we have passed several days without Jamie throwing one of his tantrums, or at least without my knowing of any tantrums, is reason for celebration. It also leads me to realise that his difficult behaviour is indeed the result, at least in part, of loneliness. A child his age should not be alone… I mean, without steady companionship. I am not enough for him any longer.'

The truth of that struck him. For two years— no, longer—practically since Jamie's birth he had become utterly involved in his son's life, setting them up as a unit apart. In the year since his father's death something was beginning to shift and it was as unsettling to him as it probably was to Jamie.

He went to the window. The study was one of the few rooms on this level he had an unobstructed view of the water. It was raining again and the horizon was blurred into the sky. They might as well have been underwater, or in the clouds. Somewhere closed in, sealed off. He moved away, towards the fire, aware she was watching him, a slight frown between her delicate brows.

Her ease struck him again as peculiar. She might be a widow, but she was still young and he was not accustomed to young women watching him with such blatant ease unless they were intent on attaching his interest.

'Jamie is a lovely boy,' she said. 'But it is natural he needs more companions. There is nothing wrong with that, Your Gr—'

She flushed, clearly uncomfortable with his title after his previous comment, making him feel even more like a churlish fool. Why the devil did he keep flying off the handle with her?

'I apologise. I should not have said what I did earlier, but I would still prefer you call me Lochmore rather than "Your Grace". No, I would prefer Benneit, but I dare say that is too informal for your proper English soul. In any case, it is rather pointless to insist on formality. As you can see the castle is rather sparsely inhabited.'

'Yes, I noticed that.' She smiled. 'It is rather nice.'

'Nice?'

'Yes. There were always at least two or three dozen servants at Uxmore and even I could not keep track of some of the under-footmen's names, they changed so often. I find this skeleton crew quite relaxing. Everyone is so…comfortable with each other.'

He laughed.

'I am impressed you found a virtue in it. Or is this another Mrs Minerva fabrication?'

'I am quite serious. It reminds me a little of the parsonage where I grew up. It was a tiny little hamlet, but everyone was very much part of our little world.'

He sat down, curious.

'How did you come to live with the Uxmores?'

'My father died when I was eleven and the living at the parsonage went to another man. My mother and I went to live with Lady Theale. When my mother died Lady Theale sent me to Lord Uxmore's household to help with the children.'

'How old were you when you went to the Uxmores?'

'Sixteen.'

Her eyes no longer met his. It was almost schoolgirl's recitation, without inflection. She might not be an actual servant, but it was servitude none the less. No wonder she had adored her Alfred—he must truly have appeared like a knight in shining armour out of any young girl's dream. And but for a trick of fate and her husband's pointless accident she would be still a contented wife and probably a mother of her own children. The gap between that possibility and her reality must rankle all the more now that it had been snatched from her.

'Is that all, Your—Lochmore?' She stumbled over the name, drawing out the last syllable as if unsure how to pronounce it, and it ended in a near purr. The hair on his nape rose and he shifted in his armchair.

'I suggest we abandon formality while we are at the castle. It is not as if there is anyone here to insist on proprieties. Call me Benneit and I shall follow Jamie's lead and call you Jo. Joane does not suit you.'

Perhaps he should not have added that, even if she herself made that point. But then she smiled, that sudden full-bloom smile that had made him first think of a garden pixie—mischievous, whimsical, bursting with life. Her lips looked fuller when she smiled, warmer and softer to the touch. Then it was furled back, but a smile remained, hovering and tentative.

'That would be easiest. But I reserve the right to resort to "Your Grace" when I see fit.'

'You mean when you wish to goad me.'

'Precisely, Benneit.'

It was only marginally less unsettling than her pronunciation of Lochmore, but he smiled at her determined grasping at his olive branch.

'Well, if you do resort to it, be warned I might retaliate with Cousin Joane.'

Her little nose wrinkled.

'I hate that most of all. I shall have to dole out my taunts with care, then.'

'That is all I ask. Or better yet, desist altogether.'

She stood, shaking out her sack skirts, and instinctively he stood.

'No, then you would have no excuse to lose your patience with me and that would make you even crosser.'

She was gone before he could respond, which was just as well. He turned to the window. The grey skies were turning to dusk and the fire was fading. It was too late now, but tomorrow he would make the effort to return in time to read Jamie a bedtime story.

Chapter Twelve

'I thought we were riding to the village, Jamie.'

'There's another path.' Jamie's eyes slid away from hers as he urged his pony onwards down the left side of the fork in the road.

Jo cast a glance back at the village of Lochmore and nudged her steed into motion, wondering what Jamie was up to. He had sulked all morning and so she had finally given in and agreed to ride with him to the village, but now it appeared he had other plans in mind.

She liked the village and it certainly looked inviting in the sunshine. The sky was as clear as a bolt of silk and the turquoise blue was reflected in the bay where a few fishing boats lingered. The rest were dots on the ruler-straight horizon separating blue from blue. Pretty cream-coloured houses lined the port and radiated out in a series of small winding roads and a wide white-watered burn spilled into the bay, marking the edge of the village beyond which a forest rose up towards the mountains in the distance.

For a moment she remained caught in this perfect image, wondering what it would be like to live in such a place. A small house of her own. Perhaps a friend or two. She was an impecunious widow, so surely social conventions would not bar her from forming friendships outside her own class? Perhaps a place like this even needed a schoolmistress? Would the Duke object if she chose to stay in his domain?

'This way, Jo.'

Jamie's impatient tones penetrated her foolish dreams, recalling her to the present and to her immediate problem. His little steed was surefooted and quite fleet for its size and after a moment Jo spurred hers on as well. Jamie was intent on something, that was clear, and perhaps it was better to indulge his silent insistence.

'Very well. Lead on, Lord Glenarris.'

He grinned at her, his eyes sparkling, and some of her malaise eased. At least one Lochmore found her entertaining.

They crested another rise and Jamie pulled his pony to a halt, which was lucky because Jo could only stare at the apparition. It was no Scottish cottage or glum castle, but a large, beautiful house built along classical lines in a pale, muted gold stone that could not possibly be indigenous. It stood on a low cliff, but the grounds fell away behind it into an extensive walled garden whose colourful wildness appeared perfectly intentional.

It was such a peculiar touch of England in the raw Scottish landscape around the castle that she felt her eyes prick with sudden homesickness, even though there was no home to pine for.

By the time she reached Jamie he had tethered his pony and was knocking on the large door that stood between twin colonnades. Her confusion increased as the door opened and Angus scowled out at them, his frown shifting to surprise as he saw Jo and Jamie.

'Mrs Langdale!'

'Angus?'

Before she could even formulate a coherent question, Jamie sneaked past Angus.

'Wait,' Angus said, but Jamie was already darting down the hallway. Jo hurried after him. She had no idea what was afoot, but she did not want Jamie to get into trouble. At the end of the corridor Jamie opened the door and rushed in and she followed, ready with apologies.

She stopped two steps into the room, all thoughts of apologies and precocious children evaporating.

It was not properly a room but a conservatory, with all of one wall constructed of tall glass windows overlooking a green expanse compassed by high shrubbery and populated by a host of sculptures of strange beasts. Her gaze roamed with awe over these creations until it settled on a rather different beast which was glaring back at her.

Benneit Lochmore stood by the mantelpiece, dressed far more finely than was his wont at the castle, and so handsome her heart gave a few stuttering beats before recovering. She turned at a movement to her right to see a young woman seated on a sofa dressed in a lovely pink dress embellished with ribbons of darker rose that high-lighted her abundant bosom and reddish-brown hair. She smiled, a little questioningly, but before anyone could speak, Jamie reached his father and tugged something from his pocket.

'Look, Papa, I found this. It's a gift for Braw Tumshie!'

Jamie's words forced Benneit to turn to his son. 'That is lovely, Jamie, but I am busy at the moment, as you can see. Angus!' It wasn't quite a bellow, but it brought Jo out of her reverie and Angus to the door.

'He ran in, Your Grace,' Angus said, his embarrassment comical on his six-and-a-half-foot frame.

'I tried to stop him,' Jo said, her throat tight with embarrassment and something she could not name. It was one thing knowing Benneit was probably visiting his mistress, it was another thing to come face to face with her. It was none of her business, but she felt breathless, even a little ill.

'That is quite all right,' the woman said, her voice low and pleasant and with an unmistakable Highland lilt. 'Hello, Jamie. How are you?'

'I am well, Lady Tessa.' Jamie's reply was wary but as the woman smiled his shoulders lowered a little. Out of her confusion a cog shifted in Jo's mind like a clock coming to life. Lady Tessa. Not his mistress, but the woman Benneit was to marry. As in the spiral staircase, Jo felt the world recede a little, her ears humming. She heard Benneit introduce her, the woman greet her and her own voice replying, her cheeks stretching into a polite smile. Then the world came back with a sharpness that planted an ache in the centre of her forehead. She wondered if she could sit because suddenly the world felt too large for her.

'Go with Angus, now, Jamie,' Benneit was saying to Angus, but just then a stocky man strode into the room, his red hair peppered with grey.

'Hello, is this young Jamie? Come say your hellos, boy!'

Jamie started at the man's booming voice and turned to face him, his hand reaching out to grasp Jo's. She clung to him as much as he clung to her.

'Papa, this is Mrs Langdale, Jamie's cousin

from England,' Lady Tessa intervened softly, deflecting her father from Jamie. 'Mrs Langdale, this is my father, Lord Aberwyld of McCrieff.'

'Ah! A cousin! Welcome, welcome. How do you like the Highlands, then?'

'Yes... I mean, very much, my lord...'

'Good, good. Well, say your goodbyes now, Tessa. The carriage is waiting and we'd best be off if we're to reach home in time for supper. We will see you again at the ball, Lochmore. A pleasure to make your acquaintance, Mrs Langdale.'

Jo mumbled something in return. She could not quite name the emotions struggling inside her, but pleasure was definitely not among them.

'I will see you on your way,' Benneit said. 'Wait here, Jamie. Mrs Langdale.'

Jamie prowled the room restlessly as they waited and Jo wanted to do the same. She kept her body still, but her mind prowled along with Jamie, approaching and then shearing away from the truth. When Benneit returned to the room he did not look at her, but went down on his haunches in front of Jamie.

'You know you only come here with me, Jamie, don't you?'

Jamie's hand reached out towards Benneit, but then fell.

'You didn't come to say goodnight or good

morning and I wanted to see you. And I wanted to show Jo the dragons. Are you very cross?'

'No. But next time you wait for me to bring you, understood? I explained to you that I will be busy for a while.'

Jamie shrugged, his mouth flattening into a stubborn line. Jo knew the proper thing would be for her to take Jamie's hand, apologise and leave. Instead she went to the window to inspect the beasts in the garden. They were larger, also constructed from driftwood and stones. And they were wondrous.

'Is that a lion?' she asked, painfully aware of the absurdity of her question.

'Angus, take Jamie to the summer parlour. I will be along presently.'

Jo's confusion narrowed into panic—she did not want to be alone with Benneit Lochmore. Not until she found her footing and chased off this strange rawness. It did not help that Benneit's surface calm shattered the moment the door closed.

'I do not believe I authorised your taking Jamie out of the castle grounds.'

She had no defence, but his anger and her confusion made her dig in her heels.

'I do not believe you did, Your Grace.'

'Don't play prim governess with me, Mrs Langdale. You are at fault here.'

'So? Dismiss me. He told me we were going to the village. I had no idea he would come here, or even what *here* is. I apologise if we have incommoded you, but if all you have to say is that I am at fault you are welcome to do so and then you may go to the devil, because you are just as much at fault. Would it really have cost you so much to come say goodnight to your son once during the last few days rather than leave us to cope with his loneliness?'

'I have been occupied...'

'Evidently.' She sniffed in disdain and he growled—there was no other name for that low rumble of frustration.

'What the devil is that supposed to mean?'

'Nothing, Your Grace. Now we should return to the castle. Jamie will be hungry.'

'Angus will feed him. Sit down!'

She was so surprised by the bark she sat.

'Since I was born, half the people on Lochmore land were forced out in clearances to make way for sheep and cattle and kelp kilns. My grandfather and father paid them a pittance to go to the Carolinas or to Canada and kept those that stayed quiet by encouraging them to build illegal whisky stills like everyone else in the Highlands. We made a king's ransom off wool and beef during the war, but then my father came to believe all credit for this success was his alone, so when Napoleon escaped from Elba he decided we were in for another profitable stretch of war and bet Jamie's future on that eventuality. While everyone was delighted Waterloo put an end to another decade of war, my father realised he had lost half of all he had gained in years. If he hadn't suffered a stroke, I might not have been able to prevent him from engaging in another clearance.

'As it was, I spent the last two years trying to ensure Jamie does not inherit an encumbered estate with a justifiably resentful populace. Now I have an opportunity to do something that could not only keep us above water, but create new work and hope. And for that I need the McCrieffs' support and some peace and quiet while I convince people who have better things to do with their funds that a large distillery in a remote corner of the Highlands is not some mad gamble, but a serious commercial concern that can turn a profit. So I beg your pardon if I am a little distracted with trying to secure my son's future and do not have time to indulge your snide remarks and Jamie's tantrums, *Mrs Langdale.*'

Jo felt about two inches high. No wonder he had looked so worn and worried. She thought of the castle running on a minimum of staff…his hesitation to hire someone to help McCreary. Her contrition cleared away the strange fog that had possessed her.

'I'm sorry, Your Grace. I did not mean to add to your burdens. I told you I can go back to England, there is no need…'

His stern look faded in a sudden smile.

'We are not in such dire straits—wool and kelp are still profitable and we've contained the worst of the damage my father wrought so we are no longer in debt, which is more than can be said for most of the clans. The McCrieffs aren't looking to marry into the Lochmores out of affection, believe me. But until I am certain we can go forward with the distillery I do not wish to create expectations I might not be able to satisfy. I want everything in place before I speak—the location, the plans, the funding and, unfortunately, the consent of the McCrieffs.' He hesitated. 'That is particularly critical, even more than I thought at first. The engineers I brought to the village confirmed my fear we need more fresh water than our own loch and the burn can provide and that means we depend on Lord Aberwyld's goodwill.'

'I see.' She did see. It was not merely clan politics or personal preference behind the upcoming marriage, but the key to Jamie's future.

'I should not be telling you any of this—no one but Angus and a representative of mine in London knows the whole of it, not even McCreary. I know I can trust you not to speak of this, but I need you to understand why I cannot be there for Jamie as I would wish at the moment.'

From two inches high she felt herself begin to expand again at his confidences.

'I will do my very best, Your Grace. But I can be of help with McCreary at least. Won't you make use of me there?'

She held out her hand without thinking and he took it and smiled, then completed her pleasant agony by raising and brushing his lips lightly across her knuckles, his breath whispering against the sensitive skin between her fingers.

He remained like that for a moment, suspended.

'You always smell of roses.' The words were only a murmur. It could have been an innocuous observation, but her body reacted as if he had somehow magically made her clothes slither to the ground, her breasts tightening, readying themselves to be touched. A burst of Jamie's laughter came from down the hall and Benneit let go of her hand and went to the door.

'Come. Angus will likely have set aside some tarts to fortify you and Jamie on the ride back. I must still review some documents when I return to the castle, but I promise to read Jamie a bedtime story today. You may commend my obedience now, Mrs Langdale.'

She preceded him out the door, but kept her head down, still too shaken to jest. She wished she could be worldly. No doubt someone like Bella would have taken such a comment and gesture in her stride, made light of it, perhaps flirted a little and moved on. He probably thought her terribly gauche, just as she was six years ago. She tried to think of something light-hearted, but instead the question popped into her head.

'Who is Braw Tumshie?'

'How do you…? Oh, yes, Jamie. Come with me. I will introduce you.'

He clasped her elbow and guided her outside, round the corner of the house to a low wall with a gate with stone steps leading downwards to a stone and wood zoo surrounded by a lush garden.

'Tumshie means turnip. The lion in the back there was named Tumshie after the shape of his head.'

The lion named turnip stood in a corner, shaded by the trees and the back of a vine-draped bower, his head a little raised as if catching a scent. His body was a combination of a gnarled trunk and slate-like stones, and his mane a fine web of interwoven branches. The eyes looked like obsidian, pitch dark but so deep she could feel their sadness. At its feet was a pile—mostly of stones, but also the broken arm of a toy, a few pieces of metal and other oddments. Clearly Jamie's offerings.

'Who made these marvels?'

Benneit surveyed the garden and for a moment she thought he would not answer.

'My father built this house for my mother. She was English and loved gardens, but her efforts to bring her plants to the castle knot garden in the inner bailey failed. She brought a horticultural friend of hers here and he identified this place as the most auspicious and she decided this would be her garden retreat. After I was born she became ill and that was when my father built this house for her in the image of her childhood home. It was outrageously extravagant, but it became her retreat and now it is mine.'

'She made these?'

'Yes. Like Jamie, we would gather driftwood from the beaches and she would make these.'

'And she painted the maps. She was very talented.'

'Unfortunately. Come, we should return.'

She touched the tips of the webbed mane.

'Why unfortunately? You should be proud.'

'Her horticultural interests were tolerable, barely, but a Duchess of Lochmore playing with sticks and stones was not a source of pride, Mrs Langdale. It was bad enough that she was English.'

'Is that you or your father speaking?'

The fury was so immediate she stepped back. She had not seen that expression before. She had seen him surly, annoyed, sometimes angry, but never furious. It was an answer in itself. He bent and picked up a stone and for a moment she had an absurd image of a biblical stoning of wayward, outspoken women, but he merely balanced it on the rump of a miniature horse. He did not speak, just stood turning and twisting the balanced stone, and she decided to press her advantage.

'Jamie was so happy to come here and he clearly adores these sculptures. He sees all this for what it truly is—a wonder. It lit him up from inside when we found the perfect treasure to bring to the turnip lion. Don't turn that into something shameful for him as he grows.'

'Do you know I considered sending you back to London in Carlisle, Mrs Langdale?'

'Only in Carlisle?'

'Blast you, Jo. Why can you not mind your own business?'

'I won't say another word.'

'I would as soon believe Napoleon is delighted

to find himself on St Helena as believe that,' he muttered, but the anger was gone and he gestured back towards the house.

Jamie jumped down from his seat by a laden table in a lovely room with a view of the sea. She smiled reassuringly at him, but it was his father's face he sought and Benneit swung him into his arms.

'Have you eaten it all or left us anything, Jamie?'

Jamie's face relaxed, his arms curving cautiously around his father's neck. Benneit sat with him on the window seat and extracted the stone from his pocket.

'Now show me the dragon's eye again. Here in the light.'

Jo sat silently as Jamie's pent-up worry spent itself in a tumble of chatter. Benneit listened, his eyes on his son, half-smiling, but there was a look in his eyes that brought a bruising ache to Jo's heart. She wondered if the sadness she saw there was for Jamie, himself, Bella, or perhaps all of them.

How much did he miss her glorious, beautiful cousin? She had always presumed he must be heartbroken to lose someone so lovely and accomplished and charming and…perfect, but with each passing day she found it harder and harder to reconcile the Benneit before her with Bella's husband.

'Will you pour, Mrs Langdale?'

She started and glanced up at Angus as he placed the tea tray on the table.

He was smiling and there was a complicity in his blue eyes that made her smile back.

'With pleasure, Angus.'

In the end Benneit chose to ride back with them to the castle. Jamie rode in the lead, stopping his pony occasionally to search for more treasures. The sun was directly overhead and the flat, flat sea looked so inviting she wished they could just keep riding straight into it.

'Can one swim here?' she said into the silence and Benneit laughed.

'If you don't mind freezing your... If you don't mind freezing. This isn't Brighton.'

She sighed.

'I went swimming once with Alfred. In Torquay. We went there right after our marriage and it was wonderful. There is nothing like it. I wish I could do that again, even just once.'

He did not answer, just paused where the path was closest to the cliff and looked out over the stretch of sea. She stopped as well, wondering if she had said something wrong. Perhaps she had reminded him of his own marriage and loss. The thought doused her pleasure.

'Lady Theale said she plans to find you a husband,' he said to the horizon.

'I beg your pardon?'

'Lady Theale said...'

'No, I heard you, I merely... Did she?'

His mouth softened once more. 'Don't glare at me. I am merely repeating what she said.'

'How generous of her.'

'She should find you a prince. You do a marvellous impression of affronted royalty.'

'No, she should find herself something more productive to do than meddle in...' She snapped her mouth shut.

'My sentiments precisely. As they were one morning three weeks ago when she dropped you on my doorstep.' His smile took the sting out of his words.

'You can always drop me right back. The moment you wish me to leave, you have merely to say so.'

'Prickly, prickly,' he admonished, laughing, his eyes as green as the hills behind him, softening the austere planes of his face. A wave of answering happiness swept through her, shocking her. It was both foreign and utterly familiar, tossing her back years and years to warm summer afternoons playing with her friends in the orchard behind the vicarage.

'That's better,' he said. 'Do you know, I don't believe I ever saw you smile once all during that Season in London, which is a pity. It is a potent entity, that smile. Were you afraid of stealing Celia and Bella's suitors away if you did?'

It was a gallant thing to say, even if it was a lie. Coupled with the sparkle of mischief in his eyes, it warmed her further.

'I don't remember much about those months. Just that I wanted to be elsewhere. Timidity is the worst way to approach a London ballroom, I'm afraid.'

His eyes narrowed as he leaned forward in his saddle, his mouth still soft in a smile that was peculiarly intimate.

'You were never timid, Jo. It would have been better for you if you had been. Knowing you now, I can see you were merely blazingly angry and resentful underneath that icy veneer. I read a travel journal of a man who lived for a year in Naples in the shadow of Vesuvius which was nothing but a still and silent mountain, but all the while he was aware that at any moment the whole of the Pompeian plane could be eradicated in a burst of fire and brimstone. He said the quiet air quivered with sheathed violence. It is intimidating to say the least.'

'That sounds horrible.' She tried to speak lightly but her voice shook. His words hurt all the worse for the surge of joy that preceded them. He eased his horse closer and reached out and grasped her gloved hand, engulfing it.

'It wasn't meant as an insult, quite the opposite. You are an impressive young woman. Under different circumstances you could have had all those shallow fools eating out of your hand.'

She snorted.

'Yes, if I had been pretty and wealthy and everything I'm not. This is a foolish conversation.'

'I thought you were a better judge of people and their motivations. If you had used an ounce of that passion and determination to win people over instead of keeping them at bay, your lack of wealth would have been overlooked, believe me.'

'But not my lack of looks.'

'There is nothing amiss with your looks. Everyone wears masks in society. I think you chose the wrong one.'

His hand was still holding hers, another breach of propriety she did not call attention to, but it was his smile, softening as his eyes skimmed over her face, that set her heart thudding fast and hard. She was old enough now to know men would at least consider most all females as physical objects, attractive or not, and there was no reason to assume his assessment meant anything more than that. Alfred had been very open with her and had answered her questions as honestly as possible and shattered quite a few of her foolish notions about love of body and mind.

Benneit's gaze lingered on her mouth, his lashes lowering to shield the winter-green-and-grey irises, and her heart went into full gallop, heat lashing up her neck and cheeks, pinching at her skin. She felt scalded, but she shivered, clamping her legs tightly about the saddle. The breeze carried his scent to her—clean soap and musk over the coolness of spring water. Her lids felt heavy, her whole body felt heavy, as if she must sink into something, lean on something. Somewhere apart she knew these sensations were utterly out of proportion with Benneit's mild show of interests—it was no more than what she had seen on Alfred's face a dozen times at the passing of an attractive woman in the village square. But that little voice of caution was growing fuzzy and weak, and her hand was already beginning to turn under his.

His gaze fell and he withdrew his hand a little abruptly, a faint flush spreading over the sharp lines of his cheekbones. He looked over to where

Jamie was ambling back towards the grazing pony. 'Come, I think Jamie has found another treasure. I hope it isn't a sheep's jawbone like last time we took the cliff path.'

Chapter Thirteen

Benneit moved between the window and the desk and back again. He should not have sent Angus to summon Jo. Perhaps she was resting. It was foolish to bother her, even if she had made the offer herself. He did not like the thought that she might be comparing him to the Uxmores, who clearly squeezed her until the pips squeaked.

Still, she *had* offered, and McCreary could use the help while he was occupied with the engineers' plans.

She had smiled as she offered, too; that soft, unguarded smile that was so sincere and warm it was like a caress. She had not believed him, but he knew his sex well enough to know that had she made use of that smile, of her tumbling laugh, of the non-judgemental understanding that shone occasionally from her grey eyes, she would have had a trail of all-too-willing suitors even without a dowry and the beauty of some of the debutantes.

Clever Langdale for seeing what others had missed. It was clear their love had overcome her defences. Instead of a dormant volcano, Langdale secured himself a sweet, giving and supportive young woman. If only Langdale been less reckless, she would still be where she deserved. In his home, his bed…

The soft knock at the door dragged him out of his thoughts.

'Enter.' His voice was a little too loud and he clasped his hands behind his back, annoyed at his discomfort. She entered and paused just inside the door, looking as neat as usual despite the ghastly grey dress.

He cleared his throat, turning his mind to business.

'Thank you for coming. A word before we begin. I have been remiss about making provisions for you after we amended our agreement to extend your stay, Mrs Langdale. Please give Mrs Merry a list of anything you need and what she cannot provide or purchase in the village, Angus can purchase on his weekly trips to Kilmarchie or when we go to Glasgow.'

'If I need anything, I can purchase it myself in the village, I am sure.'

Her words were stiff, but her cheeks turned a little pink and her discomfort relieved some of his and he smiled.

'I see how it is to be. Every offer of goodwill on my part will be politely rebuffed, but if I tell you I do not need your help with Jamie or the accounts you will regard it as proof of my obstinate insularity. Double standards can be very annoying, Mrs Langdale.'

She didn't disappoint him. Her eyes crinkled at the corners and the pixie smile bloomed.

'Are you trying to embarrass me into accepting your largesse, Your Grace? All this sheep rearing has clearly made you believe people are just as easily herded.'

'I would say you have more characteristics of a goat than a sheep, Mrs Langdale. A mule even. Two very stubborn animals.'

She laughed. 'Mrs Merry and Beth have already provided me with all I need for my stay, even a pair of stout boots and a thick cloak, so you need not worry. Now show me the ledgers and we shall see if I can offer anything half as useful in return.'

He stood aside as she went to sit at his desk.

Clearly the grey-eyed pixie would not willingly accept any favours from him, which meant she would likely find it hard to accept the dresses he had commissioned from Bella's old seamstress in Glasgow. Hopefully they would arrive soon because he was tired of seeing her in these sacks.

Perhaps he should even tell Mrs Merry to accidentally spill tar on these grey horrors and then

Jo would have no choice but to accept the new gowns when they came. Though Jo Langdale might be stubborn enough to remain in her chemise just to make a point.

Unfortunately that thought led to a memory of that moment on the ship—her wet skirts caught about her legs, the elegant lines revealed...

His senses sank their teeth into the memory— bringing back the scent of the sea air, the crash and hiss of the waves, and then the sudden unwelcome sting of lust and the stretching of his muscles as his body readied itself to reach for her, to clasp about the curve and line of her ankle and move upwards.

Perhaps it was not a good idea to be concerning himself with her wardrobe. Those grey horrors were an antidote to any misplaced ideas. Or at least they should be.

She was leaning over the ledger, one elbow propped on the desk and her forehead on her palm as she reviewed the entries. Her hair was drawn into the usual severe bun, uncovering her nape and just a few soft inches of the sweep of her shoulders. She did not have Bella's perfect milky white skin. In fact, he remembered Bella once saying it was a pity her cousin was so sallow, blaming it on a childhood spent out of doors like a village urchin. He had been too enamoured with Bella during that summer in London to feel more than a twinge of conscience at Bella's occasional cutting remarks, writing them off as the natural bias of someone who was so extraordinarily beautiful she strove to raise the world to her standard. Now he wondered if Bella felt some envy for her unfortunate cousin, or at the very least resentment that Jo so evidently refused to adore her as everyone, including himself, had.

He did not think Jo Langdale merited the term sallow. Her skin was a few shades darker than ivory, a faintly warm colour that would probably take the sun well.

'Do you freckle?'

Her eyes flew up and he felt his cheeks warm in embarrassment. Had he really asked that aloud?

'I mean, if you are to spend time out of doors often with Jamie… Perhaps Mrs Merry might procure you some…cream. Bella was always in a fright about freckles.'

She touched her cheek with a look of bemusement, as if the freckles were already spreading like the measles.

'I don't… Well, I do freckle a little, but I don't use creams. I never have. It does not bother me.'

'Never mind then. Disregard it. Do the numbers make any sense to you? Do you think you can review the tallies?'

'Certainly. Your steward's hand is very neat. Yours is quite legible, too, Your Grace,' she added and he smiled.

'You needn't spare my blushes, Mrs Langdale. I don't aspire to Mr McCreary's calligraphic heights. I reserve my patience for other endeavours.'

She leaned back, looking up at him with curiosity and again he felt the strange dislocation. She looked too comfortable in his chair, despite being half-lost in its size.

He stepped back.

'May I leave you with the ledgers, then? I have some business to see to in the village.'

'Of course, Your Grace.'

'Good. Thank you. Don't overtax yourself.'

Her mouth curved, slowly. She could not possibly be aware of his discomfort but he felt peculiarly defenceless, like a child before a headmistress.

'Goodbye, then,' he repeated and retreated before his mouth, mind, or body committed any additional gaffes.

Outside in the forecourt as he swung on to Lochlear's back he glanced up at the window of the estate room. He must truly be unhinged to allow a little grey-eyed pixie to unsettle him like that.

Chapter Fourteen

'"Ou forgot to thow me Fou-ah.'

'And you forgot to swallow before you spoke, Jamie,' Jo replied, not looking up from her book. Jamie responded with a snorted giggle and an audible swallow.

'You can't scold if your eyes are laughing, Jo.'

It was such an adult, perceptive thing for a boy of four to say she could not help laughing.

'Quite right. It was Foula, yes?'

'Yes. Let's go to the Map Room.'

She enjoyed the Map Room almost as much as Jamie. The map of the known world painted on one wall between stacks of bookshelves was even more elaborate than the one in London. It was surrounded by depictions of beasts, both real and mystical and not very accurate, as there appeared to be monkeys off the coast of Wales and what looked like an elephant poking its trunk in the direction of France, while a bear was lying on its back, its paws balancing or scratching at Ireland. She particularly liked the dragon off Zanzibar that Jamie had mentioned in Glasgow, a great scaly monstrosity with eyes like owls glaring back at them. Benneit's mother had clearly been talented.

Jamie rushed forward, pointing to a blue and brown blob along the western shore.

'I made this. Can you guess what it is?'

'Is it a ship?'

Jamie crowed with pleasure.

'You guessed! I will be captain and will sail all the way here…' His finger traced a line across the wall and ended near a triangular shape on the continent of Africa. 'This is a pyramid.'

'Just like in *Desert Boy*,' she approved.

'I never should have bought that book at Hatchard's,' the Duke said behind them.

This time she was not surprised by his sudden arrival. Perhaps his scent reached her before she even realised it—the hint of wind and rainy glens and warm musk.

They might be living in a castle, but in every other respect she imagined Lady Theale and the Uxmores would disapprove of this very informal approach to rearing the next Duke of Lochmore. The Uxmores always insisted on unstinting formality and even at Langdale they dined in state every day. At Lochmore they most often dined in the nursery at a plain wooden table with an unshod four-year-old boy, a dog that looked like the canine version of the long-haired Highland cows that filled the fields, and increasingly often, with the Duke who often arrived wet and wind-blown, alternately dressed in his riding clothes or his shirtsleeves. Once he even came dressed in a traditional kilt after a village meeting. He had apologised for his dress, but she had secretly thought he looked magnificent with the orange and blue plaid fabric about his waist and slung over his shoulder.

'But you love that book, Papa!' Jamie's brow furrowed with worry.

'Of course I do, master explorer. Perhaps I don't want you sailing away.'

'I *will* come home, you know.'

'Good. Where are you sailing now?'

'Jo was going to show me Foula like she promised in London. I've looked everywhere from here to there.' He jumped up along the western coast of Scotland. 'I followed the letters just as we said. F-O-U-L-A. But I cannot find it.'

Benneit swung him into his arms. 'Keep going.'

She watched their profiles. He was dressed in riding clothes, but his cravat was already half-way undone and his hair was ruffled from the wind…or perhaps a woman's hand… She might have been mistaken about The House, but there was no saying he did not have a mistress some-where nearby.

It is none of your business if he does, she reminded herself.

It wasn't the first time these foolish thoughts and suspicions came to taunt her. But they were still less disturbing than the way her body leapt to attention every time he entered a room, like a wan flower suddenly bathed in a ray of sunlight breaking through thick curtains of clouds.

She berated herself for her foolishness, but still she did not look away, absorbing the sight of him just as that plant absorbed the light. With each passing day he was moving further and further away from her memory of the man who had married Bella. Or perhaps she had changed—she was no longer embarrassed by how handsome he was, but she found it harder and harder to look away from his powerful, austere face with the faint aquiline line of his nose and the shadows beneath the sharply defined cheekbones. The man she met six years ago had been charming and smiled more, and yet had been lesser. She did not quite understand this contradiction. But she, too, had been young and arrogant in her own way, defensive and prickly, as he had said. The change in the man before her highlighted everything that had changed in her.

'There! There!' Jamie all but lunged out of his father's hands, reaching for the spot high above the Scottish shore, but Benneit held him easily, his face relaxing into a smile which just like the Scottish sun was rare, but when it came was breathtaking. Jo turned away again to inspect the desert beneath her fingers, soaking in the quiet discussion between them until Nurse Moody appeared in the door. Jamie baulked at going with her, but at his father's promise he could dine downstairs that evening he clapped his hands and agreed to be led away. Jo moved towards the door as well, but Benneit's voice stopped her in the doorway.

'Mrs Langdale. Jo.'

She turned. It was dark outside now and without a fire in the room he was nothing more than a collection of shadows and harsh planes. For a moment he seemed part of the now murky painting on the wall, a figure stepping out of an image of the world that was both promising and terrifying. He moved towards her, out of the shadows, the light of the sconce lamps in the corridor touching the angles of his face with gold. He looked distant suddenly, once again removed from Benneit Lochmore who joined Jamie and her for their simple dinners. He looked like a threat.

'Your Grace?' Her voice shook a little, but not enough, she hoped, to be noticeable.

'I wanted to thank you. I've just been with McCreary in the village and he was telling me, again, how helpful you are. It occurred to me we are perhaps beginning to presume too much upon your generosity. When you are not helping keep Jamie out of trouble you are to feel free to spend your time as you like and go where you wish.'

She raised her chin, a little piqued at this return to formality after the comfortable rapport that appeared to have developed since their visit to The House.

'I am perfectly capable of making my own choices, Your Grace.'

He sighed, a harsh exhalation that was more weary than impatient, and her defences crumbled. She was prickling again.

'I am not being taken advantage of, Benneit. I enjoy sitting with Mr McCreary—I find numbers relaxing. They are so very…undemanding.'

The harsh look on his faced melted into the smile that did so much damage and he moved forward. In the light coming from the doorway she could see how tired he looked. In another life, another body, she might have had the temerity to trace her fingers down his lean cheek, to comfort and soothe. But she was only Jo and she just clasped her hands and waited.

'That is a novel way of looking at accounting. For myself I find numbers annoyingly demanding, especially when they insisted on heading in the wrong direction after the war. I am very glad the accounts have stabilised.'

'Mr McCreary said there might yet be a revival in the prices of wool and kelp, but that struck me as hopeful.'

'Since their substantial rise in the past was the outcome of war, I prefer to pursue other plans to help Lochmore prosper. Meanwhile I am very grateful for your help with McCreary, I am afraid he is tiring more and more easily.'

'He is still very alert, but he could use some assistance. Perhaps you could hire a young clerk when I leave. I believe it would prove an economy in the long run and that way you would be freed from overseeing him. Alfred used to say he enjoyed life far too much to mar it with matters that bored or distressed him. I found it an admirable approach to life. Up to a point, of course.'

'Up to what point?'

'Well, by the time we wed he was quite deeply in debt, trying to expand his stables with very little attention to the cost. I did my best with the accounts and was quite hopeful we could balance out over time. And probably we would have, had he not died so suddenly. Still, at least he did enjoy his horses very much while he lived.'

'And left you in debt.'

'To be fair, the debtors could not touch my

settlement, but nothing remained after the debts were settled and the entailed estates went to his cousin.'

'I am sorry, Jo.'

She shrugged. 'I am still far better off than I was before my marriage so I have no reason to repine. You will be relieved to hear that despite your concerns on other fronts, and despite the falling prices of kelp and wool, according to the accounts the estate is still turning a nice profit.'

'I am relieved to hear it. I would rather not end up like your Alfred.'

'Dead? I sympathise.'

'No! I meant in debt... Really, Mrs Langdale, you have a most inappropriate sense of humour at times.'

'Raise your voice an octave, call me "My Dear Joane" and you would sound just like Lady Theale.'

He straightened, but the stern line of his mouth wavered.

'Are you doing this expressly, Mrs Langdale? You do that with Jamie, too, you know.'

'Do what, Your Grace?'

'Try to distract him from his woes. I assure you I can handle mine. I do not need to have magical mice dangled before me.'

'I wasn't...'

'You most certainly were. And I thought we agreed you would forgo calling me "Your Grace"?'

'You reverted to calling me Mrs Langdale first, I was merely being prudent and following suit.'

'Did I?'

'You did. I notice you do so when I vex you. Which is often.'

His smile formed slowly and her heart pinched at the affection in his eyes. It should have warmed her, but it was like a slap, waking her with her foot poised off the edge of a cliff, wondering how she had gone so far. She didn't want affection, she wanted to touch him, press her palm to the hard expanse of his chest and...explore him.

He must have seen something on her face because he shook his head and cleared his throat and she stepped back from the cliff's edge.

'Speaking of prudence, Mrs Merry informed me that my aunt announced she will descend from her tower for dinner tonight which means we will have dinner in the hall. If you wish to claim the headache and avoid meeting Mad Morag, you have my permission. Unfortunately I cannot do the same. Her forays are as rare as a full week of sunshine, but if baulked of her prey, her hunger only increases. Will you join us?'

'I admit to being curious about her and a little

sorry for her. Mrs Merry and Beth only sigh and roll their eyes when she is mentioned. Surely she is not so objectionable?'

'I will leave you to be the judge of that. Feel free to exercise your Great Grey-Eyed Stare on her as much as you wish.'

Chapter Fifteen

'Hamish never permitted children at the table,' Lady Morag announced as Ewan helped her into her chair on Benneit's right. Benneit sent Jamie a reassuring look, but Jamie was occupied with something under the table and Benneit noted the suspicious snuffling there and sighed. Morag had never approved of dogs. Or of anything he could think of other than whisky.

Without Morag's presence he might even enjoy having dinner in the Hall with Jamie and Jo. But the way Morag was eyeing Jo he didn't doubt his aunt was gathering ammunition for an attack. Perhaps it was best to draw her fire in advance.

'My father might not have approved of children at the table, but he is dead, Aunt Morag. I make my own rules now. In fact, I might rethink who is and who isn't permitted at the table.'

'Impertinence!'

'I agree,' Benneit replied. 'I am Lochmore now, Aunt Morag. Kindly remember that. Ewan, serve Lady Morag some of her favourite so she can drink to my health.'

She snorted, but held out her glass readily

enough. As soon as it was full she turned to inspect Jo again and Benneit braced himself. But Jo merely sat with her eyes wide and as clear as pools of silver and Morag visibly faltered for a moment before recovering.

'I don't like your dress,' she announced in her gravelly voice.

'Neither do I,' Jo replied and Jamie giggled. To Benneit's surprise Morag sniggered as well, casting him a sly look.

'Have Benneit buy you a new one. He's been well trained at that. His Selkie certainly had enough dresses to clothe all the women to Glasgow and back.'

'She thinks my mother was a Silkie,' Jamie whispered to Jo. 'That's a seal person who steals Scotsmen. Which means I am half-seal.'

'Selkie,' Benneit corrected, happy to entertain any distraction. 'A silkie is a chicken from China with soft fur and black skin and bones. I saw one once in a fair in Cambridge. Some people say they are born of a rabbit and a hen.'

Jamie's eyes widened with wonder.

'Is it true, Papa? Can a chicken be born of a rabbit?'

'No, Jamie. Nor was your mother a Selkie, though I know that disappoints you. She was merely English.'

'Bad enough,' muttered Morag. 'It's time Lochmores stopped bringing brides from all corners of the earth. It all started with that Frenchie gel back when. Best marry a clanswoman this time, boy, not another Englishwoman or that gel McCrieff is parading for you.'

Both Benneit and Jamie frowned at the old woman.

'Does Aunt Morag mean Tessa McCrieff, Papa?'

'I don't know what your great-aunt means some days, Jamie.' Benneit said deliberately and Morag cackled and dug into her soup.

'I am taking Jo to the bay again tomorrow, Papa,' Jamie announced. 'Could you come this time?'

The last two words struck hard, as did the lack of conviction in Jamie's voice. It was like Flops's faint pawing at his boot when he joined Jamie for his meal in the nursery—wishful, but resigned to being denied scraps. Benneit mentally ran through all the tasks that awaited him, but there was such a plea in Jamie's voice he shoved them aside.

'Yes, Jamie. I promise.'

Jamie bounced in his chair with a little hoot and a sharp bark under the table alerted Morag to the presence of Flops, providing her with a whole new line of attack. But surprisingly the rest of the meal wasn't as hideous as he had anticipated. Jo met Morag's occasional shots across her bow with her quiet humour and Morag was betrayed twice more into her sniggering laugh, though her malice was never far from the surface and by the time the plates were cleared Benneit was only too happy to retire before Morag decided to bring out the heavy guns.

'Finish your pudding, Jamie, and I'll read you a story before bed.'

'Can Jo listen, too?'

Jo shook her head. 'Tomorrow, Jamie. If you don't mind I will retire early tonight. Our adventures have made me very sleepy. I am not a hardened explorer like you.'

Jamie's mouth sagged at the corners and Benneit steeled himself, but his son merely turned back to his plate. Lady Morag stood.

'I'm done, too. Too much excitement. And I don't like the dog sniffing at my shoes. Filthy things, dogs.'

'That is our cue to retire, Flops. Come, Flops,' Jo said quietly and the dog shuffled out from under the table and panted up at her. 'Goodnight, Lady Morag. Your Grace. Lord Glenarris.'

At the door Lady Morag waved her on and Jo, with a glance back at Benneit, left the hall.

'Got the dog doing as she says, too, eh?' Morag

said as the door closed behind Jo. 'Too clever by half, Miss English.'

'Goodnight, Aunt,' Benneit replied, but Jamie leaned forward, his elbows on the table.

'It's good to be clever, Aunt Morag. Why do you say it like it's bad?'

'Clever is good,' Morag answered. 'Too clever comes back to bite you, boy.'

Jamie giggled.

'Jo doesn't bite. I like her. Please be nice to her so she'll stay, Aunt Morag.'

Lady Morag shrugged.

'I won't be nasty. That'll have to do. She won't stay, though. Won't be room for two women when the McCrieff wench moves in.'

Benneit watched the door close behind her, keeping a firm hold on his temper.

'Shall we go upstairs, Jamie?'

Jamie hopped down from his chair, beaming.

'Yes, let's, Papa.'

As they left the dining room Benneit took Jamie's hand and the boy leaned his head for a brief moment against his arm.

'Don't worry, Papa. I shan't listen to Aunt Morag. I don't think she is half as clever as Jo. Will you marry Lady Tessa?'

Benneit's heart gave a convulsive thud and then paused for a little too long.

'I don't know yet, Jamie,' he lied. 'Would you like having brothers and sisters?'

'I don't know. I think so. I would be a big brother then, wouldn't I?'

'You would.'

Jamie fell silent until they reached the nursery. He stopped in the middle of the room as Benneit went to take the book from the shelf.

'Shall I have to leave my room?'

Benneit turned in surprise.

'What?'

'If you have another boy,' Jamie clarified.

'No, of course not. There are plenty of rooms. Your room is yours, Jamie. Come here.'

Benneit sat on the bedside and Jamie sat beside him.

'What if I don't like them?'

'I think you will, most of the time. Sometimes you won't. I never had brothers or sisters and I always wished I had. I was very jealous of your mother because she had two brothers and two sisters. She probably would have told you that there were some days she did not like them because they could be annoying, but she always loved them. Just as she always loved you.'

'Did she?'

'Good God, yes. You were too young to remember, but never doubt that. Never doubt that I love you, too, above everything.'

'More than your own papa?'

'More than him. That is what happens when you have children.'

'Then why aren't I enough?'

Benneit's throat clenched at the need and fear squeezed into that simple question. He wrapped his arm around Jamie's shoulders.

'I know it is hard to understand, Jamie, but I want you to have more than I had. Brothers and sisters will be part of you for your lifetime. You will have to trust me that they will add more to your life than take away from it. Imagine—you can take them down to the bay and show them your treasures and read stories with them and teach them how to find everything on the map.'

'Like you and Jo do with me.'

He gave Jamie's arm a little rub and picked up the book.

'Like that. Do you remember where you reached in the book?'

'Jo put a leaf in to mark our spot. Right there.' He pointed to the protruding tip of a dried leaf. 'Don't forget to put it back after you read so I can tell her where to continue.'

'I won't forget, Jamie.'

'You will come with us tomorrow to the beach? You did not just say that?'

'I promise. Now hush and listen.'

Chapter Sixteen

Benneit stood on the big flat stone that lay at the foot of the rock fall, watching his son and Jo sifting through a clump of dark brown kelp.

For the third day in a row.

Somehow after joining them the day following the disastrous dinner he found himself promising to join them the next day. Today he didn't even have the excuse of having promised. He had been on his way to the stables when he saw them on the beach and here he was.

He was not accustomed to being herded by a pocket-sized pixie and yet that is precisely what was happening. Though the world was knocking at his door and the fate of Lochmore hung heavy on his shoulders, here he was, spending a third morning this week exploring the bay.

And enjoying himself.

To be fair, since Jo had relieved him of the need to sit with McCreary over the accounts, the least he could do was spend some of that freed time with Jamie.

He wasn't quite sure what he thought of Jamie's insistence Jo accompany them even when he was present. He should find some politic way of reminding Jamie, and her, that she would not be staying. In a couple of weeks she would be gone and it would be only him and Jamie again. At least until he married.

He looked past them to the sea. It was calm today and the sun was shining. His project was proceeding apace, the engineers had approved the location and plans, and the banks received the investors' funds. What had seemed a very precarious gamble just weeks ago now appeared not only feasible but sensible. He had everything to be grateful for and no reason to feel as if the world was closing in on him.

He turned his gaze from the horizon to the woman standing with his son on the beach. The hems of her skirts were dark and heavy with sea water and her hair was a tangle of wisps as the north wind made a mockery of her prim coiffure. She did not look much like Mrs Langdale, but more a girl herself, caught up in Jamie's avid search for exotic discoveries. She looked like part of the Scottish landscape—an unyielding stoicism which hid a raw wildness. It was a peculiar combination. *She* was a peculiar combination. He had not understood her six years ago and he was not certain he was any closer today.

Not that he had bothered trying to fathom her

peculiarity when he had met her that year he fell in love and wed Bella. But even then he had been aware she was different, a cuckoo in the cushy Uxmore nest—strange and strange-looking with her unrelenting grey eyes that would dip downwards in mock modesty. He had always felt uncomfortable around her. Rather as if a whole Greek chorus had entered the room and everyone was tensely awaiting its verdict.

She was definitely still a cuckoo, or a changeling, but at least now he could see that he had been quite correct to feel uncomfortable around her. All that thinking and feeling tamped under her prim exterior… He only wondered how she had kept her tongue safely between her teeth among the Uxmores.

'Papa, look!' Jamie held aloft what looked like a curved piece of metal, covered in slime and barnacles. 'It's a giant's soup bowl from the Mosquito Coast!'

He met Jo's laughing gaze and smiled.

'I'm not eating out of that, thank you, Jamie.'

Jamie laughed and set it aside, plunging elbow deep into the mess of kelp. Jo stood, shaking out her skirts. They flopped wetly against her legs and she sighed, wiping her hands on them.

'Beth and Mrs Merry will despair of me. Yesterday my other dress was rent from the brambles near the copse.'

'Throw the blasted thing away,' Benneit suggested and Jamie giggled.

'You said blasted, Papa.'

'So I did. But you are not allowed to say blasted until you are one and twenty.'

Jamie nodded and inspected Jo's dress.

'Papa should buy you a new dress like Aunt Morag said.'

'Excellent thinking, Jamie. A consensus is forming.' Benneit considered and rejected the idea of telling her he had already asked Mrs Merry to provide Angus with measurements the very day she agreed to stay at Lochmore. She had made no request, but it was clear she had almost no luggage when she arrived and it was unfair she had to stretch her meagre wardrobe for a whole month. Besides, he would not mind seeing her in something other than these grey sacks.

'Nonsense. This is a perfectly serviceable dress,' she replied.

'Try for a little conviction, Mrs Langdale.'

'Well, it is. Cousin Celia kindly had three such dresses made for me the winter I came to stay with her and they are very useful for travelling.'

'Cousin Celia wouldn't know a kindness if it popped out of her morning cocoa and bit her on the nose. She was securing your guilt even as she made you wear this unsightly uniform.'

Perhaps that was a trifle harsh, but she did not seem offended, she merely sighed and detached a strand of kelp from the hem.

'Are you talking about Aunt Celia, Papa?' Jamie asked and at that Jo sent Benneit a frowning look.

'No, your father was talking of another Celia, Jamie.'

'Is she my cousin, too?'

Benneit planted his hands on his hips and grinned down at her.

'Ah, the pitfalls of falsehood. Shall I bring you a shovel so you can keep digging, Jo?'

'Will you buy her a dress, then, Papa?' Jamie insisted, sticking to the essence of the matter.

'I will, Jamie. Several. So you may both frolic in the kelp to your heart's content.'

'Nonsense. Oh, look!' Jo exclaimed, extracting a long silver tube from the mess. Jamie squeaked.

'Treasure!'

Benneit frowned and jumped down from his perch on to the mud.

'Show me.'

'No, I found it and so it is mine,' Jo said, holding the tube away from his outstretched hand. 'And I decide it goes to Jamie.'

Jamie took it with glee, turning it in his hands and brushing away the mud and clinging kelp.

'It's a flute!' Benneit said.

'I knew that,' Jamie answered.

'I thought it was a unicorn's horn,' Jo said in disappointed tones.

'Did not!' Jamie said.

'Well, I hoped it might be. Do you think it is made of real silver? Perhaps it belonged to the mermaid queen's musicians.'

Benneit tapped it.

'Tin.'

Jamie blew on it and a spray of slimy mud spattered down the side of Jo's dress.

'Sorry, Jo,' Jamie said contritely as she wiped at the goo.

'I think it's an improvement,' Benneit said, inspecting the damage. 'It looks like a map of Italy now. And there is Elba. That's where Napoleon escaped from, Jamie.'

'Oh? Where is he now?'

Benneit put his hands on her waist and turned her, pointing to a speck just below her posterior.

'On that island there. St Helena.'

Jo moved away from his grasp, her cheeks hot with embarrassment. Benneit considered apologising for stretching the jest, but it was pleasant to see her so flustered.

'We really should return. The water is rising,' she said and Benneit swung Jamie back on to the rocks. On impulse he turned and took Jo by the waist, swinging her up as well. With a gasp she steadied herself against him, her fingers brushing down the sides of his neck as she leaned her hands on his shoulders, sending whispers of warmth over his skin and tightening his hands on the soft curves of her waist. For a moment he held her between the sand and the rock, her lips parted, revealing lovely white teeth and the tip of a pink tongue that made his tingle with a need to test the sudden conviction she would taste sweet, warm, a little spicy...

She pushed against his shoulders and he raised her the last few inches to deposit her on the rock. She turned and made her way towards where the rocks descended again to the sand. He did not follow right away, until the encroaching waves licked at his boots and he cursed and leapt after them. They continued in silence until he took Jamie's hand and guided them towards the cliff path.

'Shouldn't we go by the Sea Gate?' Jo asked.

'Papa only goes by the cliff path by the chapel, don't you, Papa?'

'I like coming in through the inner bailey,' Benneit answered, avoiding Jo's questioning gaze.

'Besides, I must stop by the stables. Would you like to take your pony out to the village with me tomorrow, Jamie?'

Jamie threw his arms wide in a gesture of such obvious pleasure Jo laughed.

'What horse will Jo ride, Papa?'

He hesitated and Jo interceded.

'You and your papa will go. I shall stay to help Mr McCreary, Jamie.'

'Oh, dull!' Jamie scoffed, but danced ahead up the shore. After a moment Benneit spoke.

'If you would like a decent horse to ride while you are here, you need only speak to Angus. As long as you take a groom with you, you do not need to be limited to rides with Jamie. I presume Langdale ensured you are a fine horsewoman.'

'It was a condition of our union. He would not propose until he saw me at a canter.'

He paused, taken aback, but then burst into laughter at the glint in her eyes.

'How did you meet?' he asked, grateful she was unknowingly smoothing over that strange moment by the rocks. 'He was not of Uxmore's circle as far as I can recall.'

She laughed and again he noticed the softening of her eyes, the tiny lines fanning out and enhancing her air of mischief.

'The first time we met it was in the worst possible place in the world—Almack's. He was in town for Tattersall's settling day and his cousin had all but forced him to attend. He arrived five minutes before they closed the doors and he told me later he planned to be late so he would be barred, but his luck was out, or rather in, as he told me later. We were introduced and we danced, but as usual I was quite dreadfully discouraging; after we wed he told me I treated him as the lowliest of worms. I didn't mean to be awful, but I was so miserable I think I was dreadful to most people I met in London.'

'Was it so bad? Most portionless young women would have been grateful for an opportunity to attend the London Season.'

She walked a little faster, her shoulders curving against the wind. He caught up with her.

'Don't run away, Jo. You can always tell me to mind my business if you do not wish to discuss something.'

'I am not running away. It is cold.'

'Liar.'

She bent to pick up a smooth grey stone, her voice barely a mutter.

'If I had been pretty, or accomplished or...or something, perhaps I would have been grateful.'

He wanted to laugh at the absurdity of her words, but the memory of her—stiff, silent, awkward—made him keep his peace. She, too, had changed through the years, but for the better, unlike him.

'You didn't tell me how you came to wed your Alfred after all.'

Her face softened and warmed once more, and peculiarly he felt the spear-tip of jealousy. It was not right that when he thought of Bella he could conjure up none of the warmth so apparent on Jo's face. He could still make no sense of what he felt after losing Bella—love and resentment and disappointment and sadness all tangled together like a mess of kelp tossed up on the shores after a storm.

'I met him again quite by accident. Celia had just given birth and Lady Theale asked me if I would attend to her.'

'Just as she *asked* you if you would attend to Jamie?'

'Well, since I was helping Cousin Philippa, who is far worse than Celia, I think she was rather doing me a favour.'

'Good God, talk about the choices of the damned.'

'It wasn't that bad. But whatever the case, it was January, and I was travelling and we slipped on the ice and broke a wheel and had to walk to the nearest inn. Then suddenly a man on horseback rode by and I saw it was Alfred, but I never expected him to remember me and certainly not fondly.'

'I gather he remembered you none the less.'

'He did. He was very kind and he put me on his horse and when we were out of sight he mounted behind me, took me to his house where he introduced me to his mother. She had a weak heart, but was very lovely, rather like my own mother. Alfred and I used to laugh that he rescued me just as in the fairy tales. There I was, stranded in the snow, well, a flurry at least, and up he rode on his white steed—which was a grey, in fact, but close enough—and swept me off my feet quite literally. I was not very good as a rescued princess, though. I was very suspicious at first. I even thought he was making an effort to promote me to his mother because he wished to find a companion for her. In fact, when he did propose, I was convinced that was what he was offering me. It took a few confused moments for him to understand we were talking at cross purposes. He enjoyed teasing me about it later.'

She smiled, lost in her memory, and Benneit looked away to the shore below them. Jamie had stopped to inspect something Flops was scratching at and they stopped as well. The sun was dancing on the choppy water. It was a rare, clear, beautiful summer day. There was no rhyme or reason to why he felt annoyed. It was almost as if he begrudged her that happiness just as the Uxmores had. That love.

'Bella painted a very different picture of your Alfred.'

'I wonder how. She never met him, after all. We never went to Uxmore.'

'Why didn't you?'

'We were never invited. Not that I would have wanted to go anyway. I presumed eventually I would have no choice, but we were in mourning and then... Well, it hardly matters. I know what they said of us. I heard it all when I returned to live with Celia.'

'But you never corrected them.'

'That would have been impolitic. Celia was always kinder to me when she could look down on me. It was so hard to return to Uxmore...'

His hand rose towards her, but she didn't see and he clasped his hands behind his back. She was not a child to be comforted. The urge to tuck her against him, the small slight form in Celia's Awful Dress, and somehow protect her from the bludgeoning of the Uxmores' condescending charity...

She did not need his help. She had found her own way to survive and hold her own. In fact, she was one of the least downtrodden women he knew. The realisation surprised him. Bella had far less independence—she had always required him as her sounding board, either of his approval or his disagreement, in order to know where she stood.

Jo was… Jo. A self-sufficient island in all respects but material. She needed nothing from him, not really. For which he was very grateful. He preferred his life pared down to its basic building stones. He did not need a grey-eyed pixie widow added to his scroll of responsibilities. There was no room for someone like her in his life.

'Come, it is time to return. I have business to attend to before I leave for Glasgow tomorrow.' He didn't wait for them to respond but swung Jamie into his arms and made his way up the cliff path. He had done his share for the day.

Chapter Seventeen

Benneit stood in the shadow of the trees at the top of the cliff overlooking the bay, watching them. He was tired from the long drive back from Glasgow to advance his plans for the distillery and for the Lochmore ball, but impulse had dragged him out here once Ewan informed him Jamie was down on the beach with Angus and Jo. A week was as long as he had been away from Jamie in a long while and he had felt it—instead of the usual dread at returning to Lochmore, this time he had been restless to come home, forcing everyone to proceed at a frenetic pace so he could keep to schedule.

He should be happy. Delighted, even. Everything was proceeding smoothly. McCrieff had approved the use of water from Loch Tyre and in a few weeks men would arrive to build the distillery and expand the village port. If all went well, in a few years Lochmore might become one of the largest distilleries in Scotland, providing livelihood not just for Lochmore tenants but for the McCrieffs and possibly other clans in the area.

He should be happy.

But as he watched them, his relief at reaching home was shoved away, replaced by a buzzing sensation, like annoyance. From up here they looked like a family of beachcombers, Angus's tall frame dwarfing them a little as he bent to pick up Jamie's discarded shoes and held his hand out to take Jamie's coat from Mrs Langdale. It was a simple, intimate act from a man Benneit trusted with his life, but for some reason it irked him.

Jamie ran up the path to the castle and Angus turned to speak to Mrs Langdale. Once again, she was not wearing a bonnet and the wind was attacking her schoolmistress's coiffure and, as Angus bent his red head towards her, she raised her hand to push back the straying flaxen tresses and Benneit saw her laugh. But when Angus followed in Jamie's wake, she remained on the shore, turning to walk back along the shore.

Benneit hesitated and descended the path. There was no real danger, but he had best be certain she didn't strand herself on the rocks when the tide rose.

He found her seated on his childhood perch, the great boulder carved by years of wind and rain into a natural seat, set high on a rocky ridge that might eons ago have fallen from the cliff side. On days like this, when the sun was shining, it would be warm and nest-like, and she sat curled in it with her eyes closed and her face raised to the sun in utter disregard of all feminine concerns for milk-white complexions. The wind had won the war against her bun and as he watched she pulled out the remaining pins, letting her hair tumble about her shoulders. In a moment she was likely to unravel further, perhaps go up in a puff of smoke, like a fairy-tale sprite.

Before he could gather his resolve to withdraw she opened her eyes and saw him. Her eyes widened and her hands flew to her hair.

'Welcome back, Your Grace. If you are looking for Jamie, Angus took him...'

'Yes, I know. I will join them in a moment. Do you like the Devil's Seat?'

'The what?'

'This rock is called Devil's Seat.'

'Really? Why?'

'You are good at stories—hazard a guess.'

Her eyes lit with interest and she snuggled a little deeper on to the rock.

'Did you sit here as a child?'

'Yes, but I am sorry to disappoint you, it was named that before I was born so you cannot lay that at my doorstep. Besides, I was usually a rather well-behaved boy.'

'In my experience anything that must be qualified with both "usually" and "rather" is suspect.

That leaves me to infer that occasionally you were a rather horridly ill-behaved boy.'

'I had my moments. Rather fewer than Jamie, but perhaps that is only my memory.'

'Well, if it is any consolation, I find that it is not in the least healthy for children to be perfectly behaved. It is usually a sign something is very wrong.'

He climbed up as well and sat on the boulder slightly beneath her. Her hands rose again towards her hair, but fell away, fisting. He repressed his smile as well as the temptation to tell her looking dishevelled suited her. If he did, she would probably have her hair back into its bun before he could blink.

'Why is it a sign something is wrong?' he prompted.

'Sometimes when children do not feel secure they are less likely to risk displeasure. They become...watchful, careful. Sometimes they do the opposite—they become thorough hellions because they gain attention only when they are horrid.'

'What were you like as a child?' he asked, trying not to show his discomfort at his visceral reaction to her words.

'Me?'

'Yes, you. I presume you were not conjured

fully grown by a magician with a penchant for pixies in grey gowns.'

'Pixies?'

'You remind me of a pixie.'

'Really? Scots must have a very different notion of pixies, then. I always thought they were rather mischievous and…appealing.'

'My notion is wholly English and that is very accurate. But you are evading my question.'

She turned towards the sea, tucking her fluttering hair behind her ears.

'Happy. I was happy.'

He waited and after a moment she sighed.

'It seems so long ago. I wish I could go back. Or I wish my father hadn't died and we could have stayed in Upper Dunstable.'

'What was it like?'

'It wasn't a large village, much smaller than Lochmore, just a couple dozen houses, but we were like a family. My father was also schoolmaster and the vicarage was always full of children. My mother was quite ill when I was young. I think that was why she never had more children and she loved having the house full with all our friends. Whenever someone could not be found they came to the Vicarage, knowing they would probably be there in the parlour or in the kitchen. Mama and Mrs Dell, our cook, were friendly rivals when it came to baking and they would spend hours trying the new recipes brought by Mrs Flitwick, the grocer's wife.'

'Your Mrs Dell must have been quite tolerant. I wouldn't dare infringe on Mrs Merry's domain.'

She laughed, the tumbling joyous sound that had struck him as so unlike the image she portrayed, but now it suited her, with her tangled hair glistening from the sea spray and her hands sweeping in wide gestures.

'Neither would I, even if I had Mama's penchant for baking.'

'Don't you?'

'Not a smidgen, I'm afraid. I did try, but I was so hopeless they banished me to help Papa in the schoolroom. I would forget to mind the time or add too much salt or confuse rosemary with thyme. Hopeless. Mama said it was because I was always daydreaming and not attentive enough.'

'Strange. You appear a pattern card of sober efficiency.'

'I learned to stop dreaming. It is not that difficult to be efficient. It merely requires some determination.'

'Do you not dream any more, then?'

'Are you afraid I might neglect Jamie if I do?'

'No. I merely hope for your sake that you have not forgotten how. That would be a pity.'

She dragged her hair into a semblance of a bun and secured it with the pins in her lap. It was lopsided and did nothing to contain the tendrils dancing about her face. Her mouth flattened, draining of animation; but not her eyes—they were damp and not from the sting of the wind. He didn't know whether to apologise for raising old dreams or to tuck her against him and soothe her. Neither was appropriate.

Then, she smiled at him.

'Thank you for reminding me. I don't think often of home. It seems so…unreal. Now, how does one descend from the Devil's Seat? It strikes me it is much easier to climb up than down.'

'You don't climb. You jump.' He demonstrated, ending in a crouch on the sand, and turned to grin up at her. She stared down at him in dismay.

'There must be an easier way. Do turn your back and I shall slide down carefully.'

'Why should I turn my back?'

'Because I am likely to end up in an ignominious heap at the bottom and I prefer to have no witnesses.'

'It would be ungentlemanly of me to leave you to such a fate. Step over on to that next rock and give me your hand.'

'Why?'

'Trust me.'

'I finding trusting no one to be a prudent way to live, Your Grace. Do kindly turn around.'

'No. Give me your hand.'

'I am beginning to see precisely what you meant by horrid behaviour.'

'Very well. Go ahead.'

He turned and waited, alert to any sounds of slippage.

'Benneit?'

'Yes?'

'I think I will need some help. It did not look quite so high from below.'

She stood with one foot outstretched, as if about to dip her toe into the water. From this vantage point he could see again the elegant line of her stockinged ankle and calf disappearing under the darkness of her skirts. His hand twitched at the sight, his body tightening.

'Benneit?'

He forced his gaze up, annoyed at this recurring foolishness. He held out his hands and after a moment's hesitation she leaned forward and placed her hands in his.

'Now close your eyes and jump.'

'Jump?'

'Trust me.'

She breathed and jumped. She was so light it was easy to swing her on to the sand as he had done for Jamie a dozen times. Like Jamie, she laughed, her gaze rising to his, all her apprehension flown in the pleasure of the moment.

'I felt like a bird!'

He was about to jest that sometimes she looked like a watchful grey sparrow, but at the moment she didn't look at all like one. She looked alight, no longer merely Jo, but Joy. Now he could see the happy girl she had been, daydreaming and helping her father with the chaos of children that must have been as drawn to her as his Jamie was.

As he was…

Her lips were parted, a strand of hair fluttering across them, beckoning. He could almost feel the soft brush of that strand against his own lips, silky warm and scented with roses. Could almost feel the slip of his fingers as he tucked it behind her ear, the moment before his mouth would find hers.

That kiss felt inevitable, as inescapable as the tide. He was already drawing her towards him, when she took her hand from his to brush away the hair flicking at her cheeks.

'Jamie will be so happy you have returned. We thought you would return tomorrow and he has been on his best behaviour after his promise to you when you left.' Her words were so practical and disconnected from his momentary loss of sense he felt a dozen times a fool for his strange lapse. He let go of her other hand and began walking up the shore with her.

'He has missed you very much,' she added after a moment.

'I missed him as well,' he answered, his throat tight against the need to ask if she had missed him, too.

Because he had.

At the foot of the cliff path he stopped. She did not look at him and he was almost glad.

'You go up by the Sea Gate, but I must stop at the stables for a moment. Tell Jamie I will join him for luncheon and that he and Flops are to leave me something to eat. I'm hungry.'

Chapter Eighteen

Jo stared at the shelves in the small dressing room adjoining her room.

'Beth...'

'Yes, Mrs Langdale?'

The maid's carefully subdued excitement was answer enough, but Jo asked the question anyway.

'Beth, where are my clothes?'

'Mrs Merry had Ewan take the other dress to Widow McManus, the one without the mud stains. She said you wouldn't be needing it now you have new clothes.' The maid's voice practically glided off the last two words, full of soulful yearning. New clothes.

Not just new clothes, but colourful clothes. Not a grey in sight, not even lavender, though there was a lilac blue folded neatly under a pale creamy yellow and, on a shelf of its own, was a gown in an exquisite pale orange shot with gold thread that glistened even as she watched, taunting her. She caught her hand halfway towards this marvel and snatched it back.

'Where did they come from?'

'Why, from Glasgow, Mrs Langdale. Mrs Merry gave Angus your measurements a while back, and His Grace and Ewan collected them now during their trip. There is even a ball gown, the orange one. Lochmore colours. For the ball.'

'For the ball.' Jo couldn't seem able to say anything of any sense. She knew the castle was preparing for a special event, but somehow it had not registered that this had anything to do with her.

'Why, yes. It is Summer Solstice tomorrow. The feud ball,' Beth prompted a little worriedly, as if Jo truly had forgotten the upcoming ball that turned the usually subdued castle into·a hive of activity.

'The feud ball.'

Beth appeared to interpret Jo's blank repetition as confusion about the concept and hurried into an explanation.

'Aye, it is meant as a time for the families to lay down arms and work through differences. Well, the old Duke and McCrieff would not always see eye to eye, to say the least, and for quite a few years there was no ball. But Lady Glenarris insisted it start again after she had the Great Hall made into a ballroom. She did love a good ball and she wore such fine gowns... This year there will be another. People will arrive tomorrow from miles and miles which is why we have extra hands from Kilmarchie and Crinan. Everyone is most excited. Here. This will be your gown.'

Beth unfolded the orange dress with reverence and Jo stared, bemused, at the soft fall of shimmering fabric. Now she could see the fine embroidery of stars along the bodice and waist and the trimming of the short, puckered sleeves.

'See how light it is?' Beth's voice sank into a whisper and Jo succumbed and touched. It was as soft as a feather and she drew her fingers back guiltily. She could not possibly accept this. Angus had explained about the ball but foolishly she had never realised she was to attend. For the simple reason that she had nothing suitable to wear.

And now she had.

Except that she didn't.

She looked down at her grey dress which, despite drying while she was on the Devil's Seat, was rumpled and the hems stained white with salt water. It was horrid and would need washing, but it was still serviceable.

And it was hers.

These dresses were...

'I'll help you out of that dress, now, Mrs Langdale. Once you've bathed I think you should wear the blush muslin. It will look very fine with your eyes and hair. I know you prefer to do your own hair, but if you don't mind, I'll dress your hair, too. I'm good, miss. I used to dress Her Lady-ship's hair and hers was almost as long as yours, though not so thick.'

As Beth went about realising her plan, Jo did what she had learned to do years ago when the world swept her along. She stepped outside her-self and allowed the current to carry her body while her mind alternately fretted and fled. Usu-ally it resulted in her mind throwing up its hands and giving in, but as she sat before the dressing-table mirror, suffering the unfamiliar tug and pull of another person's hands in her hair and staring at the familiar yet foreign woman being formed in front of her, her ability to divorce herself evap-orated.

'That looks much better. You look right lovely, Mrs Langdale.' Beth sounded surprised, which stung nerves already raw and jangling.

'Yes. Thank you, Beth.'

It was only as Beth went towards the dressing-room door, Jo's old dress draped over her arm like a depleted sack of flour, that a spark lit deep inside Jo.

She was angry.

'Beth. That dress. When it is clean I want it back.'

'But, Mrs Langdale...'

'It is *mine*, Beth.'

Beth glanced down at the dress she held.

'Of course, Mrs Langdale. If you wish.'

Jo nodded. At least Beth understood. Benneit Lochmore on the other hand… He might mean well, but she was angry. He might have better taste, or more money, or better intentions than Cousin Celia, but she was angry.

Very angry.

It felt so good to be so angry.

Halfway down the stairs she spotted Angus just exiting the estate room and hailed him. He stopped and stared as she descended the last stairs.

'Mrs Langdale…!'

She ignored the admiration in his voice.

'Where is he, Angus?'

His brows rose into the fall of his ginger hair, his eyes darting to the estate room, and he shifted as if to block her passage.

She moved past him and opened the door. The Duke and McCreary were bent over some papers and Lochmore looked up with a frown. As with Angus, surprise blanked his expression.

'I would like a word with you, *Your Grace.*'

Mr McCreary scrambled to his feet and hurried past her with a murmured greeting. Lochmore leaned back in his chair, his hand playing with his quill, the feather moving round and round in slow, tipsy circles as she approached the desk. It only occurred to her as she stopped that he had not risen on her entry. He appeared to realise it at the same time because he dropped his quill and stood so abruptly he bumped into the desk, which gave a protesting squawk against the floorboards.

'Yes?'

'I am not a serf, Your Grace.'

'I… No, you are not a serf, J—Mrs Langdale.'

'You appear to have forgotten that small fact when you took upon yourself to dispose of my…of my whole wardrobe and have Angus—*Angus*—give my… How *dare* you?' She was sputtering with fury, but she could not help it. She felt she was quite literally steaming.

'I did no such thing. I asked Mrs Merry to dispose of the evidence of Celia's spite. And unless wearing those hideous sacks was part of some secret plan of penance, you should be thanking me for doing so.'

'You arrogant…high-handed… I should be hitting you over the head with a piece of Jamie's driftwood!'

'Go fetch some. I'll wait right here. Better yet, use one of these ledgers. Lord knows they are dense enough.'

She did not know what to do with herself. The image of launching herself across the desk like a vicious beast came to mind, as did sitting down in a puddle of perfect muslin and crying her heart out.

'You look lovely in that gown. Why are you so upset?' It was the softness of his tone, and the true puzzlement beneath, that broke her.

She marched to the door, but the words left her anyway.

'I expected better of you.'

Somehow he reached the door before her. He was looking a little angry himself and also, more surprisingly, hurt—rather like Jamie when she scolded him.

It wasn't his fault. He was too much the Duke to understand the emotions of someone like her.

She picked up the fabric of her skirt, the cloth so lovely beneath her fingers it cracked her heart all over again as part of her begged her not to be so petty, so stiff, just to take for once and expect nothing else.

'It *is* lovely, lovelier than I have ever had. But it is no better than Celia, even if it was done out of pity and not spite. You walked right over me, Your Grace. Just like everybody else.'

Even as she spoke the words, watching his face harden, she knew she was a fool for ever voicing something so revealing.

'That was not my intention,' he answered. 'You

have been a good friend to Jamie and I thought it only proper to show a sign of appreciation. I thought you would be pleased.'

She abandoned her foolish quest.

'Thank you, Your Grace. They are lovely. All of them. Please thank Angus for me as well.' She continued towards the door and, after a slight hesitation, he moved aside and she left.

The door closed behind her and Benneit resisted the urge to open it again and slam it as hard as he was able.

Of all the ungrateful, petty, aggravating, impossible, nit-picking...

What the devil was wrong with her? Any normal female would have been gushing with thanks and admiration. Bella would have certainly showed her approval of such a gesture. Had demanded it often enough, in fact.

For a moment when Jo had entered the study, he had suffered a moment of complete disorientation. He had known immediately it was Jo and yet he hadn't recognised her. It was amazing what a decent gown and a different arrangement of hair could effect.

As she strode towards them, her chin up, her cheeks warm with colour—anger, he realised now—and her grey eyes shining—with fury, evidently—for a moment he had a mad image of her coming right up to him and demonstrating her appreciation in a very physical manner.

It was only a momentary thought. His rational mind had immediately rejected the idea that the proper widow Langdale would indulge in such a gesture, even for a brace of new gowns, but the image lingered and took a while to be beaten back under the barrage of her accusations. That juxtaposition made it all the worse.

I expected better of you.

Well, he had expected her to be happy that he had taken the time and effort… Well, told Angus and Mrs Merry and Beth to take the time and effort, with his money, to make her happy and a little more comfortable while she stayed with them. That was the very last time he bothered on her account, that was certain.

In fact, it would serve her right if he had Mrs Merry give all those new gowns as well to Widow McManus. Let her stay in her shifts and see how she enjoyed that! Her trips down to the beach with Jamie would not be quite so comfortable.

His mind generously offered up that image. Now that he had a better idea precisely what lay hidden beneath the grey sacks, it happily proceeded the next step to imagining her in even thinner muslin and that muslin conveniently dampened by the licking waves and plastered against her by the north wind. It also removed Jamie from the image so that she stood alone on the beach, very straight, looking up at him where he stood on his rock, her eyes as grey and deep as the sea.

'Hell,' he muttered as the image filled him with unwelcome heat. He shut his eyes harder and tugged at his hair again, but the tide was rising, swirling her skirts about her legs, and she wasn't moving, so naturally he bent down to help her up on to his rock and to safety as he had that day on the beach. Except that this time he did not let go, he was standing on the rock with her, and it was a very modest little rock and he had no choice but to hold her quite close, one hand sliding over her warm curves to cup her bottom, pulling her closer as his head lowered to taste that lovely pink bow of a mouth that kept torturing him…

He shoved his hands through his hair again, pulling at it in frustration.

'Benneit?'

'What?' he growled as Angus stepped into the study and closed the door.

'Is aught wrong? Did you have words with Mrs Langdale?'

'Why?'

'I came by her and she thanked me for the gowns and I said it were you, not I, that should be thanked and she looked fit to cry. Not like her at all. Knew she'd crack at some point. You can only fit so much whisky in a cask before it starts to leak.'

'What the devil does that even mean? And, no, I did not have words with her, she had words, and plenty of them, for me. Far from thanking me, apparently I am merely another petty, inconsiderate slave master and she a meek and put-upon serf. Meek! She's as meek as the worst of the McCrieff juggernauts! If ever I've seen a woman falsely advertised, that is Mrs Joane Langdale. She won't rest until she has the whole of Lochmore dancing to her tune, as subtle as it is. No wonder the Uxmores wanted her shunted off to the Antipodes. And to think, I felt sorry for her and was thinking my sister-in-law Celia a vindictive little cow. What a fool I was. Well, I can safely send my conscience scurrying back to its cave. That is the last time I exert myself on behalf of that ingrate.'

Angus's brows climbed higher and higher into his brow as Benneit's tirade advanced.

'That bad, eh? Still and all, I did tell you not to send her own clothes away until she was ready.

People with damn all in the world can be picky about what they have.'

'You did not...' Benneit paused at the memory that Angus had suggested precisely that. 'I cannot abide people who say "I told you so".'

'Aye, people who think they know better than others can be a right nuisance.'

'Are you trying to pick a fight, Angus?'

'I thought you could do with a round or two out in the yard. You're wound tighter than a top lately.' Angus inspected his ham-sized fists and grinned. 'I think we take our differences outside. You strike wide when you're angry and I've a score to settle with you over our last bout.'

Benneit looked down at the books.

'McCreary will cry if we don't finish all this before the end of the month.'

'McCreary will cry if you snap at him like that. Besides, you owe the servants some entertainment, they've scrubbed the castle from tower to gate getting all ready for the ball.'

Benneit tugged at his cravat.

'A few quick rounds back of the stables. And don't let the young fools bet above their means.'

'I'll have a word with the lads. Oh, and I'll try and spare yer pretty face. You don't want to show a black eye to the McCrieffs.'

'I'd try and spare yours, too, if only I could tell it apart from your arse.'

'Just for that I'll have you flat on yours, young lad.'

'We shall see, old man. Lead on.'

Chapter Nineteen

'Jo! Come see. Papa is winning! I think...'

'Winning what?'

Jo moved towards where Jamie was leaning against the nursery window. For a change, Flops was alert, half-standing with his paws pressed against the window by his master's side, his huffing breath clouding the glass.

She followed their gaze to the stable yards, where it looked like the whole of the castle and quite a few of the temporary staff taken on ahead of the ball were gathered around two men dressed in nothing but buckskins and boots. The two moved about the open circle created by the wall of servants. It might as well have been a dance, elegant and light, but she could feel the force of it even at this distance. The late afternoon sun gleamed orange and red off their bare chests and arms, dancing and gliding along their perspiration-slicked shoulders.

The only man she had ever seen without his shirt had been Alfred. He possessed good arms but he had been boyishly slim and his chest as bare as a boy's. Benneit and Angus were built on a larger, rougher scale, but though Angus was yet larger, it was Benneit who caught and held her gaze.

He is beautiful. Utterly, utterly beautiful, her heart and body agreed, throwing a sack over her mind and shoving it into a closet as it tried to remind them of his flaws.

His body was long and elegant, with broad shoulders and a shading of dark hair across his chest tapering downwards, making her fingers twitch with the need to test that silky arrow. His muscles were as defined as a museum statue, though they looked much warmer—sun-kissed and slick with sweat that would glide under her hands...

Her palms were hot and tingling with the imagined sensation—her fingers curving over the bulge of his bicep and into the cool hollow at his elbow before finding the hair-roughened, sinewy strength of his forearm.

She could see the rise and fall of his chest, the trickle of sweat on his cheek and neck. Every line was enhanced by the tension in his body as he moved slowly around the circle, half-facing Angus who was doing the same. She could have sworn she caught his scent from here, closed window or not—cool and musky, the sea and the male animal prowling. She was hot with it and it was hard to breathe. She leaned her hand on the cool stone by the window and when Jamie spoke, she was shocked to realise she had forgotten his presence.

'They're looking for openings,' Jamie explained. 'Papa's lighter on his feet and faster, but Angus can pick up an oak with his bare hands and break a bone between his fingers.'

Jo's stomach clenched, her fear beating back the treacherous heat a little. She was still angry and hurt, but however much she had wanted to throw something at Lochmore, she really, really didn't want anyone hurting him.

'Oh my goodness!' Jo exclaimed in shock as Angus swung what looked like an enormous arm, but the Duke shifted aside, coming up hard against Angus who bent over and stumbled sideways. There was a muted mix of roars and groans and Jamie clapped his hands.

'Right in the pudding box! Gave him a leveller!'

'Jamie! Why on earth are they fighting?'

Jamie snorted in disgust.

'It's not fighting, it's sparring. One day Papa will teach me, too. No one in all the Highlands can take him down, not even Angus and he's as strong as a boulder. One day I'll be just as strong and just as fast. Ah, flute…'

'What now?'

'It's over,' Jamie said in disappointment.

Jo didn't answer, just pressed a hand to her racing heart and watched the two men as they clapped each other on the back and Angus gave a not-so-light pummel on Benneit's shoulder. Benneit was smiling, no, grinning, his face warm with life. This was neither the Duke nor Bella's suitor. She did not even notice as Jamie hurried out, but stood there watching until the two men disappeared from view. She peeled her perspiring hand away from her racing pulse and pressed it to the cool windowpane, but that only made her feel hotter, her lovely dress suddenly an ungainly sack about her, weighing her down. The thought of being bare, of feeling a warm, large hand settle on her shoulder, of being able to touch…

Something scraped at her shoe and she gave a little yelp, but it was only Flops. He gave a small answering yelp and buffed her foot with his paw. She had rarely seen his eyes and had not once heard him bark, but as his looked up at her, his angora-soft fringe falling back from his eyes, she could see they were black and very mournful, as if he knew something was very wrong with her. She breathed in and out until the strange sensations abated and then bent to stroke him until he tired of her and went in search of Jamie.

Chapter Twenty

'Your Grace.' Jo's voice was a little too sharp as she called out and she clenched her jaw, trying to calm her jumping nerves. Benneit stopped, his hand on the knob of the study door, eyeing her warily.

His hair was wet and dishevelled. He had evidently bathed after the fisticuffs and, though he looked weary, there was a lingering lightness in his movements and his eyes were more green than grey. It reminded her of their colour when he had picked her up on the beach the other day, the strength of his hands on her waist, how close they were for that moment before he put her down. His eyes had been as deeply green, then—jade with shards of emerald, the grey beaten back into a rocky rim. She could recall the heat of his body inches from hers, the itch of anticipation that something...

'Yes, Mrs Langdale?' he prompted and she looked down, focusing on her words.

'I wished to apologise. I was ungrateful and ungracious.'

He crossed his arms and winced.

'I owe you an apology, too, Mrs Langdale. Angus was right; I should have consulted with you. In my defence, I presumed you would continue to reject my offer of new clothes.'

'You presumed correctly.'

'Well, then I'm afraid I don't truly regret my high-handedness. If you still wish to throw something, please do so at my right side, Angus has already tenderised the left.'

'I saw. Jamie watched from the nursery.'

Colour spread over his lean cheeks and he swiped a hand over his face, as if testing the closeness of his shave. He looked so human when he blushed, she relaxed a little, then a little further at his grumbled reply.

'You'll probably say I should be more careful he doesn't witness such things.'

'No. He was so very proud. That cannot be bad.'

He stood back and motioned towards the study and she entered, far too grateful for this little show of reconciliation. Inside, she moved towards the window, too unsettled to remain close to him, her heart both racing ahead and stumbling like a drunkard down a hill. Before she could think the words rushed out of her.

'Tomorrow is the ball. Will you be making the

announcement? If so, you should prepare Jamie. He should hear it from you.'

He remained by the door.

'The announcement?'

'Your engagement.'

He walked to the desk.

'The only announcement is that we are breaking ground with the distillery. As for…the other, we have reached no formal agreement yet so there is nothing to tell Jamie. However, the plans for the distillery will give people more than enough to talk about.'

Her relief was so extreme and so foolish she held herself still in her cage until her heart settled. It meant nothing. In another week or two she would return to England and melt from the Lochmore consciousness like the dew in Jamie's deserts.

'He knows, though. Not merely from your aunt's comments. He hears the talk—here and in the village. He is a child, but he is surprisingly wise for his age. He even told me he knows it is because of him.'

'He told you that?'

'He said you wished to give him a family.'

'Was that all he said?'

She hesitated.

'I did not pry, you know. He talks when we are on the beach. Whatever comes to his mind. I merely listen.'

'I am not accusing you of prying, I merely wish to know… He does not often speak to me of such matters. He did after that horrific dinner with Aunt Morag, but since then, every time I tried to broach the subject he shies away.'

She heard the ring of steel in his voice. It was not resentment this time, but a slash of pain.

'Sometimes I think he sees me a little as he does his mermaids or Flops—he can speak freely because he cares less. You are the most important thing in his world and it is never easy to speak of truly fateful matters to someone in that position. He said he knows you wish him to have a brother and a sister so he can play with them and show them things. He said he hopes they will like maps and exploring, but that they must find themselves another dog because Flops is his.'

His mouth curved, but he still did not look at her.

'Thank you for telling me. Where is Jamie now?'

'Upstairs with Nurse Moody. They are preparing Flops for the ball tomorrow. He has not yet accepted they will not be attending.'

'Poor Flops. That does not bode well for Jamie's temper when the truth sinks in that he will not be at the centre of the festivities. Tomorrow is likely to be challenging in more ways than one, Mrs Langdale. Are you prepared for the worst?'

'I am, Your Grace. Is Mr McCreary about? We are setting a fine pace with the accounts and I am hopeful we might soon complete the review.'

'He has gone to the village on some business of mine and I am about to go as well so you are welcome to the study.' He went to pull out his chair and after a moment she went to sit down, pulling the ledger towards her.

He did not immediately leave, and she looked up, her heartbeat heading downhill again for no accountable reason. He smiled, but it was not the easy smile of a moment ago.

'You look much better than McCreary does at my desk.'

'It is the dress, Your Grace. Perhaps you should review McCreary's wardrobe as well.'

He laughed and shook his head, his drying hair brushing the collar of his coat. It had grown since she had seen him in London. Time was passing, and each moment was becoming precious. If she was a brave woman she would stand and...and do something.

Instead she pulled the ledger to her and bent over it and stared blindly at the numbers. It felt like an eternity before the door closed finally behind him. Then she set to work.

Chapter Twenty-One

Everything was ready for the ball.

The hall gleamed, the sconces were all equipped with candles, the passage to the Great Hall, usually bare, was laid with deep blue carpets and the Minstrels' Gallery at the end of the hall readied for the orchestra arriving from Kilmarchie. Mrs Merry was at her imperious best, her voice ringing up and down corridors as she held sway over the horde of servants hired for the occasion.

The Duke had every reason to be content with the state of his household. Except for one small issue.

Or rather one small boy and a rather serious issue.

'Where the devil is he?' Benneit's growl sent two temporary footmen into retreat down the hallway. 'Have you found him, Jo? Angus?'

Angus wiped his brow with a handkerchief the size of a tent and Jo shook her head.

'Nurse Moody said his best shoes and his tartan coat are missing. Clearly he still plans to attend the ball, despite your interdiction,' Jo offered and tried not to flush as Benneit's glare turned on her. Angus jumped into the breach.

'I searched the towers and those servants we can spare are looking outside, lad. Other than having Mad Morag throw an ewer at me and tell me not to come back unless I'm bringing a bottle, I found nothing.'

'Blast the boy,' Benneit cursed, raking his fingers through his hair. 'As if we have nothing better to do today than search high and low for him.'

'Perhaps…' Jo stopped short. Suggesting the Duke should have allowed Jamie to attend the opening of the ball after all was not likely to be a productive contribution at this point. Instead she searched for something practical to do. 'Perhaps we should check the cellars.'

Lochmore rounded on her.

'How many times must I repeat myself? No one enters the cellars and certainly not Jamie. He might be spoilt, but he's no fool. He's run off outside the castle walls. And why the devil are you still wearing that grey dress?'

'I will go and search the copse.' Jo turned away, resisting the urge to tell Benneit what she thought of him and his manners. Angus trudged alongside her.

'I'll go to the rock fall. You mustn't mind Lochmore in this mood, lass. He's worried,' Angus added unnecessarily.

'I know, Angus.'

'He didn't mean that about the dress.'

She laughed a little bitterly.

'Yes, he did. But he was in a foul mood even before he noticed my dress and before Jamie's tantrum and disappearance.'

'The present keeps moving closer to the future and he knows he can't avoid it.' He sighed, adding, 'He was always a stubborn boy, a heart of gold, but stubborn.'

'Jamie is definitely that.'

'I meant Benneit.' Angus smiled. 'Good luck, Mrs Langdale.'

Once she ascertained Jamie wasn't in the copse Jo followed the path towards the north bay, but without any real expectation of finding Jamie there. So even when she saw the flash of orange from Jamie's plaid coat laying casually on the stone near the cliff gate, her mind still rejected the possibility Jamie had gone down to the bay itself. She picked up the coat and promptly dropped it.

On the highest point of the rise of boulders past the first line of the rocks, sunlight gleamed off a black oval. She'd seen it only this morning when Jamie had produced his dress shoes so proudly, convinced he could yet manoeuvre his father into allowing him to attend the ball.

The waves were already licking at the base of the rocks and she moved forward without thinking. She could not see beyond the boulder, but he might be there, sulking, oblivious to the fast-rising water. Only two days ago they had walked past here with Angus on the cliff path and not two hours later none of those rocks had been visible beneath smashing, frothing waves.

'Jamie!' she yelled again and again, but the wind and the waves made a mockery of her cries. As she watched, a wave smashed against the rocks, sending a white spray into the air. The shoe slipped sideways several inches.

She picked up her heavy skirts and ran the rest of the way down the cliff path.

Benneit stopped on the top of the cliff path, picking up his son's discarded tartan coat and folding it with a frustrated curse which faded as his gaze caught on a movement below.

Perhaps it was the way she let her shawl flutter away, like a bird set free from captivity. Or perhaps it was the madness of her next move.

His heart lurched in shock and denial as he watched her move into the waves.

'Jo!'

Even as her name burst from him in a mix of outrage and terror he knew it was pointless. She would hear nothing but the beat and hiss of the surf. Already it was about her thighs, catching and tugging at the grey fabric, the waves snatching higher and higher, pushing her back even as she forced her way through them towards the underwater ledge marked by froth swirling like boiled milk.

He ran. Vaulting over boulders and cutting the last section of the path in half by leaping a good eight feet down to the sand. He stumbled but shoved to his feet again and continued towards the water, stopping only to discard his coat and rip his boots off—from long experience he knew the waves were best faced unencumbered. He didn't bother yelling. Anyone mad enough, or desperate enough, or lost enough to head into those waves willingly would not turn simply for a command.

His teeth clenched as the water rose around him—snapping cold and vicious. He could see her struggling, turning her face from the waves that reared at her like stampeding horses even as she plunged on, heading for the boulders that still jutted dark grey out of the rising sea. If by some strange strain of madness she thought that way safety lay, she was about to discover how wrong she was. If she meant to end her life, she was within moments of achieving that aim.

He stopped thinking, shoving his way through the icy water, tearing free of the grasping tentacles of kelp that lashed and tangled about his legs. She was almost to the boulder when he saw the seventh wave. It was always the largest, though not always the most dangerous if you knew how to ride it. But coming at her it would smash her against the boulders and crack her like an otter cracks a mussel.

He lunged, reaching for whatever he could grab. His hand closed on the cold fabric of her dress and he heard her cry out even as he dragged her under. She struggled, but he dug his hand into the fabric and held her down as the wave sucked at them, almost crushing them on to the stones beneath. As soon as he felt the weight of the water roll over them he shoved to the surface, pushing towards the shore without letting go his hold on her. She kicked and tried to twist out of his grasp, but he kept going as if she was nothing but a net full of fish.

The water was rising fast and soon he would lose his purchase on the rocky bottom. The waves kept coming, picking up weight. Soon the big wave would hit again, he could feel the backward surge as it gathered itself, coming at them. This time he pulled her to him, wrapping her against his body as he plunged. He felt her hands fist on his shirt, her head pressed to his chest as she curled into a ball as they went down. Even in the chaos and fixed determination of the moment he admired how quickly she had grasped the object of these plunges. In fact, all fight seemed to have gone out of her. She stayed below the water until he rose. They were just steps away from the ledge that marked the safe point.

'Almost there,' he yelled above the surf and though she shook her head and did not look at him she moved with him. The backward tug when it came surprised them both. Her eyes shot towards him as she rocked under the beat of a wave. He tugged at her arm impatiently. In a few moments the water would rise and even the ledge would offer no salvation. They had moments at best.

She looked back, reaching down, and he realised what was wrong. He planted his feet apart and shoved her hand away, grasping her skirt and tugging. The fabric was thick in his hands, scratchy in the water, but his efforts seemed to wedge it even more firmly between the rocks.

'The dress from hell,' he cursed, turning his back and pulling her against him as a wave came slamming down on them. He could feel her wriggling, trying to tug at the fabric with rising panic, but instead of joining her he grasped the modest bodice above the row of neat buttons and wrenched it apart. One of the buttons snapped him on the cheek as it flew off and the front of the dress fell open. He dragged the sleeves down, gathering her under her arms and hauling her out of it like a toddler, half-dragging her on to the ledge. The waterlogged dress surged on the wave like an animal carcass, grey and sullen, and then was sucked down as the water crashed into foam.

He kept hold of her, her body now slight and cold with only a soaked chemise as cover. On the ledge the waves were still only waist high and she stumbled ahead with him, the sea dragging at their legs, but no longer in charge. They finally reached the sand beyond the rocks and she stumbled and he sank down on his knees beside her, their breath audible above the roaring surf. He grabbed her shoulders, turning her to him, every other emotion shifting into a rockslide of fury.

'Are you *mad*? How *dare* you? How *dare* you do that?'

'Jamie… Oh, God, Benneit… Jamie!' Her voice came in rough gasps, hardly recognisable. 'His shoe was on the boulders out there. I tried to reach… Why did you stop me?'

Her fingers dug and twisted into his shirt and

there was so much agony in her eyes it cauterised his anger like a fiery brand.

'Jamie? Jamie is at the castle. Angus and I found him hiding outside the stables. I came to find you and then I saw you head to your death, you little fool.'

'He is safe? Are you certain?'

'Of course I'm certain. I told you he wouldn't go far. Unlike you, he has more sense than to stay in the bay when the tide is rising.'

'But his shoe…'

'He told me had thrown them into the sea. It was his sign of protest. You should have realised that.'

She was staring at him, disbelief and hope warring in her eyes. She had not removed her hands from his chest, they spread wide as if to push him away, but she didn't. She didn't appear aware of anything but some internal battle; certainly not the fact that she was clothed in nothing but a flimsy and now transparent chemise that clung to her body and left absolutely nothing to the imagination.

It settled one debate at least. Under Celia's horrors was a work of art. Her breasts were simply perfect, as if a master artist had decided to create a treatise on perfect proportions. The cold had gathered her nipples into two unmistakably rosy peaks under the fabric and he could almost feel how they would fit against his palms—the soft curve of sea-slicked skin and the hard pucker of her nipples pressed to the heart of his palms... Beneath the chilled outer layer of skin he felt a surge of fire, the beating of drums.

He forced his gaze away, but they only swept down, following the sheer fabric as it hugged the curve of her waist and hips and fit snugly over the darker triangle between her legs. Despite everything—his fury, his fear, his shock—his body heated and readied, fixing its attention on this unintended invitation.

Hell. This was the very definition of unwelcome.

'Thank God.' She sat back on her heels, covering her face, a shudder coursing through her. Her hair was a matted tangle and a piece of kelp was wrapped around her arm like an exotic bracelet. If not for the goosebumps and the simple chemise, she looked like a figure out of one of Jamie's tales of the sea. A mermaid cast on to land, a Selkie come to capture a mate.

The wind lashed at them and his wet buckskins were uncomfortably tight over his unwanted arousal. It should have been an effective antidote to the surge of lust, but it wasn't. He doubted a snowstorm would be effective against the chaos roiling inside him. In normal circumstances he could push aside the increasingly frequent flashes of desire this impossible woman sparked, but now neither his mind nor his body co-operated and this weakness fanned his terror-driven fury.

'You wouldn't be thanking the Lord if you knew how much I want to box your ears right now. Have you gone stark, staring mad? If you thought Jamie was in the water, you should have fetched me.'

Her hands fell away, her face suddenly fierce.

'Fetch you? Did you really expect me to leave him to the sea while I made my way to the castle? There was no time!'

'I expect you to behave with more sense than a four-year-old!'

She closed her teeth with a snap and struggled to her feet. He saw the precise moment she realised her state of undress. Her eyes widened, a flush blooming upwards from the centre of her chest like dye.

'My dress!' Her voice cracked, her eyes filling with tears.

It was so absurd he laughed. She had nearly died. They both had, yet the loss of that horror which she admitted hating had the power to reach her.

'That is the only good thing about this fiasco.

It's gone down to the depths of Hades where it belongs. If you had been wearing one of the new dresses we both would have had an easier time of it. Let that be a lesson to you to be less bull-headed, Jo.'

'Oh! You are... You are hateful, Benneit Lochmore!' She stalked away towards the path and he retrieved his discarded coat and followed, watching the way the fabric clung to a posterior as beautifully shaped as her breasts. This woman was made to be clothed in nothing but the sea. It was utterly wrong to be noticing her now, after what they had survived, or perhaps it was unavoidable. Whatever it was, it had him by the groin.

'And you are singularly ungrateful. You do realise I saved your life, don't you?'

She stopped, folding her hands over her chest, but did not turn.

'I do. Thank you. I'm sorry.'

As far as admissions, thanks or apologies went, hers were abysmal, but he kept silent, his mind firmly on other things. Her elegant ankles were peppered with grains of sand and he watched them strain and stretch as she made her way up the path and kept his eyes from straying higher. But just before the crest she stopped abruptly. Unprepared, he bumped into her, his hands seizing the opportunity to clasp her arms. Despite the breeze, her skin was already warmer than his hands and the temptation to see if that warmth was evident elsewhere was so strong he forced himself to step back.

'I can't go into the castle…like this,' she said, her voice still rough and strained.

Like this. God help him, she clearly had no idea how spectacular she looked 'like this'.

A married woman had no right to be so innocent.

He detached his gaze from the way the wet chemise loved her breasts and reached to remove the strand of kelp that clung to her arm.

'We could make you a kelp costume but I refuse to climb back down to the bay to fetch some. Don't worry, my coat will be sufficient cover and you can enter through the tower door. If you are so unlucky as to be seen, tell them the truth.'

'That I am a fool?'

He smiled at the return of Jo, uncertain he was glad for it.

'That you were foolish, but very brave. I am not ungrateful, but if you ever do something like that again I will send you to your room for a week with nothing but dry bread and a book of sermons.'

Her laugh became a hiccup and then a sob and she pressed the heels of her palms into her eyes.

'I was so scared…' she whispered. 'I didn't think.'

'I know. Hush. You are safe now.'

He didn't think either as he gathered her to him, wrapping his arms around her. She sagged against him and he felt the shudders of released tension course through her, filling his body with ideas of other shudders it was desperate to explore.

It was madness, unwanted, but it was undeniable. Right now, cold, wet, uncomfortable, exhausted from the strain of escaping the surf, he felt utterly alive and intent only on the sylphlike body pressed against him.

He wanted her.

No, he was starving for her.

It was not so very wrong, was it? She was a widow, experienced. Why shouldn't they enjoy the little life allowed people in their position, with their limitations.

'Jo,' he murmured, and she shuddered again which gave him a perfect excuse to tighten his hold, splaying his hand lower. Too low. It moulded over her backside and before he could even stop himself he raised her against him, her abdomen pressing the cold cloth of his buckskins against his blazing erection. It should have cooled him, but it only added to the erotic contrast and a groan burst from him.

'Jo.'

Her hands pressed against his chest, as if readying to push away, but she didn't move. With a slow, trancelike motion, she tilted her head back. Beyond her the sea still roared, but the grey of her eyes was calm and deep, darkened by her dilated pupils. He forced his hands to ease, but her fingers curled into the wet fabric of his shirt, her nails dragging it against his skin. It hurt, his whole body curling around that sensation as if struck, his breath hitching and his arousal hardening in an agonised surge of lust. Her lips parted, her body shifting against the unmistakable sign of his need. His hands caught her waist, trying to still her movement, but somehow they pressed her closer and her lashes dipped, colour blooming over her cheekbones like sunrise. He cupped her cheek in his hand, gathering that bloom against his palm, his voice urgent as he tried to penetrate her trance-like state.

'You have just given me one of the worst scares of my life and the only thing I can think about with any clarity is kissing you senseless. So go to the castle now, Jo. Please.' He shouldn't have added the plea; it sounded as desperate as he felt.

Her hands unlatched from his shirt, sliding down to his abdomen and he groaned as his muscles contracted under their passage.

'You want to kiss me?' She sounded more shocked by that than by anything that had preceded it and he gave a weak laugh.

'I want a hell of a lot more than that, but at the moment I would swim a mile in those waves for a kiss from you. Which is why you need to go. Now.'

Benneit wanted to kiss her. And more.

It made little sense, but the hot, hard length of his arousal pressed against her was undeniable and, as she searched his eyes, she saw it was true. Danger and anger did strange things to men. If she was sensible, she would heed Benneit's warning and hurry away.

She did not feel sensible. Her body was hot and cold and tingling as if she was too close to a fire after a bath, the hairs on her arms and nape rising towards the heat, her breasts heavy and aching.

They had almost died… *He* had almost died because of her. But they were alive and he wanted to kiss her, no matter why. That was all that mattered.

Her palms dragged against the chill, wet fabric covering his chest, rising to press against the tense sinews at his nape and into his dark, wet hair. It tickled the skin between her fingers, clinging to her hands as she flexed her fingertips against his scalp, rising on to her toes, leaning into his hard, lean body because hers was shaking with anticipation and fear.

Her lips touched his gently, but the sensation was anything but gentle—it stung her numb lips and set her body ablaze like a splash of oil on fire. For an eternity they stayed frozen, their hands holding each other, their lips touching, the only movement their shallow, careful breathing; she could feel his tension in every inch of contact between them and she knew any moment it would take him away from her. The moment would pass before it truly began.

A kiss from you...

She curled her fingers into his wet hair, latched on to him like strangling kelp and kissed him with every feeling that lived inside of her. She tasted his tongue with hers, loving the contrast of textures—his lips were silk over marble, the rougher rasp of his tongue, firm and demanding against hers, the scrape of his teeth on her throbbing lips sending shivers down to her nipples and to the thudding heat that was expanding between her legs. She had never kissed like this, but she could not stop.

A deep, guttural groan coursed through him and he abandoned his temporary passivity under her caress, his arms tightening and his hands moving over her as if he could absorb her, as unstoppable and threatening as the waves that almost took their lives.

'I warned you, Jo.' His voice was a growl of thunder, but she shook her head, trying to press even closer, her hands anchoring in his shirt as if he might escape her. But he didn't try, he just deepened the kiss, parting her lips again, tasting and suckling her lips and tongue in a searching cadence that had her whole body swaying to a foreign rhythm, like a clumsy child trying to follow a new dance. He was possessing her, encompassing her, drawing her soul out with each sweep and caress of his mouth and tongue, stripping away plain little Joane Langdale and leaving only the hot, live core of her need.

'Benneit...'

Suddenly she felt his hand directly on her chilled skin, her chemise a damp tangle about her waist, his fingers splayed on her thighs as he raised her, pressing deep into her soft flesh. She tried to draw back, shocked by her own hunger, but his other hand was deep in her hair, his fingers splayed against her scalp as his mouth sank to her throat, suckling and sending unbearable shivers down her body like streaks of lightning—sharp and slashing. His lips followed their path, but when his breath swept over her breast it became unbearable and she squirmed, trying to meet or fight the crashing sensations. He did not let go, teasing her hardened nipple into a frenzy of pleasure with his lips and tongue and the subtle scrape and pressure of his teeth. Between the thud of surf below and the keening of a gull above she heard her own whimpers of need, as foreign as the sensations gathering inside her, beating at her nerves like the waves had beaten at her body. She wanted to act, but she could only cling to him as he unravelled her, afraid that if she let go she would plummet off a cliff of her own making.

'Benneit...'

It was hardly more than an agonised moan, but she should have kept silent because he stopped, his hand burrowing deeper into her wet hair, his fingers twisting as he pulled her head back, his eyes narrowed and gleaming like one of the mythical beasts she imagined prowling the mountains high above the clouds. If she could have thought, she would have tried to shield herself from that gaze because surely he saw everything. Then his gaze shifted, moving slowly over her face, resting on her parted lips, making them throb harder. She felt his breath on the damp heat of their bruised surface, imagined the sting caused by her hair as the wind whipped it against his lean cheeks, as if she were taking part in the battle evident in every inch of the body pressed against hers, in the tension along the fingers that cradled her head, that were cupped over her bottom, holding her to him. Alfred had never touched her there, had even hesitated before his hands closed on her breasts, and she felt ashamed at how much she liked Benneit's touch, his fingers pressing deep into her flesh there, how vivid and scorching the sensation of his mouth on her breast through the dampness of her chemise. How right it felt...*he* felt...

Her shudder became a moan, half of need and half of shame at the foreign forces beating inside her. He breathed in, his arms tightening and finally his head sank back to hers, but as his lips grazed hers with the impact of steel on steel he froze. Then she heard it, too.

'Lochmore! Where are ye, lad?'

Angus's voice carried above the sound of the surf and she pulled away, shocked and scared.

'Angus, *mac an diabhal*,' Benneit cursed in Gaelic, his voice as raw and shaky as she felt inside.

He picked up his coat from where it lay discarded, and draped it over her shoulders, closing it with one fist. He did not look at her as he spoke.

'The guests must be arriving. I will go ahead and send Angus back and then you can slip in by the tower stairs.'

She stayed where she was as he disappeared up the path, hugging his coat to her. It smelled of him, warmth and musk and the sea. She shuddered, the cold reaching up from the ground straight into her heart and she pressed her face into the fabric to stop the tears.

'Oh no.'

Her words were a whisper, but all her longing and the feeling of hopelessness were in those two syllables. She was not fool enough to read emotion into Benneit's passion. Danger did odd things to men—even usually placid Alfred reacted strangely when she was once thrown from a horse—it had been the only time they had made love outside the bedroom and before bedtime. But then they reverted to the almost decorous ritual of coupling he had established on their wedding night—in bed, in the dark. She should not be fool enough to read anything into Benneit's kiss.

She pressed her face into the soft folds of his coat to breathe the warmth of his scent, knowing the coat had a better chance of a future with him.

Oh God, but her heart ached.

Chapter Twenty-Two

It had to be done. And swiftly. Leaving a thorn in the flesh led to festering and rot. In a few short hours he must face his guests and his future. But right now he must face the consequences of his abject stupidity on the cliff path. He remembered all too well Mrs Langdale's discomfort in the ballrooms of London. It would be unfair that the first time they met after his transgression would be in the Great Hall surrounded by all his guests. It might be easier for him, but it would be the coward's way out.

He knocked on the door of her parlour, steeling himself.

'Enter.'

She was seated in the embrasure, holding a book and the afternoon light was so bright about her that he could not make out her expression. It made this easier.

'Mrs Langdale.'

'Your Grace.' Her voice was as flat as the first day they met, but now he knew how unnatural it was. He cleared his throat and launched into his speech.

'What happened earlier was completely my fault. I never should have taken such advantage of your vulnerability. I did not even thank you properly for your show of bravery on Jamie's behalf, however misguided. He has already been punished for disappearing, but tomorrow I will make it clear to him his behaviour could have resulted in tragedy.'

'Oh, but you cannot tell him!' Her outward calm vanished in a flash. She surged to her feet, her eyes wide and shocked, and the book thumped to the floor.

'Naturally I must punish him for putting you in harm's way, however unintentionally. He should learn that his actions have consequences.'

'No! You cannot use my foolishness as an excuse to discipline him! He is far too young to worry a person's life hangs in the balance of his actions. He could never have guessed I would make such a mistake simply because of his coat and shoes. He is *not* heedless.'

'No? Then what the devil would you call it when he throws a tantrum and sends the whole castle into a panic the day we are trying to prepare for the one event a year where we have to expose ourselves to half the Highlands?'

'Fear. He knows what is happening. He knows his world is changing and it frightens him. He is hardly more than a babe. Please. Please, Benneit. I am begging you.'

Her hands were clasped in front of her, her lips parted and her cheeks warm with colour and he wanted... He looked past her.

'Oh, very well. I won't tell him. I dare say you think the punishment I imposed on him already is inhuman enough,' he said drily. 'How will the lad survive without his beloved jam tarts until tomorrow? But next time try to think before you throw yourself into the waves or from the cliffs, will you? I shall see you downstairs for dinner.'

He left her parlour before the frustration licking at him like fire at a witch's skirts engulfed him and made him do something or say something even more foolish. His nerves and his will were frayed to breaking and the temptation to continue their interrupted embrace was like a swarm of maddened bees inside him.

He paused halfway down the stairs, realising he had not even apologised for his outrageous behaviour on the path. He was damned if he was going back to her to do so. His life was complicated enough as it was—the last thing he needed was the pint-sized pixie needling his conscience, subverting his libido and taking complete control of almost every aspect of his life.

Why had he ever suggested she stay a month? Another week of this...

Dear God, he would be a gibbering wreck by the end of it. Now that he knew what she looked like underneath her grey armour, now that he had tasted her...his hands and body could feel her even now...

'Daingead,' he cursed as he made his way to his bedchamber. In a few hours he would be welcoming the woman he was to marry and he was as hard and hot as an oak in a forest fire for another woman. Not even at the height of his infatuation with Bella had he felt so torn, so utterly at the mercy of something he did not even understand.

Chapter Twenty-Three

'What?' Beth exclaimed and then flushed at her very unservile exclamation. 'But, Mrs Langdale, you *must* go to the ball! What of your beautiful dress?'

'I have the headache. From the cold water,' Jo said with dignity. She had been forced to tell Beth what had happened, at least part of it, to explain her salty, dishevelled and dressless state. Beth had muttered something about Jamie's tantrums, but had said nothing else as she had ordered up a hot bath and had set about redeeming Jo's hair from its salty tangle.

Beth planted her fists on her hips and surveyed Jo, her dark eyes like coals from the pits of hell.

'I've not slaved an hour over your hair for you to sit in your room and sulk because the laird gave you the scold you deserved, lass! There's been enough tantrums at Lochmore today!'

Tears stung Jo's eyes, but she drew herself up.

'I am not sulking. I am tired.'

Beth did not argue. Perhaps recalling her position, she merely curtsied and left the room, but the door closed with a distinct snap and Jo sank back on to the chair in front of the mirror. She could not explain it to Beth.

She had no idea how long she had sat there when the door bounced open and Benneit strode in without even knocking.

Jo stood and straightened her shoulders. She had been expecting some response, but not a personal appearance from a very irate Duke. Especially not after the events of that day.

It was not at all helpful that he looked utterly, breathtakingly handsome. She had seen him in a short kilt before when he was about the castle and the estate, but this was clearly full ceremonial dress, the orange-tartan kilt drawn over the dark blue coat and white shirt, its contrasting colours stretched across his formidable chest and over his shoulder, making him look even larger than usual, and the deep, burnt shades of orange accentuating the green of his eyes and his raven hair. She had thought him magnificent enough in evening dress, but the Duke of Lochmore in a long kilt was something else entirely.

The annoyance on his face faltered and his forward motion flagged. He stopped in the middle of the room, his gaze raking over her from her head to the tips of her kid slippers peeking from beneath the high embroidered flounce.

'Your Grace?' she prompted as he remained silent.

'I…' He took another step forward and stopped again, the frown returning. 'What is this about not coming down?'

'I have decided it is quite unnecessary.'

'Unnecessary? What on earth does that have to say to anything? In less than an hour half of the Highlands will be gathering below.'

'Precisely. One person more or less will hardly be noticed.' She did not add—certainly not *this* person. 'I am perfectly happy staying…'

Benneit drew himself up, clearly struggling to hold the reins of his temper.

'The point is not to make you happy, Jo… Mrs Langdale. The point is that you are Bella's cousin and it would be considered da—deuced odd of you to be hiding in the nursery while I entertained our neighbours, especially when they all naturally expect to see you. And Mrs Merry will be mortally offended that after all the effort she and Beth went to regarding your dress you might as well be feeding it to the sheep. If you wish to sit down to breakfast tomorrow with that on your conscience, then go and hide… No, that is *not* an option. You will come down right now and smile at the guests!'

He looked on the verge of stamping his foot

like Jamie. She wished he would, because his upward spiral of annoyance was unravelling her discomfort. This, she was familiar with. The impossible embarrassment at the events on the beach receded, revealing the simple truth—she did not want to stay in her room. She wanted to go down into the light and the laughter, dressed in her beautiful gown. She might soon lose everything she cared for, but she could take some of it with her, gather her memories like Jamie gathered treasures, and for that she must be brave.

'Very well.'

'You will?'

She looked at herself in the mirror.

'You are right. Mrs Merry and Beth would be very offended. It would probably affect Beth's enjoyment of the ball.'

'I had not realised she is attending the ball as well.' There was that reluctant smile in his voice that always made her mouth want to curve in response. This time she allowed it.

'Every servant in the castle house takes part in it, even if only by listening to what the footmen report when they go to the keep to fetch more food and wine. And Beth is very possessive of this dress, having had such a say in its creation. Apparently she has even asked Ewan to tell her who dances with her dress.'

'You, I hope.' His smile flashed, easing the glower further.

'I am merely a vessel. Her dress will be the attraction. As such whoever dances with me becomes Beth's possession.'

'Good God, that is mawkish. I hope Mrs Merry is keeping a tight leash on Beth's imagination. I don't want her falling into trouble.'

'Beth is far too clever. She knows the difference between a dream and a loaf of bread. She has her sights on Angus.'

She did not add—*far cleverer than I.*

'Does she? She will have her work cut out for her. He is convinced he is not marriage material with his scars.'

'She is patient. And determined. She will wear him down in the end.'

'I hope so.' He hesitated and then held out his arm. 'Come.'

She went, stepping into the lie that he wanted her there, that she looked lovely in her borrowed gown, that unlike those horrid balls years ago she would not be invisible, unremarked, overlooked. That she was not merely an impecunious widow-cum-governess invited to the ball as an act of casual kindness, but the Jo that Jamie saw in her—wondrous and wise and worth caring for.

Her head dipped and she watched the tips of

her slippers. They were the only thing she wore that were originally hers and they were a little scuffed. There would be no hiding them, not even under her lovely dress.

He stopped abruptly at the head of the staircase and she wavered and almost slipped on the top stair. His other hand caught her at the waist.

'Steady. Not even falling downstairs will be acceptable as an excuse not to attend. Look at me. Are you crying?'

Oh no. She could feel the tears straining to slide down her cheeks. She had not counted on sympathy. She was not experienced enough with it to counter it as she did indifference and criticism and anger. She shook her head.

He led her back to her parlour and her heart and mind raged. She had won her battle not to go to the ball, but she didn't want to win. She did not quite understand what was growing inside her, but it was fierce and hot and it wanted to go to the ball. With him.

'Here, look at me.' His voice was soft and she closed her eyes and shook her head, but he raised her face and she felt the cool press of linen on her eyes and cheeks, absorbing her tears.

'Is it so very bad?' he asked. 'I know you never enjoyed balls when Bella was coming out, but it is different now. You aren't Miss Watkins, being shunted between relations. You are Mrs Langdale, and my guest. I won't allow you to be slighted, you know.'

'That isn't it.' She touched her fingertips to her eyelids, stopping the tears. She was growing weak. In the past she never would have allowed this to happen. It was his fault.

'Then what?' His voice was so gentle it ached.

'It is foolish.'

'Tell me anyway.'

She grasped for something, anything to say. Strangely what came was the truth, just not the whole truth.

'I never had pretty dresses when I married Alfred. His mother died a week after the wedding and we wore mourning, and two weeks before the year was up he fell from his horse. I thought... I wish he might have seen me in such a dress...'

As the silence stretched on she forced herself to look. He was very close, she could see the peculiar grey-green of his eyes, the colours of the cliffs and sea beyond.

'I am sorry for him, too. But he was a lucky man to have you even so briefly. A smart man, too.'

He raised her hand, just touching it with his lips, his hair dark against the pale orange of her skirts. His words rang inside her like the vibrations of a bell and she fisted her other hand against the impulse to touch the silk of his hair. It was not an effusive testimony to her transformation by the dress, but it struck her as so much more personal. Like Alfred, though in a different way, this man saw her. It was not enough, leagues and leagues from what she craved, but it still warmed her.

'Thank you, Benneit.'

His hand tightened on hers as he straightened, but he dropped it and stepped back, holding out his arm as he had before.

'You are welcome, Jo. Come. Now more than ever I will not allow you to hide. Once I do the perfunctory dances with the dragons and their offspring, we will share a dance for your Alfred. Tell me you can waltz.'

'Yes, Your Grace, I can waltz.'

'Good. Your fate is sealed.'

Chapter Twenty-Four

It had been foolish to worry.

He watched Jo standing between Donald Mac-Gregor and Duncan McCrieff and wondered again at her transformation. She was laughing, her cheeks warm from the dance and her lovely mouth curved in an enticing smile. The two men were both leaning towards her like rods of metal towards a lodestone, clearly enchanted. She was nothing like the stiff and repressive girl of six years ago—the simple green bud had released the lush rose bloom within and the insects were circling, he thought with a stab of resentment, trying to feel happy for her.

'She's wearing Lochmore colours.'

He turned at his aunt's raspy voice. Her scent of whisky usually warned him she was within hailing distance, but he had been distracted.

'She is part of Bella's family.'

'Aye, but she isn't a Lochmore any more than that spoilt piece of spun sugar was.'

He laughed at the absurdity of calling Bella anything so whimsical. Morag grunted.

'Fair enough. She was hard as nails, your countess. But still spoilt. The McCrieffs won't like another of your Englishwomen wearing orange, you know.'

'Since when do you care about clan politics?'

'Since Hamish died. He never had the nerve to dislodge me from my tower, but a new mistress might. Not a McCrieff, though—she would respect Lochmore heritage and not try to clear out the inconvenient womenfolk like your previous wife would have done had she outlived Hamish. So if you must wed it might as well be a McCrieff. Your English widow will have to go, though. Lady Aberwyld won't like another young woman living here once her daughter is made Duchess, especially not if she sees you watching her that way.'

He resisted the urge to move away from Morag and her bitterness. She was and had always been ruled by her fears.

'Mrs Langdale never intended to remain at Lochmore beyond a month. She has her own plans. When I wed…' The words ran dry, soaked up by a throat as parched as any of Jamie's deserts. It was inevitable, it was already in motion. Every movement of the guests in this great grey room was a testimony to that wedding-to-be. The melding of the tribes, the burying of hatchets, the creation of a new future for Jamie. It was as unstoppable as any Greek fable told—running from your fate served no purpose but delaying the inevitable.

'Aye. When you wed. That bone is sticking in your gullet, isn't it?' Morag said, her voice ripe with spite.

The music began again and he moved away from Morag. Hell was not always fire and brimstone. Sometimes it was a well-appointed ballroom with the music spinning you closer to the rest of your lonely life.

He deserved a little escape from his fast-approaching fate, he told himself as he approached Jo. He was almost upon her when Malcolm and Donald nodded in his direction and she turned. The fairy-light fabric spread and gathered again about her legs and gold glinted in the embroidered stars along her bodice. He already had a very fair impression of her breasts from their interlude on the beach path, but under the warm glow of the candlelit chandeliers he could see how perfectly they curved above her bodice. They would be warm and soft and fit into his palms and... God in heaven, he had better stop now or his erection would pitch a tent in his kilt.

'You promised me a waltz, Mrs Langdale.'

'Unfair! I was trying to convince her of the same, Lochmore.' MacGregor laughed.

'You've already had a dance and that orange clashes with your tartan, MacGregor,' Duncan McCrieff said with ponderous joviality. 'Besides, I'm the better dancer.'

'Nevertheless, as host I claim precedence. Mrs Langdale?' He held out his hand and, though her smile was a little forced, she came to him. He wondered if perhaps she was interested in either of those foppish fribbles. She had every right. Perhaps it would even suit her to secure herself a husband here rather than attempt to strike out on her own as a schoolmistress. It was certainly a more sensible choice and he had no right to object, certainly none to feel such a burn of jealousy.

'Enjoying yourself?' He tried to keep his voice level, but she noticed the edge, her hand twitching under his where he held it to his arm.

'Very much, Your Grace.'

'I gather from your becoming colour they have been plying you with compliments.'

'Everyone has been very kind.'

'Was that kindness on exhibit there just now? It looked like something far less uninterested.'

She tried to draw her hand from his arm, but he pressed it there more firmly. He was being an ill-tempered idiot, but it was beyond him. He did not like those men fawning over her and he did not like not liking it. Perhaps if he said nothing...

'Why are you angry, Your Grace? Is something wrong?' She spoke softly, with real concern, which only fed his self-disgust.

'Damn it, Jo. Why can you not get angry when you ought? I know I am behaving like an ill-mannered idiot.'

'Yes, you are, but my dress is lovely and has danced with many lovely kilts and coats and so I forgive you.'

She smiled and he wished they could just stop. Stop everything. Send everyone away. Or go back to the day before he was fool enough to step across the line in the sand. He didn't want this.

'I trust Beth will be pleased with your dress's performance.' He smiled. 'MacGregor certainly seemed pleased, or was that his kilt?'

He had not expected her to catch the lewd import of his comment, but her eyes widened and she burst into her gurgling laughter. He was so tempted to pull her out on to the terrace, spread out his kilt on the grass and bare her beautiful body to the moon and stars and his touch and taste.

'Jo.'

He didn't know what she heard in his voice, but her laughter faded. For a moment everything faded but the deep grey of her eyes, the soft sweep of her lips, halfway between a smile and bemusement. Then an ache, deep inside but as sharp and stinging as a blow from Angus's fist, spread through him.

He took her arm.

'They are striking up a waltz. Come dance with me.'

'Oughtn't you rather—?'

'No,' he interrupted her, moving her firmly towards the dance floor. He did not want to think in shoulds and oughts. He wanted this. Her. Now. It would be over soon enough.

Jo felt the guests staring as he drew her on to the dance floor and her gaze settled on his shoes and her slippers as they moved to the lovely music. She did not recognise it—it was light and dreamlike, as if the composer had crawled inside her head and heard a long-lost dream of hers. And the more recent dreams of Benneit, smiling at her...touching her... She had seen him dance often enough six years ago—tall and handsome and perfectly matched with Bella. It made little sense that he was dancing with her now, his hand warm on hers through her glove, his fingers shifting slightly on her waist as he guided her.

'Are you counting your steps? You don't need

244 Unlaced by the Highland Duke

to, you dance beautifully.' There was a smile in his voice, but also something else she could not read. Was she embarrassing him?

'I'm sorry. I was listening to the music. It is so lovely. There is something so...wistful about waltzes. Sometimes I think they should be danced with eyes closed.'

'If everyone did that it might wreak havoc on the dance floor.'

'That is a very practical consideration, but not at all relevant to daydreams.'

'Ah, this is daydreaming Jo. What tale would unfold behind your lowered lids?'

She shook her head, embarrassed to have even said as much, but he continued.

'You could do that now—close your eyes and dream away.' His voice sank and there was heat in it, but also a raw edge that brought with it the memory of that brief, wild embrace on the cliff path; the aftermath of fear and fury and the grasping at life.

She didn't tell him that this time she did not want to close her eyes. That there was no daydream that could outdo this moment. It was a dream come real, but with the bitter twist of all such dreams—it was still out of reach and all the more vicious for that chasm.

She did not want the moment ruined by bitterness so she kept her smile and forced herself to look up.

It was a mistake. She had been warm before, but the look she saw in his eyes seared her skin. Until this moment she was convinced the kiss on the cliff path was mostly the outcome of anger and frustration. But in this civilised setting she could not mistake the stark desire in his eyes; it reached out and grabbed her like a dog sinking its fangs into a rabbit. Then his thick black lashes lowered and he smiled as well, but it was not an easy smile.

'You can dream of Alfred seeing you as you are now,' he said, his hand tightening on hers and his other sliding lower on her back. She stumbled against him, her leg brushing against his, and another bolt of lightning ripped through her, as if they were two pieces of flint, incapable of contact without the threat of fire. Her ears were ringing with it, her breasts heavy and almost foreign in a bodice now too tight.

'I'm sorry, Jo, I should not have said that. I didn't mean to hurt you.'

He sounded angry with himself and she forced a smile.

'It did not hurt. I don't wish to dream of him. I am happy as I am right now.'

His hands softened on hers, his thumb shifting

to brush the heart of her palm, but if he meant to soothe her, it had the opposite effect. Even that tiny caress poured heat through her, making her arm shiver. How could he not know what he was doing to her? What every word and touch were wreaking? She was accustomed to thinking that her thoughts and emotions and very existence were invisible to the world, but surely some of this storm inside her must be visible?

'I am glad.'

He didn't sound glad, he sounded as raw as she and she made herself look up again, even at the risk that he might see what she was feeling. She was greedy, she wanted to capture this image in her mind—his hand holding hers, his body so close to hers she felt his heat engulf her like the waves had, and just as dangerous to her well-being. But mostly she wanted to fix in her mind the stark lines of his face and the green storm within his eyes. They were narrowed and shaded, but she could see the fierce heat was still there. Unwanted but there and she felt a primitive shiver of victory.

'Jo.' His voice was so low she felt rather than heard the word, as it reached her through his hands on her and the air around them. She could hardly feel her feet on the floor. Had no idea if she was dancing or suspended in his arms like a rag doll. All she could do was feel him, that she was already part of him.

Then the music slowed and the world returned—noisy, colourful, buzzing with words and laughter and the scuffing of shoes on the floor. It sounded strange, unrelated to her. When his hands left her she made her way towards where Ewan stood overseeing his small army of footmen. She had to be useful. Useful was where she was safe.

But she had not quite reached Ewan when a tentative voice behind her stopped her short.

'Mrs Langdale?'

Jo turned and smiled reflexively at the woman who was to become Benneit's wife.

'Lady Theresa.'

'Could I beg you for a moment's help? My ribbon has become hopelessly tangled and every time I try to loosen it, it draws tighter. I don't want to bother Mama or my sisters because they will preach I have been carelessly clumsy once again.'

'Of course.'

She led the younger woman to a small room by the withdrawing rooms which Mrs Merry had prepared for just such eventualities. A sewing kit was open on the table besides a tray of refreshment and three lovely fans that might once have been the Duchess's. Lady Tessa picked up one of the fans and unfurled it absently in a shimmer of sky-blue silk.

'I was hoping to see Jamie. But he will be coming with Lochmore when they visit us. You will come, too, won't you, Mrs Langdale?'

'I don't believe so, Lady Theresa.'

'Oh, do come and please call me Tessa. Theresa sounds so prim and I always hated that name. I was named after my aunt and she is frightful, but thankfully she lives in Aberdeen. Are you enjoying staying at the castle? It is much larger than ours and I always found it a little...intimidating.'

The ribbon, a lovely pink silk threaded around the high waist, had tangled into a knot under Lady Tessa's arm and Jo removed her gloves to work it free. This was a servant's task, but for some reason she did not find the young woman's request insulting. This was not one of Celia's commands as requests, but a transparent manoeuvre to have a tête-à-tête and Jo wondered why. Surely this lovely girl, with her voluptuous figure and hair the colour of a sunset, would have no reason to be concerned about the presence of a widow well past her first blush, with no countenance or fortune?

When the ribbon was freed Lady Tessa sank on to one of the chairs with a sigh and adjusted a thick curl of hair. Its colour was not quite as red as Angus's, something between amber and auburn, and though it should clash, Jo had to admit she would look marvellous dressed in the Lochmore colours. Far better than Jo herself.

'Thank you, that is much better.' Lady Tessa smiled. 'Did you know my maid is Beth's cousin by marriage? She said Jamie dotes on you. Will you be staying at Lochmore or must you return to England?'

Jo hesitated as she would before walking across a chasm balanced on a plank. Perhaps she was wrong about this woman's guilelessness. Perhaps she had seen the truth on Jo's face during the dance.

'I agreed to remain here a month, that is all, Lady The—Tessa.'

'I see.'

Tessa's shoulders slumped and her tone was so despondent Jo was surprised into honesty.

'Why do you ask?'

'You must know what is being said, about the alliance, and I was rather hoping there might be someone here who might be a friend.'

'If you are to wed, I would imagine your husband would be that friend,' Jo answered, her heart thumping like a great drum, and Tessa's smile was wry.

'It is not that kind of alliance. Lochmore is a good man, but... Was your husband your friend?'

'Yes. But I know that is rare. Still, your family is not so very far and you will make new friends perhaps, and then there is Jamie and eventually...'

Her resolve to be cool and calm sank under the weight of her horror at the picture she was painting. She did not hate this woman, but she would happily see her erased from the face of the earth. She stood.

'We should return, Lady Tessa.'

The younger woman sighed and stood as well.

'Yes. Sometimes I wonder how it is that women have not yet overturned the world. There is something dreadfully wrong with it.'

Jo's pain melted a little.

'That is very true. Perhaps one day they shall. Perhaps one day your daughter will.'

Tessa smiled.

'Or yours.'

Jo shook her head but didn't answer.

Just before they regained the Great Hall a hand closed tightly on her elbow and she turned in surprise to face Morag.

'Shoo, girl.' Morag waved a hand at Tessa. To give Tessa credit, she sought Jo's confirmation at her dismissal, but Jo smiled reassuringly and

Tessa continued, glancing back once over her shoulder before entering the Great Hall.

'Secrets between the Is and the Will Be?'

Jo tried to focus on the slurred voice and the bloodshot eyes and not on the venom.

'Shall I ask Mrs Merry to help you to your rooms, Lady Morag?'

'I know my way. This is *my* home, whatever the two of you are conniving. Setting up to share my nephew? I saw the way the two of you danced. Dancing! There's another name for that! Well, don't think you three can conspire to send me away from my tower!'

'He will never send you away, Lady Morag. Trust me, it is not something he would do. Why test him, though?'

The filmy brown eyes cleared for a moment.

'I don't know if I want her here.'

'Whether you wish it or not, his honour is pledged.'

'Aye. Whether *you* want it or not. I don't like seeing Aberwyld in these walls.'

For a moment there was nothing but sincerity in Morag's rough voice and Jo recognised a kindred pain.

'I am not particularly fond of Lady Aberwyld either,' she said, thinking back to the dour woman she had encountered that evening.

Lady Morag dropped her arm and stood back, a mixture of viciousness and pain in her lined face. 'Clever little miss, aren't you? It won't save you, though.'

'I know that, Lady Morag.'

'I don't want her here. My father wanted Mc-Crieff to marry me, did you know that? To bring peace between the families. But then *she* sank her claws into him and he forgets all about me. Fat lot of good it did him.'

The pain was so vivid Jo felt horrified with it— would she, too, be so torn decades later? Tangled in these feelings for Benneit? Before she could even think of a response, Mrs Merry appeared in the corridor, her surprise turning to a frown.

'I'll see you to your room, Lady Morag, and Beth will bring up a nice toddy. Mrs Langdale, Angus would like a word with you. He's by the great staircase.'

Jo nodded with relief as Mrs Merry led Morag away, then went to find Angus. His face was calm as always, but immediately she tensed.

'Angus, what has happened?'

'Now, dinna worrit, Mrs Jo, but Jamie's ill and is calling for 'ee. Looks like to cast up his accounts.'

She nodded and picked up her skirts, heading up the stairs, her heartbeat swift. Angus's broadening brogue was a clear sign he was more concerned than his words indicated.

'Where does the closest doctor or surgeon reside, Angus?'

Angus grimaced, his scars twisting even further as he strode up the stairs beside her.

'Doctor Harris is gone to Edinburgh this week so there's only Dr Mitchell and he'll be deep in whisky this hour. We don't send for him after the sun sets unless we send for a priest, too. I don't want to worry Benneit… His Grace…unless we must. Tonight of all nights.'

'Well, we shall see first what is ailing Jamie and then decide.'

Nurse Moody was in the room when Jo entered, bending over Jamie's bed. Jamie himself was curled up into a ball at the corner of the bed and she saw immediately this was not merely one of his nightmares. His face was chalky and his forehead glistened with sweat, his eyes tightly shut.

'I want Jo!' he moaned and she hurried forward.

'I'm here, Jamie.'

'My pudding box hurts! Worse than in the carriage…'

She sat down beside the little ball and touched

his forehead. He was cool and one worry erased itself.

'Was he asleep?' she asked Nurse Moody and the older woman shook her head worriedly.

'I don't rightly know, Mrs Langdale. I heard him moaning and I came.'

Jo ran her hand down his clammy cheek and her fingers snagged on a red substance at the corner of his mouth. For one horrible moment she feared it was blood, but without thinking she raised her fingers and sniffed at them. Before she could comment a harsh shudder ran through Jamie.

'Angus, the basin, now!' she called and to his credit Angus grabbed the basin quickly enough and she had it under poor Jamie's head as his body heaved. For several moments the only sounds were his dreadful retching and choked sobs, mixed with her murmurs as she tried to calm the little boy. When the retching settled into shudders, she handed the basin to Angus who took it with all the fastidiousness of a London dandy and hurried out. Nurse Moody handed her a dampened towel and she bathed Jamie's face as he lay exhausted and shuddering.

'Jamie! What is wrong?' Benneit burst into the room and Jamie gave a little wail and burrowed into his pillow.

'Hush, Benneit,' Jo admonished.

'Don't hush me, what is wrong?'

He sank on to the other side of the bed, turning Jamie towards him, his face as pale as his son's, though less grey. Jamie moaned and a tear squeezed out of the corner of his tightly shut eyes.

''m sorry...'

Benneit turned to her, his face pale and fierce.

'What happened? Tell me!'

'Too many tarts,' she replied, bathing Jamie's forehead and cheeks. 'You needn't worry, Jamie. No one is angry with you.'

'Tarts?'

'I believe Jamie didn't want to wait until his punishment was lifted to sample Mrs Merry's jam tarts. To be fair, they are delicious... Sorry, Jamie, I should not have said that,' she amended as the little body heaved. Benneit cupped his son's face in his hands, his profile tense and hard, and Jamie began crying weakly.

'I feel awful, Papa.'

'Hush, Jamie, don't worry,' he murmured, stroking the damp curls back from the boy's brow. 'It will pass.'

Jamie shook his head, crying harder. Jo thought of leaving them, but did not move. As if sensing her hesitation Jamie's hand crawled from under his blanket and tucked itself under hers. Benneit directed her a hard, angry look, as if either his son's illness or this gesture were transgressions on her part, which perhaps they were.

He is merely scared and a little jealous, she assured herself. But it hurt more than it ought, especially after his chivalry that evening and the moment of raw heat during the dance. It hurt, but not enough to convince her to leave.

They sat in silence. At some point Benneit took the damp cloth from her and soothed Jamie's face. Eventually the shudders calmed and Jamie's body stretched out, inch by inch, his eyes fluttering open and a little colour returning to his cheeks.

'I'll never eat tarts again, Papa,' he whispered, his voice raw. 'Ever.'

Benneit set aside the cloth and smiled.

'Not for a while, at least, little turtle. Can you sleep now?'

'I'm thirsty.'

Benneit glanced past her towards where Angus and Nurse were seated by the door. He gently put down Jamie's hand and stood.

'I will return directly, Jamie.'

The three disappeared and the room sank into silence again. Jo watched Jamie's quivering lower lip.

'Did I ever tell you about my dog Bumblebee?' Jo asked.

'You had a dog named Bumblebee?'

'Well, he wasn't strictly mine like Flops is yours. He belonged to the farmer down the lane, but I made believe he was mine and he was certainly of no use as a sheepdog. He was far too small, for one thing, and the only thing he chased were butterflies and bumblebees. But he had one skill no other dog ever had...'

She let the words hang until Jamie detached his eyes from the door and looked at her.

'What could he do?'

'He could talk to other animals, especially donkeys. He used to jump on the back of the farmer's donkey and ride it down to the pond where there were the most flowers and butterflies. I think cats understood him, too, but they ignored him so I was never certain.'

Jamie's mouth softened into a smile so like his father's her heart became a tightly clenched fist before releasing with a sigh.

'I think they understood. Cats are smart.'

'So they are. Well, one day...'

Halfway through her elaborate tale, Benneit and Nurse returned with a cup of a brew smelling of chamomile and mint. Benneit raised Jamie gently and spooned the tea into his mouth, waiting between each sip. There was a methodical rhythm to his motions and again she noted he was surprisingly unawkward in his care. He had done this before, set himself and Jamie apart from the world. She was an interloper.

Jo again considered leaving but did not move. She glanced over to where Nurse sat with practised patience by the wall, expecting to receive the usual blank stare or some sign of condemnation at her insistence on staying. To her surprise, Nurse's wrinkled visage softened into a smile, her blue eyes bright and warm. It startled Jo so much she smiled back and then looked down, as embarrassed as if she had been caught staring at Benneit.

When the cup was empty, Benneit eased Jamie back down into the bed and covered him, and they sat as Jamie lay with his eyes closed, his breathing settling. Soon Jo felt the tell-tale twitches in Jamie's legs against her thigh that spoke of sleep, but it was only when he breathed the single shuddering breath as he entered deep sleep that Benneit stood. Jo followed him and Nurse into the corridor.

'I'll sleep with the door open to Jamie and call you if he wakes,' Nurse Moody said and returned to the room.

Jo glanced at Benneit and then down at her crumpled, water-stained skirts. Her beautiful dress was ruined.

'You should change your cravat if you mean to return downstairs, Your Grace.'

He caught her hand as she passed, his gaze serious as it swept over her.

'Thank you.'

'Pray, do not be foolish.'

'Is showing gratitude being foolish? Why did you not send for me, though? I only learned he was ill when I asked Ewan where you were. You should have told me Jamie was ill. I told Angus the same.'

'I did not want to take you away from your guests, at least not until I knew what was wrong.'

'It is not your place to decide that.'

That struck harder than any whip, in particular after the intimacy formed in Jamie's room during the past hour. She tugged away and proceeded towards her rooms.

'Wait, Jo. I did not mean it like that...'

'Your guests are waiting, Your Grace.'

'No, they are not, I said my goodbyes when Angus went to fetch the tea. Now it is well past midnight and they have all no doubt retired. This isn't London.'

'Goodnight, Your Grace.'

'Wait. Jo, I am grateful, truly, but Jamie is mine to care for. For his own good he should not become too dependent upon you. If you care for him...'

She had opened the door to her room but at those words she rounded on him, choked with pain and rage far more potent now than it had been two hours ago as she watched him with Tessa McCrieff.

'*If* I care? How dare you? You may go to hell, Benneit Lochmore!'

'Hush. Stop yelling. I did not mean to upset you.' He crowded her into her room, his hands raised.

'I am not yelling! You didn't mean this and you didn't mean that and you didn't mean anything, but you are just plain mean! I hate you!'

He gave an odd laugh which was worse than all his words and she sank even lower in her unaccustomed and childish tantrum and tried to shove him back into the corridor. He took a step back, but planted his foot, covering her hands with his and her shoving amounted to nothing and all her powerlessness rose to the surface like Jamie's tarts and she began to cry.

'Jo. Please don't. Ah, Jo...' He let go of her hands, but only to wrap his arms around her and though this, too, meant nothing, she sank against him and let her weariness and pain win.

'I didn't even think of you,' she babbled. 'I only

wanted to go to Jamie as quickly as I could. I didn't mean to come between you and you are cruel to think that.' She wailed, then rendered herself even more ridiculous by adding, 'And my beautiful dress is ruined and Beth will be disappointed in me as well.'

'Jo. Please don't cry, I am so sorry, lass. I was scared, and I'm a fool when I'm scared. Hush, darling, please...' The words were warm against her temple, his lips brushing the sensitive skin there, and she shivered, breathed in, utterly confused.

The words, the warmth and strength of his arms around her made no sense. Or only made sense to that part of her that had dreamed this. *Darling?*

An endearment that meant nothing at all. He wanted her to calm down and stop making noise. That was all.

The same applied to his hands shifting lower, shaping the slope of her waist, tightening on the softness of her hips. *Just comfort, Jo.*

She had a harder time explaining away the shudder that pressed his body against hers, or his voice wrapping around her name as it had for that strange timeless moment during the dance.

'Jo...'

She froze. Raised her hands and wiped her wet face with her fingers and searched for the lie in the urgency she read in the tension of his body against hers. His embrace was no longer comforting—it was demanding.

It must be a lie.

She forced herself to lean back, to look up into his face and see the pity and contrition his words had evoked, but instead she saw what she could not mistake.

Fire.

She had never imagined a man would look at her like that. Not even Alfred, who loved her, had ever looked at her with such concentrated fire, with a tension that slashed lines of shadows and darkness into his austere face.

His hands rose, cupped her face, his thumbs brushing across her cheeks, sliding on the remnants of her tears. His touch was gentle but his voice was rough, an underground scraping that rose up from her feet and shattered her as it went.

'Tell me to leave now, Jo.'

'Why?' she asked, without thinking, and he sank against her, wrapping himself about her, a laugh coursing through him and adding to her destruction.

'Why? No reason. No good reason. Tell me to stay. Please, Jo.'

'Stay. I want you to stay.'

He groaned, his hands moved from her hips to

her backside, raising her against him. She felt it then. He was hard and hot and the contact drove back everything but awareness. What was no more than a dream minutes ago was now the very centre of her existence.

'Oh, God, Jo. I've been wanting to touch you for ever. I can't bear it any longer...'

His words echoed her thoughts and she ignored the lie. It didn't matter. What mattered was that he wanted her now. Even if it was only because of fear and loneliness and frustration. Right now he wanted her.

'Then touch me, Benneit.'

She waited for him to pull up her skirts, press her back on to the bed as Alfred did on those rare occasions he took her when they were not already in bed. He always felt guilty later and she usually felt...incomplete. She did not want to think of Alfred now, but she could not help it. Her body was alive and straining for something, but her mind was scurrying away. She wanted Benneit, but she knew in a few moments he would be sated and then he would leave and she would still be there, even more alone.

Then she realised Benneit had stopped and panic set in. She did not want this, but she did not want him to go away. Her hand fisted on his kilt and she leaned against him.

'Benneit, don't stop…'

'Hush,' he breathed against her ear, his lips a heated slide against it, sending ripples over her nerves like warm water. 'Slowly. Let me touch you. I need to feel all of you.'

The words touched her, reached inside her, a strange dark promise and demand. He kissed the lobe of her ear, a light brush of skin on skin, but it made her shoulder rise involuntarily and he kissed that as well, moving slowly towards her neck, lingering on the silky skin below her ear, so gently it felt like the caress of a breeze. Then, just as gently, he touched his tongue to her earlobe, closed his teeth on it and suckled.

A dam of liquid heat burst inside her, her palms flattening on his chest, ready to push away, but instead they pulled him towards her, as she angled her head to capture every nip and sweep of his mouth as he unravelled her. But he didn't match her urgency—his hands caressed her back, drawing her deeper into the slow, swaying rhythm of his mouth as he continued to explore. It was a sweeping possession, like the furling and unfurling of the waves in the south bay, but underneath was all the raging fierceness of the sea that had nearly destroyed them and it was terrifying and exhilarating. He swept her into his rhythm, into the scorching sweep of his mouth and tongue on her body, breaking her into elements, finding places that had never meant anything to her before this moment, but now made her shudder and cling, whimpering for something she knew he held, but withheld.

'I've found your rose, an Autumn Damask, right here.' He breathed in, the air cool on the skin at the base of her neck. She shivered and he guided her arm around his neck so he could bring her closer, moulding her body against his with a shuddering sigh of satisfaction, as if this was what he wanted, just this meeting of bodies.

For a moment he held her there, only their breathing shifting their bodies against each other, but it was not a peaceful embrace. The silence and the stillness was merely a stage for the swirling heat that had caught them on the cliff path and in the dance—it was there, still raging, gathering force. When he spoke, his voice measured but harsh, she knew he felt the same.

'I should leave, but I can't. Not if it is left to me. You will have to say the words, Jo. Choose.'

She didn't want that burden, she wanted him to shoulder it. But there was enough of her own conscience still alive to recognise he was trying to show her some respect. Because he could offer no more than this. She would have to choose.

'I need you here tonight, Benneit. Please stay with me.'

The words unleashed the fierceness he had shackled so firmly, his hands pulling her hard against him. His mouth was no longer soft and coaxing—it slanted over hers, taking her fully, his tongue teasing and touching places that made her body clench halfway to release before a single layer of clothing was removed. She wanted him to hurry, to slow down, to combust and take her with him... She was cold and hot and everywhere at the mercy of his hands as they explored her body, tightening impatiently on her buttocks as he raised her against him to deepen the kiss, his tongue tracing hers, suckling and tasting, and everything poured through her to lash at the burning, dampening flesh between her legs, turning her skin to liquid warmth until she was shaking, about to crest the waves.

She felt everything, but hardly noticed as her dress and stays fell away, followed by the heavy folds of his kilt. She only realised she was half-naked when the backs of her legs met the coolness of the bed. He leaned her back until she lay there, with him standing between her legs. He pulled off his shirt, holding it in his hands as he looked down at her and her legs tried to close but only managed to press against his as he stood there.

His thighs felt like rock against the inside of her knees. As hard and warm as the Devil's Seat in the sun. He tucked his hand under her knees, raising them so that her feet were braced on the edge of the bed, then shocked her by brushing a light kiss on her thigh, even as his hand curled under it, his fingers caressing the soft skin, slowly moulding and kneading as he slid the edge of her chemise upwards, his mouth trailing in its wake, a whisper following a whisper.

The fire was behind him, gilding him with a garish halo and leaving his face in darkness, but between soft, feathering brushes of his mouth along her leg his eyes rose to meet hers with an obsidian glint like those of a panther.

'You like to be touched...' His breath glided down her thigh, settling on the damp, pulsing centre between them like a rippling wave. The chemise followed inch by agonising inch, but his hands and mouth stopped mid-thigh despite the heat gathering unbearably at the pit of her stomach and at the core of her arousal. It was a deep thudding burn and her teeth dragged at her lower lip as if that could somehow alleviate the rising discomfort. He smiled and leaned forward, brushing his lips very lightly over the rise of her hipbone, his words slipping and sliding over the quivering valley between her hip and navel, and downwards…

'Yes. I will do that, too, but first I want to see you. All of you. Do you know how much I wanted to take you there, by the cliff? Strip off that last, damp petticoat that was wrapped to you like a second skin. Warm you with my body, inside and out. Taste you… Everywhere…'

His hands had worked the chemise about her waist, his fingers tracing quicksilver burns from her hips to the valleys beside them, the roughened pads of his fingers abrading the skin above her pale brown curls, cutting off her breath and driving her hips up as she tried to catch and capture his fleeting but devastating caresses. Her eyes drifted shut, trying to block out his animal beauty, protect herself from him.

'Look at me.' It was between a purr and a growl, but it was definitely a command. It was the stilling of his hands that made her obey. If surrender was the price she had to pay for him to continue, she would pay it. He leaned one fist on the bed beside her, sinking on to the knee that rode between her legs, so close to the apex of her thighs she could feel its heat at her core, the pleasurable abrasion of the silky hair on his thighs on the bare softness of hers. Her legs clamped hard on his knee and she tried to slide towards him, but then he finally bent to kiss her, his mouth as gentle as his hands at first, just skimming her tightly held lips, sending a starburst of sensation with each sweep. He smoothed the chemise over her breast, languorously skimming the fabric around the swell, torturing her with the drag and shift of the fabric against the aching, sensitive peak.

Her own hands came out of their dream state, rising to press against the heat of his chest. She moaned at the contact and she felt his harshly indrawn breath against her mouth. Before he could pull away, her teeth caught at his lower lip, caressing it with her tongue as if it was her own. He answered with a groan, his hand tightening on her breast, his thumb flicking its already hard crown, and her body rose to meet his, her fingers dragging down his chest, sliding up and back, feeling every line she had stared at with such hunger, watching him in the stable yard. Seeing everything without vision, just through the sensation of hard muscle, corded sinew under silky dark hair, sheathed bones and sudden soft dips of flesh that made him shiver under her touch. The kiss deepened, his tongue and lips no longer playing, but demanding. With each plunge and stroke the heat at her core expanded and contracted and she tried to pull him down to her, but he took her hands and anchored them to the bed, the firelight dancing and glittering on his heaving chest as he drew back.

'Not yet, not until you are coming apart with it.'

'I am…' she gasped.

'No. When we step off that cliff I want you with me. With *me*, Jo.'

She shook her head. Who else was there? There was no one in this world, nothing, but him.

'Slowly now,' he whispered and she laughed at that absurdity. Slow? He must be mad. She was already dying, there was no slow. But she, too, wanted to make this last into infinity and she kept her eyes open as he leaned over her again, easing off her chemise and drawing the pins from her hair with excruciating care. Her eyes teared as a pin snagged, the pain only adding to her quivering agony, and he pressed brief, light kisses to her eyelids, the crest of her cheek, the corner of her mouth in a trail that was almost innocent but for the gentle lick of his tongue at the corner of her mouth, coaxing her open, to dip along the seam of her lips and inwards.

'This is how I will taste you there. Soon.' His words were like silk drawn over her burning body. She did not know how she knew what he meant—it was outrageous, but the heat between her legs flared, her legs closing convulsively against his knee where it was still braced on the bed between them.

'Yes,' he murmured as his mouth and hands continued mapping her body, shifting lower and lower, 'You can feel me there already, can't you?'

'Benneit!'

She was nearly crying with need by the time he pressed a light kiss to the valley beside her hipbone, nuzzling there as his fingers continued brushing and stroking the soft down of hair, sliding through it and down the cleft between her legs. It was a single scorching line, light but definite, and she felt her dampness under his fingers. She didn't understand any of this. It was so different from how it had been with Alfred and yet so much more right. Some residual shame made her try to pull away, but he only took advantage of her movement to nudge her thigh with his shoulder, his tongue a caress, his breath a tangle of hot and cold on her shimmering skin. Shock held her still, but then his tongue gently brushed the sensitive nub at the apex and she squirmed to escape the coil of almost unbearable heat that simple caress unleashed.

'Don't run from me, Jo. I won't do anything you aren't ready for. I promise.'

He moved up again, his mouth nuzzling and caressing her breast and though he let her close her legs, his hand remained resting on the downy hair, his long fingers curved against her flesh so that she could feel their pulses meeting, pouring through her. When he nudged her legs apart again with his she was so awash with warmth she just exhaled on a long sigh as his fingers opened her, sending whiplashes of pleasure dancing between his teasing mouth on her breasts and the swirling, coaxing slide of his fingers at her core. When he shifted lower again, his mouth retracing its path, she didn't have the will or the shame to resist. She was no longer herself, she was nothing but what he found in her—light, life, heat... This time when his mouth found the slickness of her arousal she didn't think at all. She had never been so present and so utterly far from reason in her life. Her hands snagged at the sheet, his shoulders, his hair and finally covered her face to muffle the whimpers of pleasure she could not hold back as his mouth and tongue and breath tortured her beyond belief, turning her skin liquid and her blood to fire. Lash after lash of pleasure burst through her and it felt impossible to continue without something terrible happening, but when the world burst in a shower of sparks and a long surge of honey-sweet joy she gave in, welcoming oblivion.

* * *

Benneit raised himself carefully on to his elbow.

She had turned over with a sated sigh after her climax and now lay half on her side, facing away from him. The fire was just a collection of embers and the orange light kissed her bare shoulder and cheek and gilded her eyelashes. She looked as soft and dewy as dawn and he was as hard as the standing stones of Inverdine and as hot as the inside of a volcano.

He smiled, letting his hand hover a few inches above the arch of her back, absorbing her warmth. He was in agony and in heaven. Her pleasure was addictive, intoxicating. He wanted to wake her and take her back to that peak of pleasure so he could watch her melt. And then do it again. And again. He should have had the forethought to take her to his room where he had a French sheath, because this time he wanted to be inside her when she unravelled so she could torture him with each undulating contraction. He still could, but he didn't want to move. He didn't want to do anything that would send her scurrying behind her grey-eyed shield.

His fingers twitched with the urge to follow the guidance of that light where her curves sloped under the blankets, but he stayed motionless, trying to absorb this new reality. It didn't reflect well on him. He had seduced a respectable widow, his son's companion, his dead wife's cousin, a woman under his protection, while half of the population within a hundred miles were guests at the castle.

There was not one way to look at this that would make it acceptable.

Well, there was one way. It had been given to him in the soft moans as he goaded her towards climax, in the sweet curving of her body against his, in the generous slide of her hands over his body, torturing, seeking, giving...

He shuddered a little in remembrance of that first moment of bliss as she had abandoned herself to his hands and mouth, as he watched the bottomless grey of her eyes awash with need and pleasure as he touched her, tasted her...

Who would have guessed his externally placid and controlled little pixie would be such a wild lover?

Well, to be fair, he was not surprised. There had been sufficient clues even for someone as obtuse as he, though she had been hidden behind magical mice and pond maids and a pixie who waltzed like an angel and who cried because her dead husband had not seen her in her lovely new dress. He pushed that thought away—he did not want to think of Jo in Langdale's bed. Which was problematic enough. Jealousy was not an emotion he was familiar with and being jealous of a dead man was...wrong.

He sat on the side of the bed and surveyed their scattered clothes. Her lovely dress was probably ruined. He would buy her a dozen more if she would let him.

He sighed. That would be a battle royal.

Still, having discovered new ways of resolving the conflicts between them, perhaps a battle would not be entirely a bad idea.

The darkness in the window had already shifted and he knew he should leave her room. There would be guests to tend to in a few hours and the servants would be up early. He drew the cover carefully over her shoulders and she sighed, tucking her hand under her pillow and rubbing her cheek on it as she had earlier on his chest with a feline purr of pleasure. A shaft of heat shot through him and he waited for it to peak and settle before he slid off the bed and collected his clothes. It was a little ridiculous to react so hotly to something so simple. Except it was not simple at all. He had been in trouble long before he entered her parlour that evening and saw her in her lovely new dress, her hair arranged into luxurious waves, her eyes huge and full of light... He did not know when this pull began. From some strange moment in the carriage heading north. From taking her hand in the dark to help her off a boulder as she dreamed of her mountains. From watching her face the elements and bare her ankles on the ship. Each moment a little pixie dart, seeping her pixie poison into his blood, making him want this...her...

God, he was aching like a green lad. He wanted nothing more than to slide back next to her, press up against her warmth, tangle his limbs with hers, his tongue with hers... Make her moan and beg and cry out in the agony of her pleasure and this time slide into her and absorb all that heat and passion with his body.

He watched the amber shades of firelight play on the rise and fall of her sleeping form and succumbed to temptation, trailing his hand from the peak of her shoulder down the smooth slope of her arm, settling for a moment in the soft crook of her elbow to catch the warmth of her pulse. As soft as it was, it latched on to him like a reverberating drum, echoing through his body. He breathed in and detached his hand, trying to call himself to order and forcing his eyes back up to her shoulder, but they glided down again, following the curve of her spine and, without thinking, his hand followed his gaze, shifting the blanket down. There was a small heart-shaped beauty mark just above the curve of her behind and his finger traced it and moved lower, cupping her bottom with his hand, his fingers splayed on her hip, slowly kneading it with his palm.

She shuddered into wakefulness, turning towards him, her hand brushing down his chest, her legs shifting towards him. He caught her hand in his, his voice as taut as he felt. 'Don't. If you move I'll do something rash. Just let me look at you for a moment and I will go.'

She looked up at him, her eyes gleaming like mother-of-pearl in the near dark. Then her leg stretched, sliding between his, before rising and coming to rest against the rock-hard length of his frustration. His breath caught and he couldn't resist sinking against her, fitting himself so he was poised against the damp heat still pulsing with her climax. Her scent—a whole lush summer garden of roses—was all around him and he closed his eyes and imagined her at The House, spread out before him as he spread her legs and tasted her to his heart's content, suckled her into mutual annihilation. He couldn't help sliding against her slickness, he could feel every one of her textures against his sensitised erection and the promise of that tight, wet fist of muscles waiting to pull him in... He cursed and shifted, but her leg just found him again.

'I don't think all of you wants to go quite yet,' she whispered, her voice wavering between embarrassment and laughter. He nuzzled the warm fragrant curve of her neck, edging his knee forward, forcing her leg harder against him, his breathing quickening at the pressure.

'None of me wants to go. Except go off, perhaps.'

'Then stay.'

Her hands rose, but hovered by his shoulders, her fingertips just grazing his taut muscles as if afraid he might indeed go off at the first contact. Then they settled, shaping his shoulders, sweeping down his arms. He held still. At least most of him did. His arousal pulsed and surged against the pressure of her leg, answering her hands as they settled for a moment on the pulse inside his elbow, then traced up the hidden skin under his arm, his ribs, her nails pressing for a moment into the taut rise of his shoulder blade. He could not tell if her exploration was the result of an innocent's hesitance or a siren's determination to demolish him. He anchored himself on his elbows, keeping as much space between their chests as possible while her hands roamed, though he longed to sink down on her, feel the hardened tips of her breasts graze his chest as he pulled her against him.

Her hands sloped down his back, drifting like a breeze, but when they reached the rise of his buttocks they fluttered and stilled. Then fell away. If he hadn't felt the quivering in every inch of her body, the shallow raspiness of her breath, he would have wondered if she lost interest. He looked up from the pulse fluttering at the side of her neck to her eyes, wide and confused.

'Did I do it wrong?' she whispered.

For a moment he just stared, too much of his intellect hovering at waist level.

'Wrong?'

'You aren't...you aren't going in.'

'Going... Sweetheart, I can't enter you. It wouldn't be safe. The only means I have to protect you are in my room and I can't even think of moving away from you right now, not even for that.'

Her eyes gleamed as they widened, her lips rounding into an *O* of realisation.

'But you still want me to touch you?'

'More than I want to breathe at the moment. There are ways to give and receive pleasure without penetration, but we don't have to do anything. Rest now.'

He kissed her, a short, quick brush on her lips,

intending to move away, but her mouth opened under his, her hands sliding into his hair, her words coming in breathless bursts.

'You touched me. It was… You want me to touch you like that? There?'

He still hesitated. He was too close to the edge for the patient tutoring she deserved. But her words rushed on.

'I want to know… Benneit. Show me how to touch you…'

He sank back, defeated, too ravenous to be sensible. He took her hand, sliding it down his chest, his back arching as her cool fingers closed on his blazing erection. Her hand leapt under his, then tightened, and he sank his face into the curve of her neck, dragging air into his lungs.

It was torture. He had never been so aroused and so unwilling to end it. Her hands were exquisite, like a silk scarf drawn over his skin, and he suffered the soft sweeps of her fingers and palm as she explored, growing bolder as he guided her. It wasn't only her hands—she was so engrossed in following his guidance she seemed unconscious of her own body, and it was doing as it willed—her legs kept rubbing against his, her toes flexing against his calves as she tried to draw him even closer. He didn't want it to end, ever. He wanted to remain at this peak of agonised pleasure for ever.

She raised herself on her elbow so her lips could brush over his jaw, over the corded tension of his neck and shoulder, kissing and tasting him as she went, and when he succumbed to the need to close his hand over her breast she gave a little mewl and her teeth nipped his shoulder, making him gasp as he fought to stave off his climax.

'Did I hurt you?' she murmured, licking the spot like a cat at a spill of milk.

'No. But you're killing me. Don't stop.'

She blew on the damp spot and shifted her lips to his chest, her hand still gliding over his erection. 'There are so many textures…' she murmured, her palm curving over the base of his arousal and skimming upwards again. 'I never realised. It feels like velvet here, but so hard beneath. And hot…'

He choked, caught between a laugh and a groan, closing his hand on hers. She raised herself, suckling his neck with sudden and total abandon, her hand following and then leading the rhythm of his body until he could no longer fight the racking shudders of pleasure. In his mind he was inside her, becoming part of her, branding both of them with his need. And then it all fell away and he was melting, they were both melting into the sea, a liquid warmth with no boundaries between them. At the edge of his reason like a storm on the horizon was just that flash of lightning and fear—that he would never find those boundaries again.

Chapter Twenty-Five

Benneit paused before entering the study. The blessed silence that fell on the castle after the last of the guests departed was purely external. Inside his head a dozen voices were sparring and all of them were coming off the worse for wear. He pushed them all into the background and entered the study. It was time to face his little nemesis.

'I would like a word with Mrs Langdale, please, McCreary.'

A look of blank panic widened her eyes, but McCreary was out the door before she could speak.

Benneit closed the door and stood for a moment, surveying her. She wore a pale yellow gown that gave her skin an ivory lustre. Evening primrose, he thought inconsequentially, pleased with how lovely she looked in her new wardrobe. And how much lovelier she looked without any clothes at all.

He must be quite mad to even contemplate what he was contemplating. Because as he watched her slightly averted face and the tension in her slim shoulders, he knew he was far from done.

He knew it was unfair to her. To all of them. The sensible course of action would be to accept what happened as an aberration and resume an amicable but respectful distance. Since his marriage to Bella he had been determined to pursue the sensible course of action and Jamie's birth had transformed that decision into a moral necessity. But still...

'I will not apologise for last night, Jo.'

'Neither will I.'

Her chin rose and he was so tempted to pull her out from behind the desk and coax her upstairs. Reminding himself that was not wise, he changed course.

'I must go with the engineers to Kilmarchie today and must stay there tonight, but tomorrow we are invited to the McCrieffs'.'

'So I understand.'

'It is only for the one night. We are likely to be back here by the following afternoon.'

'Good. Enjoy yourselves.'

'The invitation includes you as well. The three of us.'

'Surely there is no reason for me to come.'

She still did not look up from the ledger. He didn't know why he was pressing. It was wrong to take her to the McCrieffs'. But he wanted her with them. With *him* for whatever time was left them together.

'I won't force you. But Lord Aberwyld extended the invitation to you as well, by name. Besides, I have engagements with the engineers and builders in Kilmarchie in the morning and so I must travel to McCrieff directly from there. Jamie will be coming by carriage and will be upset if you remained behind and...'

'Oh, very well. You have made your point,' she interrupted, frowning. 'Is there anything else, Your Grace?'

'No.'

'Good luck in Kilmarchie, then, Your Grace.'

He finally moved forward and she leaned back in his chair as he came around the desk. It really was uncanny, her ability to show absolutely no expression, but he knew her well enough now to see the small signs—the dilating pupils in the grey-ocean eyes, the careful flattening of her soft lips. He placed his hand on her wrist where it lay on the ledgers, his fingers seeking and finding her pulse. It echoed his, an angry beating at the walls. He might not be able to read her emotions, but he could read her body. This pixie was as passionate as she was deep.

'I am not leaving until we clear the air.'

'There is nothing to clear. You have nothing to apologise for. I am neither an innocent nor a fool.'

'I agree. I won't lie and say I regret what happened or that I do not wish to repeat it. But while I am gone I want you to consider what *you* wish during the time that remains of your stay here. I will respect whatever choice you make.'

He stroked his thumb over her wrist and she leaned further back in his chair, strands of flaxen hair clinging to the dark embroidery. He pulled the two visible pins from her bun before she could react. Her hair slid down to rest on her shoulder.

'Benneit!'

He ignored her hoarse exclamation, pulling the last pin from the tangle and placing it on the desk.

'I want this image in my mind tonight.' His voice was as hoarse as hers, his throat tight as heat streaked through his body at the thought of unfurling her further, from the yellow dress that reminded him of the primroses that sheltered below the wisteria vines in the garden at The House. He raised a long strand of her hair, breathing her in, his cheek just an inch from the heat of hers. He could feel his voice echo against her throat, his breath shallow.

'I want your scent with me when I think of you tonight, Jo. Think about that when you slip into the bed we shared come evening. I'll be miles away, but thinking of touching you, tasting you...'

'Stop.'

Her cry was one of pain as she clasped his nape, her cheek pressing against his, her breath hard and fast. The force of her fingertips against his flesh was painful, but it was as welcome as a full surrender. She was still so tightly held, so much Joane, but he wanted Jo to come forward as she had last night in her room, to tell him she wanted him.

He pressed his mouth to the hollow just below her ear, his tongue capturing her flavour. His hand traced down the other side of her neck, tickling the edge of her bodice before gently settling on her breast, a light, feathering touch that soon felt the answering hardening of her nipple. He wanted to see her bared to him in full daylight. He wanted to make love to her under the sun and sky. With each sweep of his hand and mouth he hardened, too, his erection a hot demand straining against his buckskins.

'Tasting every inch, Jo. Every inch of skin you can see and every inch you can't.'

He let his hands sink lower and when he pressed it against the apex of her thighs she rose against it with a breathy denial. His hand fisted on the fabric of her skirt and he closed his teeth gently on the petal-soft lobe of her ear.

'Will you think of this when you touch yourself tonight, Jo?'

'What?'

'I want you to touch yourself and think of me tonight.'

'Touch myself?'

Her voice was lost and fading and his sanity was following fast, but he drew back at that, keeping his hand on her thigh, gently kneading. Her eyes were dark and her mouth was warm with colour, as if he had already kissed her senseless, but there was no recognition. Last night he had been too caught up in his own arousal to think about the peculiarity that her husband had never introduced her to what he would have considered basic intimacies between a man and a woman. Still, he knew many of his peers regarded intercourse with their wives on a different plane than that with their mistresses. Or perhaps Alfred might have been as innocent as she before their wedding.

Whatever the case, he felt a surge of atavistic satisfaction. He might not be able to keep this passionate lover for himself, but he could at least be the one to initiate her to the gift of pleasing herself. It was selfish, too—he hated thinking she might one day have other lovers, that someone else would tap her passion. He should wish it for her, but right now he couldn't. So if she learned with him the joy of pleasing herself, perhaps he could fool himself into imagining she did not need another man.

It was selfish, greedy, unfair, but undeniable.

He wanted to keep her.

He pushed the thought away before it sank its teeth into him.

'So, we will have to do something about that when I return, *mo leannan.*'

'What does that mean?' she whispered.

He leaned his forehead briefly against hers before moving away. He had no right to say those words to her.

'I will tell you when we return…'

He fell silent as the spectre of the McCrieffs rose again.

'Goodbye, Jo. Take good care of Jamie.'

'Of course I shall.'

He made it to the door when her voice stopped him, a little breathless and more than a little enthusiastic.

'Do you mean it is possible to do…that…for myself?'

He curled his hand hard on the door frame.

'Are you expressly trying to kill me? Yes, of

course it is possible. If it wasn't, there would hardly be sermons denouncing it, would there?'

Her eyes widened.

'Oh, is *that* what it means?'

He rubbed his jaw, so tempted to drag her out of his chair, haul up her skirts and do something about the raging fire in his buckskins. At this rate he would come before he made it out the castle gates.

'If there wasn't so much riding on this meeting in Kilmarchie, I would take you upstairs and show you precisely what it means.'

She clasped her hands together, her cheeks flushed.

'You should leave, then.'

'Yes. Tomorrow I will meet you and Jamie. And when we return...'

He fell silent and forced himself to leave before he lost all sight of his priorities.

Jo returned to Benneit's chair at the desk. She brought the maligned ledger back to face her and stared at it blindly.

In less than a day her life was transformed. She was a magical mouse and her Summer's Solstice transformation was far better than any devised in her mind. Benneit had saved her life, danced with her and shown her a level of bliss she had not the slightest idea existed. It was thrumming through her like a chaotic mixture of the elements, jostling and dragging her towards what was either heaven or hell and she did not care. By some wondrous magic he wanted her. Perhaps the magical Minerva existed after all and had placed a spell on him? She laughed at the absurdity, but it was only marginally less fantastical than the thought that he wanted her…and with such passion. Or did all the women he enjoyed feel just this heat? See that blaze of lust in his eyes as they mutated from jade to razor-edged emerald?

She shut her eyes and brought back the image of Benneit leaning over her, his gaze and then his body scorching and devouring. It might be wrong, but she wanted it so very badly. She wanted him. She wished he *had* taken her right here in the study. Anywhere he wished.

Another image came—of Benneit with her on the Devil's Seat, the stone warm and hard beneath her bare back, the grating of sand as their legs… She breathed deeply, blinking it away.

He was breaking through every one of her defences, but she still ought to be careful with her fantasies. She would see him tomorrow, but it would be in the home of the woman he was already pledged to, formal engagement or not. She must not begin to imagine a future with him. He was offering her a very temporary affair, that was all. He was on edge, concerned about his future on so many levels, and she was conveniently there, a distraction.

Worse, a convenience.

A convenience, again.

How useful you are, Jo. How accommodating, how soberly utilitarian, how...stupid.

Falling in love with Benneit Lochmore was the very definition of stupidity.

In love.

There was no hiding from that truth any longer. It wasn't only the joy he gave her, it was him. He had brought her back to life, like a house re-inhabited, doors and windows set open to the world, light streaming in so she could see herself and, strangely enough, through his eyes she liked what she saw, even the flaws of faded carpets and outmoded furniture. She wanted so desperately to do the same for him, make him see himself as she saw him—complex, generous, troubled, honourable and so full of the feeling he kept it deep underground, like a shameful secret. She wanted to make him happy.

She might be stupid, but she was also blissfully, foolishly alive. And terrified.

Chapter Twenty-Six

This carriage ride from Lochmore to McCrieffs' was utterly different from the ride from London just a few weeks ago. *She* was different. She had grown up more in these weeks than in the past two years.

Jamie was different, too. He leaned against her unashamedly as they wove stories together about the stark countryside they passed. Her heart ached, but she didn't once consider putting him away from her. She knew it was wrong of her to go to the McCrieffs', but she did not want to lose a single moment of Benneit's and Jamie's company.

'There's the McCrieff keep!' Jamie bounced on the carriage seat, looking very neat and proper and grown up. He had not even kicked off his shoes and he reached up to touch the hair Nurse Moody had slicked to one side. She looked out the carriage window at the structure now partially visible as they came down a rise. She could not see much of the keep through the window, but though it looked smaller than Lochmore, it gave the same impression of heavy stone and glum foreboding.

'Oh, and there is Papa!'

Jo turned to follow his pointing finger and saw the men on horseback coming down from the rise behind the keep. Benneit was immediately recognisable, taller and much darker than the other men. Her body lit from inside with a harsh snap of nerves, crowding with memories of his body, his touch. She turned to inspect Jamie, busying herself with him and calming her breathing as the carriage drew to a halt.

'Papa!'

Jamie launched himself at Benneit as he opened the carriage door and over Jamie's dark hair she met his gaze, warm with pleasure and, despite her pain, she smiled back. In her mind she closed that circle by reaching out and taking Benneit's hand. In a world of her making that would be her right. This would be her family. But it wasn't and within moments she was being led away by a maid while Jamie and Benneit remained with the McCrieff brothers.

It was early evening when the same maid helped her dress and led her downstairs. Her dress was pale lilac blue, a colour suitable for a widow but still youthful, and she knew it enhanced rather than dulled her grey eyes. She could not compete with Lady Tessa on any scale that counted, but she would at least not appear a complete dowd.

'Jo! We waited for you.' Jamie rushed up the steps towards her and her throat tightened with pleasure and pain as she saw Benneit at the bottom of the steps. She had been prepared to enter alone and remain alone and this consideration warmed her as much as the banked heat in his gaze as he watched her descend. But he didn't speak and she couldn't.

In the hall they were greeted by a bluff hello from Lord Aberwyld and a more subdued greeting from Lady Aberwyld. There was no mistaking the animosity in her gaze before she turned from Jo to smile at Benneit and Jamie, and Jo was relieved when their attention was caught by a cheer rising from a group of children playing in a corner of the large hall they entered. A young girl, perhaps eight, beckoned to Jamie.

'Jamie! Come!'

Jamie's body angled closer to Jo even as his hand slicked his hair again. Jo caught Benneit's frown and though she was not certain it was in response to Jamie's shyness or to his move towards her, she bent a little towards him.

'What is her name?' she whispered.

'Beth. Like our Beth,' he whispered back. 'There are many Beths.'

'What are they playing?'

'Spillikins. I am good at Spillikins. Ewan and Angus play with me.'

'Say your hellos to Lord and Lady Aberwyld before you go with Miss Beth, Jamie,' Benneit said and Jamie came forward, but at the last steps as he approached the great bearded figure seated on an armchair around which the room appeared to rotate, he clasped Jo's skirts. Even when she sat he remained by her side, his hand fiddling with the embroidery on her skirt. Benneit stared straight ahead and Jo was caught between the need to hug Jamie to her and guilt that he was clinging to her so obviously.

'So, boy,' McCrieff intoned, his voice a vibration throughout the room. 'Gave your papa a scare the night of the ball, didn't you?'

Jamie turned scarlet, his fingers tightening on Jo's dress as the Earl burst into rumbling laughter. Lady Aberwyld leaned forward and smiled.

'I'm glad you are well, Lord Glenarris. Beth, take him to the children.'

'That's right, go and play,' the Earl interjected. 'This is a children's house, as you can see, Mrs Langdale. He needn't hang about your skirts. 'Twill do him good. Right, Tessa?'

Tessa McCrieff was seated by her mother's side

and she smiled over at Jo with the same cheerful sweetness as at the ball.

'He had a grand time when he was here last. It takes a few moments though, Father. Don't press.'

'Press? I never press, girl! Where's my whisky?'

Jamie cast a look of entreaty at Benneit, but when Beth approached he went with her, eyes downcast, and Lord Aberwyld watched them with satisfaction.

'Too shy, that boy. Needs toughening. He'll get that here.'

'Beth will take good care of him, Your Grace,' Tessa said softly.

'Aye, she's Duncan's eldest and already a natural mother, that one. Like our Tessa here.'

'Papa!'

McCrieff laughed and began talking of the clearances, though by the look on Benneit's face the man's views on that topic were hardly more welcome to him than his views on his son. But with some deft manoeuvring he shifted McCrieff to a discussion of the progress made in Kilmarchie regarding the distillery and Lord Aberwyld's sons joined in.

The next day Jo hardly saw Benneit or Jamie. He was out with the men and she remained with the women, discussing family matters and the changes in fashion now the war was over. They might be hundreds of miles from Uxmore, but other than the Highland accent and the heavy stone walls, they might as well have been in Oxfordshire. It was utterly familiar to Jo and already foreign after the ease that had become part of her life at Lochmore.

The worst was how much she liked Lady Tessa. Jo had secretly been hoping that her pleasant behaviour at the ball was a ruse like Lady Aberwyld's veneer of politeness, but Tessa was genuinely nice. She would, as her father advertised, make a fine mother. A fine wife. Jo wished she could be happy for Benneit that he would wed someone as generous and warm as Tessa, but she wasn't noble enough. She liked Tessa, but she hated her from the bottom of her aching, weeping heart.

She wished the afternoon would arrive so they could depart, but the day dragged as they pored over the latest *La Belle Assemblée* fashion plates, lingering on one of a wedding gown with striped muslin skirts and flowers at the gathering of the sleeves. There was a round of tittering and meaningful glances in Tessa's direction and Tessa's rounded cheeks heated, but she ignored them, turning the page to a lovely evening gown of lilac sarsenet over a white underskirt and three elaborately braided flounces. The moment passed, but Jo's misery deepened and she went to the window. The view was blocked by a tight clump of trees, but she stared at it none the less.

'I wish they would not do that,' Lady Tessa said as she came to stand by her. 'That is all they can talk about since Papa and Lochmore spoke months ago.'

Jo clasped her hands together and managed a smile.

'That is understandable.'

'Is it? I am not certain I do understand. I feel like a prize cow on her way to the fair.'

Jo's smile faltered.

'Don't you like His Grace?'

'I like what I know, which is not much. We have not spoken often. I like him best because of Jamie. I tell myself that anyone who is so good to his son must be a fine man.'

Jo nodded, but couldn't answer, and Tessa continued.

'He called for you last night, you know.'

'What?'

'Jamie. Beth told me he woke and called for you and she came to comfort him.'

Jo was grateful for the gloom that obscured her harsh blush at her misunderstanding.

'She should have sent for me.'

'She is accustomed to tending to the little ones. She will make a far better wife and mother than ever I will. He is very attached to you.'

'He is a wonderful boy. He will come to love you very much.'

Tessa touched the windowpane. Beyond it evening was swallowing up the landscape and Jo could see their reflections and the blur of people behind them. She wanted this over. She should not have come to the McCrieffs' and now it was too late.

'Did you love your husband?' Tessa asked. Jo should have evaded her intrusive questions, but she couldn't even do that. Everything was too late.

'I cared for him.'

'That is not the same.'

'No. Not quite the same.'

'Why did you marry him?'

'We were good friends and he made me happy even if I did not love him.'

'Did he love you?'

'Yes. Perhaps in time my feelings would have deepened. I think they would have. I was not very trusting to begin with—of myself or others. It takes trust to truly love someone.'

Tessa nodded, tracing a finger through the sheen of condensation forming on the pane.

'It is peculiar—I know we do not know each other, but I can talk to you. I wish you could stay. I know that is impossible, but I wish you could. I wish…' She turned back to the room. 'We are being summoned. Come.'

Jo followed, heartsick. She never should have allowed Benneit to convince her to come to the McCrieffs'.

Tessa did not subject her to more confidences, but she remained close to Jo, almost protective of her, especially when Lady Aberwyld indulged in thinly veiled snipes about Jo's lack of youth and looks and her imminent departure. Jo was immensely relieved when it was time to leave, but the carriage ride was hardly any better. Jamie was full of his visit, his palpable pleasure adding great boulders to the weight on Jo's heart. She hated her jealousy, but controlling it was beyond her. She would just have to endure this as well.

Jamie finally fell asleep just as they passed Lochmore village, his head slipping on to Jo's shoulder, and Benneit gathered the boy on to his lap, his hand brushing her arm accidentally. She tensed, but Benneit merely looked out the window into the falling darkness as afternoon slipped into dusk. She leaned her head against her side of the carriage and closed her eyes, weary and miserable.

'Tired?'

Benneit's voice was a murmur and she forced herself to straighten.

'A little. They were very nice.'

'Yes.'

'Jamie felt at home.'

'Yes. Thank you for coming with him.'

'Thank you for inviting me. It was pleasant,' she lied.

He did not speak again.

When they reached the castle it was already night and, though Ewan and Angus came to greet them, Benneit raised Jamie to his shoulder and took him upstairs. She knew she wasn't needed, that following him was a form of self-flagellation, but she did so anyway. He did not send for Nurse Moody, but brought a nightshirt from the wardrobe and dressed Jamie himself while she placed Jamie's clothes on a chair. Then she left the room before temptation strangled her. She just reached her door when she felt him behind her, the words a murmur that flowed under her skin.

'Will you come with me, Jo?'

She tightened her hand on the door knob.

'No, Benneit.'

'You are tired.'

'Yes, that, too, but that is not why. I cannot do

this. Perhaps if I had never met her, or knew… I cannot.'

He leaned his hand on the wall. She did not look at him, but she could feel the tension coursing through him, the sheer bulk of his presence overshadowing her, pressing her into no more than a core of need around a howl. Her hand was boiling on the doorknob. It would surely melt or crack under the pressure of his silence. She turned it and pushed open the door but could not move.

'Jo.' His voice, full of dark heat, acted like a spur even as his hand rose towards her and then she was inside her room, the door closed behind her, before she could betray herself. She stood there, hardly breathing, her palms pressed against the cool wood door for ages and ages, until the scrape of his boots marked his departure.

Chapter Twenty-Seven

The most effective hell is a twisted version of heaven, Jo told herself as she followed Jamie up the cliff path.

The week since their return from the McCrieffs' was outwardly no different from the week before the ball. She and Jamie explored and read. They went more often to the village and twice with Angus and Benneit to The House where Mr Warren and Mr Carruthers, the engineers, were staying to assess the village port. Jamie was enchanted with the engineers' tools and tales and they treated him with kind tolerance, giving him little tasks which he carried out with enthusiastic concentration. Jo was happy for him, happy for the pride in Benneit's eyes as he watched his son, but also utterly miserable.

She could not help turning to Benneit when Jamie sparkled with pleasure at his successes or frowned with interest as he listened to the engineers' explanations. It was as instinctive as the lurching of her heart whenever Benneit appeared, joining them suddenly on the beach, or in the nursery, or when a summons arrived from The

House to join him and the engineers for nuncheon.

She paid for those moments. Benneit never again asked her to come to him, but he was torturing her.

She did not know if it was intentional, but it was unbearably effective. He spoke to her only when necessary, but when he joined them on the beach he would sometimes take her arm to help her over the rock fall, or grasp her waist to pull her away from the rising tide.

He was always polite to her and sometimes she thought he had accepted her rejection in good form, perhaps with a bit of piqued pride. But sometimes, when his fingers took her arm, she felt a ringing tension in the body next to hers, the kind of beating pressure like the waves crashing against the cliffs below the castle.

He never looked at her in these moments as she struggled to keep from turning to him and weeping out her need and pain. His eyes remained blank and his mouth a straight, uncompromising line. But sometimes, after she moved away, she would feel the sharp green jab of his gaze in her back, like a blade piercing her. Sometimes it felt like hate.

On each occasion of these brief touches, she was shocked by the speed with which her body clamoured for more. The heat was like a wild animal inside her—Benneit's touch unlatched its cage and it leapt through her, hot and desperate, leaving her insides scratched to ribbons as he turned away, his face a mask.

He never returned with her and Jamie through the Sea Gate tunnel but would walk back along the beach and up the other path to the stables. She would turn and watch his solitary figure on the sand, his dark head bowed, his hands deep in the pockets of his coat as if cold despite the unseasonably warm summer weather.

Once, she turned back and he was still watching them and, though she could not see his expression with the sun in her eyes, her breath had stopped. It was all her own invention, no doubt— the confusion, the agony, the bone weariness of holding it inside. To imagine she saw any of her own suffering in the dark figure standing so still on the sand was folly. Yet, she almost moved towards him when Jamie called to her impatiently, reminding her of the world.

And it became harder, not easier, as the days passed.

On the day that marked a month since her arrival at Lochmore, she went with Angus and Jamie to The House to bid farewell to the engineers who were departing for Glasgow for a couple weeks to oversee purchases. Benneit was already at The House and when they came through the gardens Jamie ran ahead in search of his father. Angus turned to her as she paused and she smiled.

'You go, Angus. I will linger in the garden a little. It is so peaceful.'

'You need some of that, lass. I'll send Jamie for you when nuncheon is served.'

Her eyes burned at the kindness in his voice, but she couldn't answer. She was not surprised Angus saw through her. There was no judgement, only sorrow in his voice, and it threatened to unravel her flimsy defences. She sat on the wooden bench in the vine-covered bower where the laburnum was in glorious bloom, its clusters of yellow flowers as bright as the sun.

She knew immediately by the footsteps that it was Benneit coming up the path from The House. She stood, wishing she could sink into the vines and disappear. She was at her breaking point; she should not be with him alone. She tried to push her way between the vines to the small path that led around the house, but the branches caught at the ribbons of her bonnet.

With a muffled curse she tugged at them, but it was too late. Large, warm hands brushed hers away, turning her. His face was as masklike as ever, his eyes hooded as he began disengaging the ribbons from their green captors. He was standing so close that if she just bent her head it would rest against his chest. His arms brushed hers as he worked at the ribbon and she watched the shifting speckling of sun on his coat as the wind teased the bright yellow flowers in the vines above them. The garden was in summer bloom, a raw jumble of flowers and trees, the scent of pink jasmine entwined with richer honeysuckle. But she only smelt him—his warm musk scent with a cool earthiness beneath it.

She kept as still as a statue, breathing him in, her hands itching with the need to rise and feel him, drag up his shirt and scrape up his skin, mould over the hard planes of his stomach and chest, the silky straight dark hair that teased a line downwards. Then the ribbons fell free, but though he dropped his hands, he did not move back. She watched his chest rise and fall, faster and shallower than before, felt the shadow as his head lowered towards hers. There was an ache at the pit of her stomach—every part of her was clenching, gathering as if for a leap across a ravine. Her own breath was non-existent.

She had no idea what would have happened if Jamie had not come rushing out, his shoes crunching on the gravel. When she dared look at Benneit again as they joined the engineers for nuncheon in the sun parlour he was as calm as always—a polite, attentive, amusing host. There was no sign that moment had been anything other than him helping her with her bonnet. Still, he came to sit beside her at the modest table, his thigh so close to hers she felt her legs sucked towards its warmth, the heat like a contagion between her thighs, rising to her breasts like a devious tide no matter what she did to try to stop it.

As they rose from the table the side of his knee brushed hers and she could not help looking towards him and he did not mask his expression swiftly enough. It was there—the tension in his mouth and cheekbones and something very like fury in his quickly veiled eyes.

When he came out to put Jamie on his pony for the ride back and Angus helped her into the saddle she dared look at him again and before he turned from her she saw not anger or resentment, but confusion and such weariness on his face that whatever part of her heart remained shielded from him surrendered.

Would it be so terrible to give and take comfort? There was so little time left. Were scruples and honour and self-respect so important?

Jamie tucked his hand into Benneit's where it rested on the saddle.

'You promised you'd come with us to the north bay when the tide is out. There will be new treasures after the storm last night.'

Benneit smiled, closing his hand on Jamie's.

'Did I promise?'

'You know you did, Papa! And Lochmores always keep their word, don't they?'

Benneit nodded, his smile fading.

'Yes, Son. I will come. I must speak to Mr Warren first, but take the horses back to the stable and meet me at the top of the cliff path.'

Jamie grinned and nudged his pony forward.

Jamie clambered over the large stones and stood poised, hand outstretched like a captain of a ship sighting land. Benneit stood a little to the side, his hands on his hips as he looked out over the waves. Jo probably should have left Jamie with him at the top of the cliff path, but now that her resolve was weakening, all she wanted was the opportunity to tell him she had changed her mind. If he was still interested...

'See, Jo?' Jamie prompted and she focused back on him. 'That's the cave where I went with Angus before London and we found the great big log washed in by the tide. I think it came all the way from the Amazon. Maybe it is still there.'

He ran ahead even as Benneit turned and reached out for him. It was a peculiar gesture, a grasping of the air, and she looked up to Benneit's face. He looked dazed and very pale beneath his sun-warmed skin. Her own agony forgotten, she turned to him, touching his sleeve.

'Benneit?'

He didn't appear to hear her, but then his gaze focused again. He glanced down at her hand and in a convulsive gesture he grasped it and moved forward, pulling her with him.

'Jamie, come back!'

Jamie stopped at the mouth of the cave.

'I want to see if the log is still there, Papa!'

'No. Come back here now.'

'I'll only look…'

'I said no!'

'But, Papa…'

'Jamie! Come back now or you'll spend the rest of the day in the nursery!'

'Benneit…' Jo began tentatively, but his hand tightened on hers, his voice a snarl.

'Stay out of this.'

Jamie stood unmoving, staring back at his father, his smile gone, his face as stony as Benneit's. They looked remarkably alike now, all trace of Bella's beauty wiped away by the obdurate glare they shared.

'Jamie.' Benneit's voice was low, but there was such menace in it Jo was not in the least surprised when Jamie continued towards the cave. Benneit dropped her hand and bounded forward as if stung. He reached Jamie in seconds, picking him up, and Jamie squirmed in his arms, his fists flailing in a silent battle. Benneit just shifted him, hauling him on to his shoulder, his arm pinioning his legs as he turned and strode back to the path. Jamie fought and cursed, his tantrum in full bloom, but Benneit ignored him, his long legs eating up the distance all the way to the castle.

When they reached the nursery he lowered him gently, but Jamie immediately kicked out, catching Benneit in the shin, before retreating to the corner by his shelves.

'Blas— You will stay here for the rest of the day, James Hamish Lochmore.'

'I hate you,' Jamie spat, flinging himself on his bed.

Benneit turned and, seeing Jo, herded her out of the room.

'You will not go to him today. I will not have him disobeying me like that.'

'I don't think...'

'Good. Don't. For once don't think and just do as you are told. He is my son and I am telling you as clearly as possible so not even you can misunderstand my meaning. You will not go into the nursery today. Just...stay away!'

He strode off down the hallway, a column of fury and something else she could not understand. She glanced at the closed door, so tempted to defy him, but instead she went to her room. She might think him mistaken, but it was not her role to make that judgement. Had she been Jamie's mother she might perhaps...

She closed her door, each beat of her heart a palpable ache. She had not expected to fall in love with Lochmore and his son.

How would she survive leaving?

She heard the cough in the corridor but it did not immediately draw her out of her brown study. The second one did, though. It was deliberate, fake and Jamie's.

She opened the door and the light spread out into the darkened corridor like a fan. At its tip was a rounded bundle. She inspected Jamie's hunched back, his arms hugging his legs.

'What are you doing out there, Jamie?'

One shoulder rose and fell.

'Won't you come inside? It is cold in the corridor.'

He shook his head.

She sighed, considering her options. She returned to her room, took a heavy shawl from her chair and went to place it around Jamie's little shoulders.

'There is a nice fire in my parlour and I was about to send for some chocolate. If you wish to join me, you may.'

She returned to her room and pulled at the bell cord and waited.

'There's a bundle at yer doorstep, Mrs Langdale,' Beth announced when she entered, her mouth prim.

'I know, Beth. Could I bother you for two cups of chocolate and perhaps some biscuits?'

Beth nodded and smiled.

She was still smiling when she returned with a laden tray.

'Still there, the bundle. Stubborn like his father. Here you are, Mrs Langdale. Mayhap this will do the trick.'

Five long minutes later the door to the parlour opened, paused and opened further. A very stubborn boy.

He did not speak as he joined her at the table,

or as he took his cup and drank with all the enthusiasm of a man contemplating entry to debtors' prison, but the chocolate went down, as did the biscuits.

'I should return to the nursery now.'

'That is probably best.'

'I only wanted to see if the log was there.'

'I know. Perhaps your father was worried, especially after my foolishness in falling in the water the other day.'

He finally looked at her.

'That *was* foolish. I would not go there when the tide is rising. It wasn't rising then.'

'Well, fathers sometimes worry more than they need. It is hard to know just how much worry is right.'

'He was angry, not worried.'

'It looks the same from the outside, Jamie. He was very angry at me when I worried him.'

He shrugged, his little shoulders barely shifting her shawl, and she was not certain she had quite made her point, but it would have to do.

'Come, I will see you to the nursery.'

At the nursery doorway she stopped and smiled.

'Your father did tell me not to go in.'

Jamie's mouth relaxed, hovering on the edge of a smile as he slipped inside, closing the door. Beth was waiting in her room, a peculiar expression on her face. Jo wondered if perhaps Beth, too, felt she was overstepping her boundaries with Jamie. But then the maid smiled and the thought fled.

'Malcolm McCrieff and his wife are below, Mrs Langdale. Stopped by on their way to Kilmarchie. Feeling at home already, the McCrieffs,' Beth said, her voice a little acid. 'His Grace requests you join him.'

There were limits. Sitting tamely in the drawing room after Benneit's tantrum while he entertained his future brother-in-law was the definition of several steps beyond her personal limit.

'I have the headache, Beth,' she said with dignity.

'I'll tell Angus. His Grace won't be happy, though. He's in a mood and it will be a wonder if he doesn't bite someone's head off before a new day rises.' Beth's sigh robbed her words of their disrespect.

Jo waited for the door to close and wondered if that would be the end of it or whether Benneit would storm up there with demands as he had at the ball. In his present state of mind he appeared capable even of that. And if he came to her room she might burst into tears.

She stood. She would not sit there waiting for the axe to fall. If he could not find her, he could not make demands and she could not make an utter fool of herself. There was one place she was quite certain no one would look for her. Just for an hour or so she could be assured of being left utterly alone.

She lit a candlestick and left her room.

Chapter Twenty-Eight

Finally. He thought they would never leave. Malcolm McCrieff would be just like his father one day—when he sank his teeth into a topic it was like sitting through the speeches of three of the most tedious orators at the House of Lords. How the McCrieff women sat so placidly while they droned on… It would drive him mad. Tessa Mc-Crieff might be lovely, sweet and the perfect wife for the Duke of Lochmore, but each step closer to his fate rang with a visceral resistance to it.

He couldn't do it.

He was glad Jo had not joined them in the end. It had been pure bloody-mindedness on his part to even send for her after his outburst which had capped the most hellish week of his existence. He had merely…

Wanted her. Whatever he could have of her. Even silent, disapproving, distant, he wanted to be with her. However much time was left he needed to be with her even if it was destroying him from inside. It was not her fault, but it felt like it was. Everything felt like it was her fault— the inescapable need to be with her, to touch her.

He had been so close to losing his control that morning in the garden. Having her so close, he could see the faint freckles on the bridge of her nose, the curve of her cheeks, the nearly transparent hairs shivering with her heartbeat at her temples. He had been so hungry for her, his blood felt like molten steel, burning its course through his veins. If not for Jamie, he might have broken right there—gone down on his knees and begged for scraps…

He picked up his glass of whisky, put it down. Perhaps he should go spend the night at The House. Get away from all of them and especially from the temptation to go to Jo's room, slide under the covers and find her soft, warm… Make her shiver as she had moments before abandoning herself to bliss. Slide his fingers over every disapproving line of her lovely body and coax it back to him. Taste her, inch by inch, until she called his name, not in condemnation, but with that breathy need for him. He wanted to be inside her when he brought her to climax. Deep inside her so that her soft moans and that cataclysmic arrival at heaven would be his.

He closed his eyes at the memory. Just thinking of her made him hard as a log himself.

Blast the woman.

He should at least apologise for his behaviour

that afternoon. Then go to his rooms and lie awake as he had every night of the past week.

But he had to see her first.

At her door he hesitated, but his body didn't and he knocked softly before he could change his mind.

'Jo?'

Silence.

He drew a deep breath and opened the door. The fire was still going, but the room was empty and the parlour beyond it as well. On the table he saw the tray, the two empty cups of chocolate and the plate with crumbs and some of his heat migrated to anger.

He went down the hall to the nursery. Jamie was there, asleep, a tight ball under his covers, a smudge of chocolate at the corner of his mouth.

Benneit sat carefully on the bed and touched the smudge gently. Jamie's eyelids fluttered open.

'Sorry, Papa.'

Benneit's eyes stung.

'No, I'm sorry, Jamie. I was too harsh. I love you, you know.'

Jamie nodded, snuggling closer, his hand searching for Benneit's, and when it was secured he closed his eyes again.

'Was Jo here?' Benneit asked, hating himself.

Jamie shook his head and yawned.

'I went to her. We had chocolate and she sent me back.' He opened his eyes again. 'She didna' disobey you, Papa.'

'Don't worry, Jamie. All is well. Do you know where she is, then?'

Another yawn cracked.

'Exploring. I went to give back her shawly thing and saw her go down the forbidden stairs with a candle. I wanted to go, too, but I remembered I was to stay in the nursery so I came back. Dinna worrit, she's brave...' he murmured and sighed, sinking back into sleep.

Benneit sat for another moment, his heart beating hard again, but for the wrong reasons.

It had nothing to do with him. If she chose to disobey his very clear...his *crystal*-clear instructions not to enter the tunnels alone and with nothing but a candle that would probably not survive the first whisper of dank sea air that pierced the walls, anything that happened to her was her own fault.

She's brave.

He found the lamp in his room and lit the candle in it, tucked a tinderbox into his pocket, cursing as he went. If he had an ounce of sense he would send Angus to find her. Or wait. In all likelihood she would return any moment. Even Jo would likely not find the tunnels appetising.

She is brave. And curious. And quite angry with you at the moment.

Any hope that thirty years had dulled the edge of his weakness was dashed within seconds of beginning his descent down the spiral staircase into the tunnels. He hated these stairs, narrow and choking and twisting into darkness. It was like being swallowed down the throat of a great beast. The world disappeared, shrinking to a small reddened pocket of candlelight glimmering on the damp stone walls.

When he finally found her he would…do something.

If he found her. If he ever escaped this hell.

She is brave.

Jamie's quiet confidence, the ease of slipping into sleep because *Jo is brave*, gnawed at him as much as this beast inside him.

They are only stairs. Only stairs. He knew where they began and where they ended. Had been up and down them dozens, hundreds of times before that horrible day and night. They would eventually end. They could not go on for ever, no matter how much every inch of his body was convinced he would never escape their stone belly.

He leaned his hand on the wall—cold and damp and rough—he could feel his heartbeat in his palm—thudding like a hammer trying to break through this prison. He pressed harder and took another step, and another, counting them.

He was pathetic, weak, unfit to be a Duke, a father. He could not even go down a stairwell without his heart thudding in his ears as if he had run ten miles. Even if he survived this hell, how would he find the strength to follow her into the tunnels?

Damn her, damn her, damn her...

The doorway. Thank God.

He stumbled through it, the lamp swinging, but his heart hardly had time to sing its relief when it shrivelled again. Even after close to thirty years he recognised everything. Not that there was much to recognise—the passage was broad but ended in darkness, making it look a mile long. He could not even see the indentation of the passage to the Sea Gate, though with it locked for the night she could hardly have exited that way.

He tried to focus on the tunnel itself, on how ordinary it was—merely a corridor like all the corridors in the castle. Darker and danker, certainly, but just a corridor. He kept his eyes on the floor and listened. Nothing.

She has probably returned already. Turn back. It will be easier going up than down. In a few moments you can be back in your room, safe and warm.

What if she is *in here somewhere? What if she took one of the other tunnels to the cellars and is lost...? What if she has fallen?*

The crypt steps were narrow and uneven. He knew that all too well. She might find herself as he had, at the bottom, unconscious...alone... afraid...in the dark.

He moved forward, his throat tight. He had no idea how long he searched or how far he descended into his own personal hell. Thirty years ago it had been cavernous, echoing, but now it was narrow and tight and every step he took felt like the walls were closing on him, would finally crush him.

But he had to find her.

Some sensible flicker in his mind finally lit into a spark and he stopped. In the silence, sound would carry far, even with these thick walls. He was a fool for not calling out her name from the beginning.

'Jo!'

The word exploded against the walls, tossed back and forth, taunting him.

'Benneit? Benneit! Here!'

He surged forward, almost dropping the lamp.

'Jo?' His voice was hoarse and he cleared his throat. 'Call out again!'

'Benneit!' Her voice shook. 'It is so foolish, I went to look at the effigies in the alcove and I tripped over the stones from the old wall and the candle fell and I couldn't find the exit and… Oh, I can see your light. This way! Oh, thank goodness, I was beginning to think I would have to spend the night here until someone realised I was missing and it is dreadfully chilly and I kept hearing things and even though I knew it was only my imagination it was terrifying. I know you will be angry at me and truly it was foolish…'

The light entered the crypt and with a little cry she moved towards him and stopped at the bottom of the steps leading down, her hands clasped at her chest in an unconscious mirror of the effigies lying on the tombs in the alcoves along the walls. Behind her he caught a glimpse of his own hell—the effigies of his ancestors, the cracked lid of the empty tomb, and the shimmering glint of the clan brooch resting on the breast of the other, inhabited tomb. He looked away, fixing his gaze on her as she moved towards him.

'I'm so sorry, Benneit. Please don't be angry, at least not until we are above ground and in front of a fire. I'm freezing.'

He placed the lamp on the floor very carefully

and took off his coat, focusing on placing it on her shoulders. Her hands rose to hold it around her and his own hand grazed hers; her fingers were frozen and his were clammy and shaking. He leaned back against the stone doorjamb.

'Benneit?'

He tried to reach for the lamp, but it was very far away. He made another effort and managed to close his hand around the handle. Her hand closed on the handle as well.

'Here, I'll take it,' she said, all panic gone from her voice and he closed his eyes, utterly humiliated but still unable to do more than stand there, his back glued to the wall, the stone cold and sharp through his linen shirt.

Her other hand closed around his and he forced himself to look down at it. It was small and fine and there was a faint scratch near her wrist. He wanted more than anything to raise it to his lips and breathe in her scent, but she was pulling him forward and they climbed the stairs which thirty years ago had felt so high he had been certain he was falling to the bottom of the earth.

He turned at the top stair of the crypt, the lamplight settling on the carved effigies of his ancestors once more. It was different from the image seared into his child's brain the moment before the candle hit the floor all those years ago. Then it had been a stark mask of dark and light with the single brooch glistening atop the occupied tomb next to the empty broken one, like a cyclopean eye of a beast rising from hell. It was an image of evil and cruelty that was seared into his mind in the sudden and absolute darkness that followed the fall of his candle. And that darkness had lasted for ever.

'Do you have any whisky in your rooms?' Her question brought him into the present. Amazingly they were already in the small parlour connecting to his bedroom and the candle on the mantelpiece was only half-gone. It had not been an eternity, but moments. How was that possible?

She took his other hand, looking up at him, her eyes wide and worried.

'Benneit? Is there whisky here or shall I fetch some?'

His hands tightened on hers. *Don't leave me, not yet.*

'In that cupboard.' His voice was as rusty as the hinges on the gates to the north bay.

'Go sit by the fire.' She drew her hands from his and he let them go reluctantly and obediently went to the chair by the fire. The warmth, his chair, his room and mostly her presence were cleaving their way through the darkness and the shuddering horror was beginning to dissipate at the edges, making more room for more humiliation. He rubbed his hands over his face, dreading what was to follow.

'Here.'

She handed him a glass and pulled a chair beside him.

'Drink.'

The welcome burn of whisky chased back more of the mist and he drank in silence, awaiting his fate.

'I should have realised,' she said. 'By the cave. Even in the carriage on the way north. It did strike me as strange even then, but I was too caught up in… I'm sorry I was so blind, Benneit.'

Oh, God, just leave me be.

'Did something happen or was it always like that?'

I don't want to talk. Go away.

He spoke anyway. 'Same as you. My candle blew out exploring the crypt. I was four, perhaps five.'

Her breath hissed inwards. 'Jamie's age. Were you there long?'

A lifetime.

He had probably slept some of it, out of sheer exhaustion, and had been asleep when they first came looking. It had been the servants' voices calling for him, but they had capped his horror—

in his child's mind the effigy had risen, a vision from hell, calling his name as it came to claim him and keep him there for ever, in darkness.

'A night and a day. My parents had been fighting, again, and I ran away. I should have made my protest clearer because my father thought I was at The House with my mother and she thought I was with him at the castle. I wanted to go somewhere that would make them angry, but then I fell down those blasted stairs and my candle went out. They never looked for me until the next day and even then it took them hours to think of the crypt. I remember it was already evening when they found me because the first thing I saw when we reached the nursery was the sunset.'

'A whole... Oh, my God. I was only there a few moments and I was ready to scream. And you were four. Oh, Benneit...'

She had his free hand pressed to her cheek. He could see into her mind. She was with that boy, another Jamie, her heart weeping for the horrified little Benneit. He was erased, reduced to that weak, terrified child. He jerked his hand away.

'I *told* you not to go there!'

'I know it was foolish, but I...'

'But you wanted to defy me. First you don't come down to our guests and then you go to the one place…the one damned place I told you *not* to go!'

'They were not *our* guests, they were your guests, and, yes, I dare say I did want to defy you, but I never meant…'

He slammed his glass down on the small table by his armchair and stood.

'You don't, do you? You don't *mean* to strip everything away, right down to the cracks and the flaws, but that is what you do time and again.'

'I can see why your fear of enclosed places makes your life difficult, but it doesn't diminish you, Benneit.'

He groaned and turned away, dragging his hands through his hair.

'Can you not leave me a shred of dignity?'

'It seems to me you have quite a few shreds of dignity. Perhaps even a few too many.'

'Damn you, Jo.'

She stood as well, her hands clasped before her, her eyes wide and worried. He wanted to chase away that worry, but he also wanted her to suffer as he was suffering. It was not possible that all the agony was his alone.

He didn't know what he wanted. He didn't know anything any more. This is what she had reduced him to. To one Great Big List of Things He Did Not Know.

Except for her. He knew he wanted her.

He laughed and turned away.

'Maybe you do mean it,' he said, not even bothering to hide his bitterness and pain. He was beyond that, beyond anything. He didn't care any longer. 'Maybe underneath all that show of understanding you enjoy watching me squirm. Torturing me like you have this week.'

'I haven't...'

'Yes, you have. Don't lie. You know how desperate I am to touch you, to be close to you, how unbearable it is just to feel your arm under my fingers, watch you smiling at Jamie, your eyes lighting up for him, for Angus, even for Mr Warren and Mr Carruthers, but you won't even look at me. You don't laugh with me anymore. Does it make you feel powerful to reduce me to this? How do I know you don't take perverse pleasure in watching me writhe in this purgatory?'

'It's not true. Benneit, you do not...you *cannot* believe that.'

'I don't believe much any longer. I have been so abysmally wrong in the past. Why not about you?'

Jo's heart was thudding so hard she could barely hear him. She was terrified and exultant all at the same time.

She could not mistake the raw heat in his eyes. It was not just anger and disgust at her and at himself, but the same cavernous need that was eating away at her.

She did not care any longer that it was wrong.

It was so natural that he appeared when she needed him. But to know he had come at such a cost to himself... How could he not see how magnificent he was? That this rescue, against his nature, against his fear, was more precious to her than anything? It was one thing to have dragged her out of the water; it was another thing entirely to follow her through the gates of his personal hell.

Her hero.

If she could have saved him that agony she would, but since she could not, she was glad she had shared it, even if he hated her for it.

She held out her hands, but he stepped back, his face still harsh with anger.

'Don't play with me, Jo. I don't want your comfort.'

'I don't want to comfort you, Benneit. I want to make love to you. I'm tired of trying to do what is right. I cannot bear being here any longer and not being yours. Please, Benneit.'

'No. I may have discovered stores of restraint I never knew I possessed, but they are all but depleted after this hellish week. I won't have your conscience on mine as well, Jo. If that is how it is to be then you had best start running. Fast. Stay or run, but choose.'

She placed her hands on his chest as she had wanted to in the garden, moving them softly upwards, her fingers lingering on the hint of roughness of his chest hair under the linen, the hard, smooth line of his collarbone.

'Every night I imagine doing this,' she whispered. 'Every night I imagine you touching me. I told myself it was enough to have felt it once, your body against mine. But that is a lie. I want you. For however long we have left. I want this.'

His hands covered hers, closing on them painfully, his shoulders hunching.

'God, Jo. I could climax just listening to you. I hear you in my dreams, feel you against me. I wake up hard as granite and with your scent lingering and I dread the sun rising because it means I must go through another day making believe I'm not aching to touch you.'

She rose on tiptoe, brushing the tense muscle in his cheek with her mouth, his stubble tingling on her lips.

'And I ache whenever you accidently touch me…' she murmured, kissing a trail along his jaw, hovering at the corner of his mouth where a muscle was twitching.

'There is nothing accidental about it. You've reduced me to the level of a green youth, brushing against you because I can't think of anything else to do.'

She leaned against him, her breasts pressing against his chest, and his arms finally went around her, hesitant for a moment before closing hard around her, a groan rising through him as he pulled her against him, burying his face in the curve of her neck. His arousal was hot and hard against her stomach and she shivered with anticipation.

'A well-endowed youth,' she gasped as his teeth grazed the side of her neck. 'And growing...'

Something between a laugh and a groan escaped him and he hauled her into his arms, striding towards his bed. He stood for a moment holding her above it, his eyes emerald bright. Then he lay her down, very gently, and bent to kiss her.

It went on and on, from soft butterfly brushes of his lips to his tongue teasing, sweeping against hers, coaxing her into a response that coursed through her body. It was in complete contrast with the desire that was flashing through her, nervous and demanding.

He neither joined her nor undressed her, just rested his fists on the bed as his mouth seduced, plundered, caressed and coaxed her until she was panting, her hands pulling at his shoulders to bring her to him, her heels pressing into the bed.

'Benneit, please. Please.'

'Soon. I want you to need me as much as I need you. I want you flayed in the same agony you reduced me to.'

'I am, I am… Oh, God, hurry!'

'Not a chance in hell.'

He undressed her just as slowly, stopping only to help her fevered attempts to do the same to him. If she hadn't seen the green flames in his eyes, the tension in the lines bracketing his mouth, she might have been afraid at the difference in their passion, but she knew his control was in accord with his need. She could feel it in the heat of his skin, the staccato rapping of his pulse. His breathing was as short and shallow as a man caught by fever and everywhere she touched she felt his muscles flinch and watched his eyelids dip as if in pain.

If she hadn't felt his tension she might have thought he was toying with her. But though she might mistrust his words, she felt a passion that matched hers in every tense line of his body and face.

When they were finally naked, his eyes stripped her again, raking over her body with an appreciation and pleasure that soothed her doubts.

'You're beautiful, Jo. Beautiful and mine.' His voice was harsh, filled with the same demanding accusation she had mistaken for hatred. She didn't even question the lie—right now she *was* beautiful. As exquisite as he. She drew him down against her, luxuriating in the slide of his body against hers, the landscape of soft and hard, smooth and rough. She wanted to absorb him, pull him into her and never let go.

'I love feeling you, Benneit, love how you feel on me, against me.'

She could not stop her hands from caressing him, stroking his chest, her nails tracing the silky dark hair, snagging on his hardened nipple, making him gasp and buck against her. He laughed and groaned at the same time, his legs tangling with hers, his hipbone grinding into the soft skin of her abdomen as she writhed against him, loving everything—the pleasure, the pain, the anticipation, even her coming destruction had a sweetness to it, like the last glimmer of a sunset.

'My wanton pixie, you will finish me before we even begin.'

She didn't answer, just drew his head down

to hers, kissing him with everything inside her, holding nothing back.

Every caress, every glide of her body against his was too much, every touch of his fingers and mouth raising her inexorably towards the promise of sweet release. She hardly even sobered when he left her for a moment, returning with something he extracted from a box, sheathing himself with it before he sank back between her legs, his hand soothing as he eased her legs further apart before entering her gently, slowly. He filled her utterly, hot and hard and so right. She didn't want him to move because it would be the end of it, but when he did she just abandoned herself to the joy of their bodies, the way his chest scraped against her breasts, the way his hand moved between them, goading her on until she was panting and begging, her legs rising to pull him in as deeply as she could. Then the pleasure became unbearable, hot honeyed waves hitting again and again as if they would never stop. She wanted to cry or yell, but could do nothing but fall as the world burst and faded. Even as she lost herself she dimly felt him move inside her, his chest heaving with great gasping breaths.

'Jo. God, Jo...'

Her name reverberated through her body with the diminishing waves of her own climax as he shook through his, his voice hoarse and grabbing her very core in an iron fist.

'Don't leave yet. It is still short of midnight. Stay.'

Benneit pulled her back towards him as Jo tried to rise, tucking her against his length, his mouth brushing her temple and then pressing a kiss to her shoulder.

'I shouldn't.'

'Why not? Are you regretting this again?' The words were brusque compared to the message of his body and she heard her own uncertainty there and shook her head. Perhaps she would later, after she left Lochmore, but whatever time was left she did not wish to ruin with regret.

'No. Though it is still hard for me. Perhaps we should not have done this here, in the room you shared with Bella.'

His arms pulled her even closer, his hand spread over her ribs below her breast. It was large and warm and both soft and calloused and her skin tingled beneath it, already wanting more.

'She was never in this bed, so that needn't sit on your conscience. You've too much there already and I can't bear adding to it.'

She ignored the future, focusing on the past, more curious than jealous about that. 'Never?'

'She preferred her own chambers. She hated the castle and demanded we redecorate and, as you can see from the Hall, I gave her free rein in most places outside my room and the study. And the crypt. Her romantic fascination with all things Scottish didn't last long when confronted with the reality. When my father told her about the mystery of the plundered tomb in the crypt she wanted to transform it into a quaint attraction for visitors, but I drew the line there.'

'The plundered tomb? Was that the one with the broken lid?'

'Yes, there is no body there and the matching brooch was missing. They were taken during a battle with the McCrieffs hundreds of years ago, but no one knows where or why. Bella felt it would be a pleasant attraction for when we entertained our English friends.'

'Didn't she know you hated closed spaces?'

His fingers stilled for a moment in their slow caress of the curve of her waist, but he didn't withdraw as she expected.

'No. My parents taught me quite effectively no good came from sharing my mental instability. I am usually better at masking it.'

'It is not mental instability. It is the natural outcome of a horrible experience. If this had happened to Jamie, you would not allow anyone to regard it in that manner!'

'I would not allow such a thing to happen to him. Why do you think I forbid him to go alone to the tunnels?'

'You cannot know what life will do to any of us. But I know you would not shame him for his fear any more than you shame Angus for his reluctance to see beyond his scars.'

'That is pure selfishness. I like having Angus here.'

She pressed a kiss to the curve of his shoulder.

'You are a monster of selfishness indeed. I knew it all along.'

His arm tightened again, his leg rising to brush against hers, but he lowered it.

'Bella certainly believed I was.'

She barely resisted the urge to snort.

'Bella was certainly an authority on selfishness. She had many good qualities, but she was spoilt from the cradle. I always envied her her certitude.'

'So did I. It was one of the things I admired about her. It was…persuasive. I wanted to be like her.'

'I thought you were rather like her,' she admitted. 'Back then. You appeared perfect together.'

She covered his hand with her smaller hand. He sighed, linking his fingers with hers.

'The bard had some words on how the world seems compared to how it is, didn't he? We were perfect for how we both wanted to appear to the world. But Bella needed someone kinder than I, someone indulgent who could calm the little girl who was afraid she would no longer be loved when she ceased to be perfect. I had no notion and, to be honest, no real will to do so. Sometimes I think it irked her most of all that I preferred her imperfections—that made them all the more real to her. Once our mutual infatuation was over we had to face the fact that we were not very well suited.'

He raised her hand, brushing her fingertips across his lips as he spoke, his breath warming the sensitive skin between her fingers, smoothing over the back of her hand.

'She married a wealthy Duke-to-be who played the London game and ended living in a social wasteland with a Scottish heathen at war with his father and who was up to his neck in estate matters. I thought once Jamie came it would create a bridge between us, but then Jamie changed everything for me. I cannot explain—the moment I took him in my arms I knew everything was different.' He laughed, looking years younger than he had this past week. 'It was like hitting a wall. My resentment against my father, the demands of Lochmore, Bella's frustration—all that faded and I realised nothing mattered as much as Jamie.'

'Poor Bella,' Jo said, and, absurdly, she meant it.

'Poor Bella, indeed. Unlike my shameful flaw there was nothing I could do to mask my love for Jamie. Perhaps if we had been in London she would have found our differences more bearable. I hoped Jamie would bridge that gap between us, but I think that very expectation only made it worse. When she went down to Uxmore that last summer and left Jamie and me here I was so relieved that when the news came of her illness and death all I could feel was guilt that I had so thoroughly enjoyed my time alone with Jamie.'

His hand stilled on her hip, she could feel the tension gathering in him and searched for some way to stave off the intrusion of reality. But he spoke first.

'What about your Alfred? Or did the accident occur too soon for disenchantment to set in?'

She wondered what she could say. She wanted to repay the gift of honesty, but not scare him out of the temporary intimacy they shared.

'There was no disenchantment because there was no enchantment. You will think me horrid—I did not marry Alfred because I loved him, but because he loved me. It was the opposite—I learned to care for him because he valued things in me others hardly even noticed. So when he died I told myself I must not lose that completely. I also feel guilty because I never loved him as he deserved. Not even as much as I think I was capable of.'

In the silence she heard the murmur of the fire and the pattering of rain. His fingers stroked her hip as they might Flops, methodically but absently. Then they stopped and she gathered her resolve. Time to regain reality. But when she moved towards the side of the bed she found herself suddenly on her back, Benneit propping himself above her, his leg sliding between hers, his erection hard and hot against her thigh. He was in shadow, but his eyes were as sharp as a panther's, narrowed and predatory. Even his words were a growl.

'You aren't leaving yet. We are not done here.'

The transition from empathy to blazing desire was so extreme her body ached, her skin tight and tingling as if it had shrunk on her. She could not stop her legs clamping around his, her hips trying to rise. Her hands rose as well, pressing against the stubble on his lean cheeks, feeling the bone beneath.

For now he was hers. His body wanted her—

as strange as it was, she knew it was absolutely true and marvellous. Somehow, for now, Benneit wanted her with a passion that equalled hers.

'What shall we do, then?' she asked, breathless, and he smiled, a panther's smile.

'You shall do nothing. You have earned your rest. I will do everything.'

'But I enjoy doing,' she murmured, touching the sharp-cut line of his jaw, the sweep of his shoulder and collarbone. Beautiful.

'Later. I want you addicted to this before morning comes and I can't concentrate when you're touching me,' he murmured against her nape, his own hand trailing lower. 'So for now I want you to keep those dangerous hands of yours to yourself, little pixie. Close your eyes and drift…'

Chapter Twenty-Nine

Benneit woke into softness. The bed was soft, the cover above him was soft. His skin felt soft. He only wished she had not left before dawn so he could sink in to her again. He didn't want to wait until nightfall again. He wanted to tell her how good he felt with her. Not good—wonderful. He felt he could walk into the crypt and take a nap there and… Well, not quite that good, but close. There was no point in chasing ghosts, as Jo had said.

In fact, a large portion of his life recently was becoming dictated by what Jo said, what she did, what she wanted. What she needed.

Amazingly, it felt right.

Unlike Bella, Jo's words and actions and wishes felt an extension of him, of Benneit, not Lochmore.

He opened his eyes, staring at the canopy.

So this was love.

Even as the words formed in his mind, a welling of heat spread upwards through his body, expanding him.

I love Jo.

It wasn't completely a revelation. It had been forming, weaving itself into his fabric with each word and look and gesture on the trip north, then put together as she explored his world, him. As she made room for him and Jamie in her thoughtful little world. As he came first to see and then realise the wealth under her cautious, watchful exterior.

I love you, Jo.

The words felt inadequate, as far from reflecting what he felt as a speck on the horizon reflected the reality of a great mountain.

Do you love me?

He swung his legs off the bed, an echo of the fear and pain of the last week pinching at his skin.

That question was more dangerous than any of his thoughts. Because if she did… How could he walk away if she did?

How could he walk away even if she did not? Even if her feelings were nothing more than lust and the kind of warmth she offered those within her circle of care.

There must be something wrong with him to feel he could not weather losing her. A woman he had only truly known for a month of his life. That it should be sitting in the same corner of himself that raged and cowered when something threatened Jamie.

Had Bella ever been there? Even at the height of his passion for her he wasn't certain he had felt she was essential to him. His father had never truly been that, and he could not reach back with clarity to his mother's loss. With Bella he found the kind of union his parents had—a mix of sexual fascination and antagonism—but he had kept most of himself apart, just as he had with his parents. With Jo he couldn't hide himself even when he tried.

Even Jamie was different—Jamie was his to care for and carry through life until he could walk alone. He wanted Jo for himself. For her. For ever. The thought that the rest of his life would stretch out without her was…

Wrong.

There had to be something he could do.

But he could think of nothing that wouldn't make Jamie pay the price for his selfishness. If not for Jamie he could have turned his back on all of this, not without pain because Lochmore was also his to care for, but he could have done it and paid the price. But how could he expect Jamie to pay that price for the rest of his life? By shaming Tessa McCrieff, he would be shaming Jamie.

It was impossible.

* * *

'Mrs Merry says the sun will hold so what must she do but decide to wash all the linen and bring three girls from the village, each sillier than the next, making sheep's eyes at Angus and Ewan when they should be hard at work,' Beth complained as she laid out the green-sprigged muslin dress.

Jo tried to commiserate as Beth prodded her into the dress but failed utterly. She treasured these bright, warm days, but it was a joy tempered with the knowledge of pain to come. All too soon they would be gone and so would she. Surely that made no sense? It felt as wrong as stopping her breath.

When Jamie came rushing in to tell her they were to go have luncheon at The House she hurried Beth along. She did not wish to waste a single moment she could spend with Benneit.

The contrast with their last visit to The House was so extreme, Jo ached with it. She and Benneit rode side by side, knees brushing occasionally, and Jamie turning back often to smile at them, as if he was the proud parent and they well-behaved children. Angus and Ethel were waiting for them with a light meal which they ate in the conservatory overlooking the sculpture garden.

After the meal Jamie curled up on the sofa and was soon asleep and Benneit took her arm, leading her into the garden.

The light-hearted happiness began to fade the moment they were alone, replaced by tension and an edge of pain. In the bower Benneit let go of her arm and moved to inspect the clambering vines and Jo took the plunge, her half-formed thoughts tumbling out.

'I was thinking,' Jo said.

'Thinking what?' He turned to her and she saw a reflection of the same tension in the harsh lines of his face.

'I told you I don't intend to return to Uxmore. I always thought I would go to London, but when we were in the village the other day I spoke with Mrs McManus and she said it is becoming harder for her at the school. Lochmore may have shrunk, but there are more children than ever and she was thinking of speaking with Mr McCreary about finding someone younger to assist her. And I thought...perhaps I might...'

'You wish to become a schoolmistress? At Lochmore?'

'It was a foolish idea. I'm sorry. I dare say it would be embarrassing to have a relation of Bella here in such a capacity.' She turned away and reached towards a cluster of buds hanging from the vines that covered the trellis above them. 'What is this?'

'Wisteria. It is one of the loveliest plants here, but you can only appreciate it once it blooms.' He guided her towards the bower where the sun was strongest. One of the clusters was a pale lavender, soft and fresh, the colour of a mythical dawn. 'They will all be like this soon and then you will see why my mother took such effort with it.'

Benneit watched Jo touch the delicate cluster hanging from the trellis, the buds shivering under her fingers and an answering shiver skimmed under his skin. In an instant he was on fire, his skin tight, tingling with the need to act, press himself against her. It was so immediate he felt dizzy with it, his breath turning shallow.

In his mind's eye he saw her naked beneath the vines, covered with these flowered waterfalls, waiting for him. But that would never be and it hurt like nothing had hurt in his life.

'It is lovely,' she murmured, her voice sucking him further under the wave of lust. He rested his hands on her shoulders a moment before turning her. Her eyes were still bright with appreciation of the beauty, her mouth the soft curve of a smile that stripped him of his defences every time. It was that smile that made her impossible to ignore, each smile as soft as a petal unfurling, but with the power to destroy his defences.

'There should be roses, too.' His voice was hoarse because it hurt to talk. 'I should have tried harder to keep them. They would be in bloom now. I want to see you surrounded by roses, find the one as soft as your mouth, as sweet as your scent so I can find you when you leave.'

Even speaking those words hurt and he pressed his hands to her cheeks, moulding his fingers over her face, mapping her, the soft curve of her cheek, the firm, stubborn chin, the long gold-tipped lashes that were shielding the cool pixie eyes, and her mouth, the generous, sweet bow that could rule his reactions and which gave her away far more than her eyes. It was parted now, her breath as uneven as his, as vulnerable as he felt, shivering like a petal in a rising wind. He brushed his fingers over it, catching the warmth of her breath.

He couldn't touch her here. Anyone could come by out and see them...

One hand slid into her hair. Without her bun it was looser and it made way for his fingers, warm and silky, made to be set loose and wrapped about him as it was at night.

'I want to make love to you in daylight, here, with the sun streaming through the vines, touching you as you touch me. I want to taste the sun on your skin, every golden gleam, every freckle, I want to make you blush so I can watch heat pour through you when I enter you, when I make you shudder. Right here in the centre of the garden so that no corner is ever free of you, of your feel and your scent. You will always be right here.'

She was shivering and her eyes were damp; he knew he was going too far, but he could not stop. Not if the whole of Lochmore and McCrieff were standing around them baying for his blood. Right now he could not, would not stop. This was his. One last moment of something purely for himself. It was not even for Jo because he could not have her, but he could have this. Jo in his garden. He would never take anyone else here. Here, with her, he was completely himself. As she was. This was Jo—perfect, lovely, clever, impossible. *His* Jo.

The kiss was hard and deep, his mouth capturing hers, his hands crushing her against him. Even as his body raged, his hands dragging at the dress that kept her from him, his mind was howling in agony that it could not be more than a moment.

How was that possible? It was all wrong.

'Jo. Oh, God, Jo. You're mine. That is why you cannot stay. You know what will happen if you stay in the village. Every day I will have to stop Jamie from coming to see you. And every night I will have to stop myself from thinking—she is so close. In a little house in the village, alone in her bed, maybe thinking of this...' His hand curved over her breast, his thumb flicking at her nipple, teasing it into a hard nub. She moaned and he scraped his teeth down the side of her neck, as if to punish her, then suckled the skin, adding heat to heat.

'I will be thinking—I can walk there now. In my mind I can see every stone and tuft of grass and stalk of heather on the way. I'll know that when your cottage comes into view I am only five minutes from being able to do this...and this... And I'll have to lie there, in my bed, knowing that you are so close and as far from me as if you were a myth. And one day, you will meet another Alfred and I will have to watch...come to your wedding... God help me, I'm not strong enough, Jo. It will break me.'

He held her against him, his lips on her hair, breathing her scent, trying to secure it in his mind.

'When I'm sane I want you to find someone who will adore you, and care for you, and love you as you deserve to be loved, Jo. I want you to have a family...' He felt her breath choke with the pain he knew she shared. He knew without looking her eyes were burning like his. 'But it's also a lie. I don't want you to ever love anyone. I can't bear to think of anyone… Oh, God, this is unbearable. I can't do this. I need to go. Angus will see you back to the castle.'

He strode away from the garden, from himself.

After a moment Jo sat on the bench, watching the purple cluster swinging a little in the breeze, like a brace of chimes.

It didn't help that for the first time she had heard a real echo of her feelings in his voice. That he might care…really care for her beyond the lust that had taken them by surprise. She knew that cleaving—the need for him to be happy and the fury that he might be.

He probably would be in the end. Content at least. There would be other children and he would love them as much as Jamie and that would bring him joy and fill his life and one day he will wake up and perhaps discover he truly cared for Tessa.

Her nails bit into her palms.

He was right. To stay would be a worse torture than leaving. It would be a slow death, especially now that she knew he truly cared. She would be so tempted to use that against him, to bring him to her exactly as he had described. To take agonised pleasure in imagining him awake as she in the middle of the night, thinking of her while another woman slept beside him. Waiting always for the next chance encounter, building her whole life around the echoes of his.

She could not stay.

Chapter Thirty

'Good day, Your Grace. Not that we are not honoured to see you again so soon after your last visit, but perhaps you should have sent word so we could prepare for your arrival...'

Caught in his cloud of shame and misery, it took Benneit a moment to realise he was unwelcome. Lady Aberwyld was looking haughtier than usual, but her hands were pleating the fabric at the edges of her tambour frame and her cheeks were flushed.

'I apologise for incommoding you, Lady Aberwyld, but I must speak with Lord Aberwyld. And Lady Tessa.'

Her eyes flickered about the room, as close to panic as he had ever seen her.

'Lord Aberwyld is out with the steward and dear Tessa is a trifle under the weather. Perhaps...'

'No, I am not, Mama.' Tessa entered the room, her voice and movements sharp.

'Tessa! Return to your room immediately. Your father forbade you to leave it.'

'I know he did, but I saw Lochmore ride up. You may have disposed of my sisters as you saw fit, but I will not allow you to do the same to me. I wish to speak with Lochmore. Alone.'

Lady Aberwyld surged to her feet, her cheeks purple with anger and fear.

'Be silent and go to your room, you ungrateful child. You have everything...*everything*... offered you...'

Tessa was nearly as red as her mother.

'Not everything, ma'am. And not what is important to me.'

'What do you know of what is important? I knew I should never have allowed you to spend that year with your aunt in Glasgow. She crammed your foolish head with girlish nonsense. This is real—you will marry Lochmore and be grateful to find yourself a bridegroom everyone in the Highlands will envy you for!'

Tessa was breathing heavily.

'I will speak with His Grace, Mother. Alone!'

'You will do no such thing! Aberwyld!' Lady Aberwyld gave a savage tug on the bell cord. 'Lochmore, you will not listen to this foolish child. These are mere nerves.'

Benneit had hardly dared breathe throughout the scene, but now he turned to meet Tessa's stormy gaze.

'Are they, Lady Tessa?' he asked calmly, holding up a hand as Lady Aberwyld began answering in her daughter's stead.

Tessa raised her chin.

'No. I told Father and Mother the night you left that I will not marry you. I shall not change my mind. We women have few enough prerogatives, but I believe we still possess this one.'

'You do,' he replied as calmly as his thudding heart allowed. 'It was always your right. I would never wish for a bride that did not come willingly. And you deserve to want that of your bridegroom as well.'

A sudden, surprising smile cleaved through her tension.

'Precisely, Your Grace. I might have been willing to live in the shadow of the ghost of a beautiful countess, but not in the shadow of the live ghost of a woman I admire. I want more in life.'

'You little fool,' Lady Aberwyld wailed. 'He might love her, but he will marry *you*. That is all that matters.'

'No, it isn't.' Benneit and Tessa spoke the words in unison and suddenly the tension in them both broke like an ice floe setting loose on the loch.

'Why did you come today, Benneit?' Tessa asked, ignoring her mother. 'To offer for me?'

He shook his head.

'To speak with you. To explain. To beg if need be. But to marry you if that was what you wanted and try to do my best by you. Jamie matters more than I do.'

Her mouth wavered.

'But that is why I cannot do it. I want someone to do that for me. To want me up to the edge of their honour.'

The door opened and McCrieff strode in, his brow lowering ominously at the sight of his daughter and Benneit, his eyes wary as he absorbed Lady Aberwyld weeping into her handkerchief. But he visibly dragged a smile on to his ruddy face.

'Lochmore!'

Tessa stepped forward.

'I told him I shan't marry him, Father.'

McCrieff gave the roar of a wounded bull and Benneit stepped between him and Tessa, but McCrieff merely raised his hands and grabbed his hair as if trying to pull it out by the roots.

'Ignore her, Lochmore, these are naught by maidenly fears.'

'I shan't marry him.' Tessa's voice was calm and final and for a moment she looked incredibly like her father—obdurate and solid. 'I shall not yield.'

'‘Tis your fault! You spoilt her, Aberwyld!' Lady Aberwyld moaned.

'I spoilt her? *I?* You were the one set on sending her to Glasgow! The girl needs town polish, you said! Well, this is what you get!'

Benneit and Tessa stood silent as battle waged between husband and wife. It raged for full five minutes before Lady Aberwyld withdrew, weeping into her handkerchief, her tambour frame bouncing to the floor.

McCrieff rounded again on his daughter, but in a moment the fury deserted him.

'Ah, child. Child… You're a fool. You would be Duchess of Lochmore! My life's dream.'

'Yours, sir. Not mine,' she answered simply.

'I'll send you away.'

'I know that. I hope somewhere not too wild. Seeing that I am already such a heathen.'

His shoulders fell.

'Will you not reason with her, Lochmore? This is your fault, you know. She thinks you are in love with that little Englishwoman. I told her it is different for men. Why, you could even bid your widow stay and we'd not say a word.'

'Father!'

'No, I couldn't, McCrieff. Neither Mrs Langdale nor your brave daughter deserve such disrespect. I would not dishonour your family or a woman I care for in such a manner.'

McCrieff sank into the chair vacated by his wife.

'You young people with this nonsense of love.

The world has become a foolish, self-indulgent place. Your father and I ought to have known better, too. Foolishness is clearly heritable.'

'My father loved my mother very much,' Benneit said with certainty, surprising himself.

'Ay, and suffered every day for it. They fought like cats and dogs.'

'I remember.'

'And that is what you want?'

'What I want matters only to me and, to a certain degree, your daughter. She is not a fool. She knows I will marry her if she demands I honour the unspoken agreement between our families. Jamie's future rides as much upon upholding Lochmore honour as it now rides upon the future of the distillery which depends upon your goodwill. I will not put his future in jeopardy, no matter the pain it will cause me.'

McCrieff's smile twisted.

'I have you at my mercy, have I not?'

'You have. I came to throw myself at your feet even if Tessa had not spoken, so do not lay all the blame at her doorstep.'

'My doorstep, you mean. I have proven a failure as a father.'

'That is not true, Father,' Tessa said, her voice cracking for the first time.

'You'll have to go away, girl. Your mother will

make both our lives a living hell for a year at least.'

'I am ready for that.'

'Aunt Maura will have to take you. Perhaps you'll mind her if not me.'

Tessa's eyes widened with barely repressed hope.

'Mama will never allow me to return to Glasgow.'

'I am still master in this house, am I not?' Mc-Crieff bellowed, thumping the armrests.

'Of course you are, Papa. Thank—'

'Be gone, girl! I don't want to see you till you're packed and ready to leave.'

Tessa didn't wait for more.

'Tell her I wish you both happiness,' she whispered to Benneit as she hurried by, her eyes laughing and full of tears.

'Twenty per cent!' Aberwyld growled and Benneit blinked, still waiting for the other shoe to drop.

'Twenty what?'

'Per cent. Of the distillery. That's my price for letting you walk away with your honour and your conscience clean.'

'You could ask for more than that, McCrieff,' Benneit said truthfully.

'I have my honour, too, Lochmore. Blast the both of you. It's like a blasted curse ever since your ancestor Ewan stole Duncan McCrieff's Frenchie bride. Every time our families look to mix their blood again, something blasts it all to hell.'

Benneit had no patience for superstition, but in this instance he had no wish to argue against anything that gave McCrieff comfort.

'Perhaps that is what it is. Perhaps we should accept fate and be content with what we have.'

'If the two of you could have done that we wouldn't be up to our necks in this bog. Ah, well, I can hardly blame you when I did something not very different when my father and your grandfather tried to create matches between your Aunt Morag and myself and between my sister and your father. It was wrong then and I'd be a hypocritical fool to play dog in the manger now. Though my present lady might not be all I hoped when I wed her, she's a sight better than your aunt, Lochmore. Come drink with me, man, before you go. If I were you, I'd take that little Englishwoman of yours south for a time while I soothe my lady wife. Now drink up and make good your escape. Oh, and I'll want the first ten cases of whisky from our distillery, mind you.'

Chapter Thirty-One

The nursery was empty and Benneit cursed. What a time for them to go wandering!

'Angus!' His bellow echoed in the stairway as he ran downstairs again. '*Angus!* There you are. Where the devil is Jo? I need to… What is wrong?'

'Am I to wish you happy, Your Grace?'

'What? What has happened? Where is Jo? Where is Jamie? Is something wrong?'

'Jamie is in the Map Room. There is nought wrong with him but a broken heart.'

'What the devil are you going on about? Where is Jo?'

'I'd say halfway to Inveraray.'

'What? What the devil is going on? Angus!'

'Don't go howling at me, Your Grace. There's a letter for 'ee in the study.'

'Don't turn your back on me, Angus. Why did she leave?'

'Mayhap she didn't wish to remain here so as to have to raise a glass for you betrothing yourself to another. You didn't even have the guts to tell her you were off to the McCrieffs! She had to hear it from Beth, who heard it from the stables. She begged me to take her to put her on the post in Kilmarchie, but I told her I'd not lend my hand to that nonsense and she said she'd walk if need be. So I had the carriage brought round. She told Jamie some fib about her family needing her and was off an hour ago. So—am I to wish ye happy?'

Benneit strode into his study.

'I'm not marrying Tessa McCrieff. I went there to beg her to release me. Blast you, you should not have let Jo leave. Have Lochlear saddled right away. I'll ride across the glen.'

The letter lay in the middle of his desk and he opened it, furious, scared, but still stubbornly elated. His heart was soaring like a hot air balloon—she would not have run if she did not care. In an hour, less if he was lucky and the glen not sodden from rain, he would reach her and tell her precisely what he thought about her running away. But first he would make it abundantly clear to her she was staying. No, first he would beg her to tell him he was not wrong in his belief that she cared as much as he did. He needed to see her when he spoke the words. See the truth in her eyes, whether it took him to heaven or hell.

He unfolded the letter and read.

Dear Benneit,

Beth told me where you have gone, so it is time for me to leave.

I should end my letter here and thank you for everything—tell you to take good care of Jamie, though I know you will. And say Godspeed and congratulate you.

But I cannot say that and I cannot stay. Not one moment longer. I know this is the right path for you, but if I were wealthy and beautiful, or even merely pretty, I would fight for you and tell Tessa McCrieff she cannot have you.

Yet I can offer you and Jamie nothing but what I am. No, even that you have taken from me. You have stripped me of my armour against the world and now instead of thinking I speak, and instead of wanting I am beginning to make demands, and this is dangerous.

If I stay a moment longer I might begin to beg when I have never, ever begged for anything in my life.

You will feel guilty, I know, even hurt, and perhaps responsible, and you will consider coming after me. But if you dare... If you dare I will blacken your eye, Benneit Lochmore.

You have your pride and I have mine. I am writing this to you because I must, and because even though we cannot be friends you are my finest friend. I will take this loss and make even more of myself now because of you—not less because of this pain I am taking with me.

Jamie is upset and hurt, but Tessa McCrieff is a good person and will be a good mother and I believe he will become attached to her. You are and will be an excellent father. The very best. Please don't ever doubt that. This is one of the things at the very top of my List of Things I Know to be Absolutely True.

Goodbye, Benneit. It will only ever be you, mo chridhe.

'Papa?' Jamie stood in the doorway. His cheeks were marked with streaks of drying tears and strangely Benneit noticed he was wearing shoes. Flops's muzzle was pressed against his hand, gently licking.

'I tried to make her stay, Papa. She said she couldn't. I don't understand why.'

Benneit covered his eyes for a moment, then strode towards Jamie, swinging him into his arms.

'It is my fault, Jamie. But I will make good. I

need to leave now and fetch her back. Don't you worry. I'm bringing her back to stay, Jamie.'

'To stay? For ever? She won't leave?'

'Not if I can help it. I must go now and hopefully we will be back by nightfall. You will be laird while I'm gone and make certain all is well and ready for our return. Understand, Lord Glenarris?'

Chapter Thirty-Two

It was perverse. It had been a beautiful sunny day for his ride out to face his doom at McCrieffs' and now that he was trying to capture his small corner of bliss, the world was leaking—the sky, the ground, the heather, his greatcoat, even his boots.

Poor Lochlear sensed his urgency and made good time across the glen even in the rain, his hooves sending up clumps of mud and heather. Despite the miles falling behind them, a superstitious fear clung to Benneit that he would never reach her, that she would disappear into a fold in the air, leaving only the memory she had imprinted on his heart and mind and body. Spirited away after the Summer's Solstice like her magical mice.

But as he neared the Standing Stones he spotted the carriage and spurred Lochlear on. Dougal heard his shout and pulled on the reins, and the carriage drew to a halt on the side of the road where a track led off towards the stones.

'Your Grace! Is aught wrong?' Dougal asked.

'Yes. You are pointed in the wrong direction, Dougal. I'll have a word with Mrs Langdale while you find a spot to turn. Take Lochlear for me, will you, Ewan?'

Ewan jumped down from the box and took the reins, his jaw slack, but Benneit ignored him and went to open the carriage door. Jo sat in the corner, very straight, her eyes wide and blank. He knew that look.

He held out his hand.

'Dougal must turn the carriage and this is a rather narrow road, so despite the rain you are safer on terra firma with me than inside.'

'Is there an obstruction on the road that necessitates our taking a different route to Glasgow, Your Grace?'

'You are not going to Glasgow. You are returning to Lochmore. If you wish to discuss this here with Dougal and Ewan as audience, I will, Jo, but I prefer not to keep the horses standing for longer than necessary in this weather. Come.'

She did not move and he sighed and began climbing in.

'No!' she exclaimed. 'Oh, very well, outside, then.'

He stepped back out and held out his hand. She ignored it and used the door to help her jump down on to the road. He motioned her towards the track to the standing stones and she strode ahead, her mouth prim and her chin up, the proud effect ruined somewhat by the mud squelching at their feet. He resisted, barely, the urge to pull her back against him, envelop her, melt her resistance and fear.

'You should not have run away like that.'

She stopped at the first of the standing stones and turned the full force of her great grey-eyed glare on him.

'I did *not* run away. Our agreement was for a month and now it is time for me to leave. I came to help you with Jamie and I have done precisely that. It is not my role to hold your hand and warm your bed as you prepare the castle for your next Duchess, Lochmore. Now that you will be announcing your engagement it is no longer appropriate that I remain at the castle. I have too much respect for Tessa McCrieff.'

'If that is your objection we are quite in the clear. There will be no wedding. She has rejected me.'

'She… She what?'

'Unbelievable, I know. I could hardly credit it myself, vain peacock that I am. She told me that on no account would she marry me.'

He smiled a little at the blank shock on her face.

'Your disbelief goes a little way to restoring my bruised pride. But only a very little way. It will need more than that.'

'Is there someone else? Is that why?'

'Most assuredly… Oh, you mean for Tessa Mc-Crieff. I'm afraid I didn't enquire, though she did appear very willing to be banished to her aunt in Glasgow for some reason. I was rather too dazed at my good fortune to take in the details. I went to throw myself at her mercy and she ended up cutting me loose with hardly a scar to show for it. I can only console myself on my good taste that had matters been different she would have made me a very creditable wife, but she also makes an excellent jilt. In that, too, I am luckier than I deserve. I'm free, Jo.'

Free.

Jo leaned back against the stone behind her. Her head was pounding, her *heart* was pounding. She felt sick and terrified of the joy that was trying to burst out of her at this reprieve.

But it made no *difference*. If Tessa McCrieff would not have him, no doubt McCrieff would toss another clan member at Benneit, or he would find some lord's lovely daughter from Inveraray or Kilmarchie—she had seen enough pretty things sighing over him during the ball. The principle was the same. All that had been bought was some more time.

But time…

With Benneit and Jamie.

She would give everything she had for this time. She had already given her heart, what did pride and honour and reputation matter next to that?

'You wish for me to return with you.' She sounded calm, which was amazing.

'Yes, Jo. You aren't leaving.'

'It is *not* for you to decide.'

He came and pressed his palm against the rough grey stone behind her.

'You do realise where you are, don't you?'

'In a field. A wet and muddy field.'

'That, too. But you have very unwisely chosen to stand within the Ring of Inverdine, *mo ghràdh.*'

She looked away at the casual endearment, finally noticing the peculiar arrangement of stones. The name sounded impressive, but it did not look very daunting. Just an arrangement of tall and very uneven stones laid out in a broad circle. What on earth did that have to do with her whole world closing and opening and ripping her heart to shreds in the process?

'So? Why unwisely?'

'Come now, Jo. You of the magical mice and mystical cats should know about such things. You cannot challenge a Highland laird in a stone circle in his own domain and expect to come off scot free.'

'I'll never be free of Scots,' she muttered and moved away from the rock, but he placed his other palm on it, fencing her in. She debated ducking under his arms but that was childish. And she didn't want to leave either ring—not of his arms, not of this magic he was spinning.

She forced herself to look up, which was an error, because even in the mist of fine rain she saw his eyes were blazing with heat.

'I'll make very certain of that, sweet Jo.'

'They will see us...'

'Dougal and Ewan are clever fellows. They will take their time turning the carriage. I wish our ancestors had planned better when they created these behemoths—they would do much better with a roof. I need a roof right now, and a bed, and a fire and some whisky to lick off your...'

'Benneit,' she moaned, half-protest, half-supplication.

'Then say yes, blast it.' That too was half-supplication.

'Of course I'll come back to Lochmore. Oh, God, everyone will think I am quite mad and I dare say I am. I should get in that carriage and go. You are not good for me, Benneit.'

'Don't say that. Please, Jo.'

He pulled her against him, his arms tight. She felt his mouth moving against her damp hair, his words muffled but filled with a pain she did not understand unless it was guilt or regret. She ran her hands up and down his back, slipping under his coat, trying to reassure him. She did not want him to feel guilty. She made her own choices.

'I'm sorry, I should not have said that. It is not your fault I am weak.'

'I'm not so gracious. It is definitely your fault I am weak, Jo. I've been in hell for weeks. Well, swinging between heaven and hell. And then for two hours riding back from the McCrieffs' I was in heaven only to find you flown. I had everything ready in my mind. Everything I wanted to tell you, finally, and beg you and then seduce you and you were gone. And for ten whole endless minutes I actually believed you wanted to be shot of us.'

He let her go and sank to his knee. The mud squelched in protest and instinctively she reached out and tried to draw him to his feet. But he merely took her hand, wrapping his around it and bending to kiss it as gently as a butterfly wing buffing a rose. The touch was gentle, but the impact was like the lightning scarring the sky—it seared her insides, lighting her from within.

'Benneit! What are you doing?' Her voice was

as weak as her will and he looked up and smiled and what was left of her senses surrendered unconditionally. If she did not have the rock behind her, she would have sunk to the mud on her knees next to him.

'I am taking advantage. You cannot deny me here inside the standing stones. It would be bad luck and we've both had enough of that. What I beg for, you must grant.'

'Benneit…'

'I'm on my knees, Jo. Well, one knee. Two would be rather precarious in this mud. If you leave—' his voice turned hoarse and he pressed her hand to his forehead '—I don't know what I will do. I should say I will manage. For Jamie's sake. I dare say I will. But I don't want to. I'm selfish and I want you with me. I need you with me.'

'I already said I will stay until…'

He tugged and she sank on to the mud.

'My dress!'

'Devil take your dress, woman. And stop saying "until". The only "until" is until I'm dead and buried. This is Scotland—I'm marrying you right here in the blasted mud. We'll have a proper ceremony so Lady Theale can gloat over the success of her machinations since I wouldn't be surprised if her devious mind foresaw this. But this is between us, here. I stole you back from the sea and you're mine and we are sealing that fact here in good Highland fashion—in the rain, in the mud and with some blasted druid's spirit hanging over these rocks and ready to topple them on us if you say nay. I love you, Jo. Do you care for me?'

He brushed the rain from his face with his sleeve without even letting go her hands, as if she might flit away if he did. It streaked mud along his beautiful cheek. The fierceness in his eyes faltered at her silence and again she saw the look that she had seen but not understood before—pain, uncertainty, loneliness. Her voice was husky with her own pain and need when she answered.

'Of course I care. How can you not know that?'

He let go of her hands and touched her cheeks, his fingers cold as they slid over her damp skin, tracing the warmth where her tears were mixing with the rain.

'Jo. I need to hear it. In your voice.'

'Oh, God, Benneit. I love you so much. I am tired of holding it inside me, but I'm terrified of letting it out. I am afraid to believe you. You think you care, but it is only magical mice and soon the solstice will be over and you will forget we were even friends. I have none of the makings of a Duchess...'

'Yes, you do, you little fool, but more importantly, you have all the makings of my wife. You have my love, my heart and far too much of my mind. The only thing you lack is some sense. As your husband it will be my duty to help you rectify that lack, as challenging as that task may be.'

'I'm too plain…'

'Stop saying you are plain. What does that even mean? That you don't look like a doll on a shelf? Well, you don't. You look like Jo and I can't stop looking at you. I have spent more time looking at you against my will, and searching for you against my better judgement, and lusting after you against my very sanity these past weeks. I see *you*. Just as you see *me*. I don't know how it happened, but I cannot imagine passing a single day without you. I cannot imagine who I am without you any more. God forgive me for saying this, but not having you would be as bad as not having Jamie. He needs me, but I need *you*.'

Benneit held her as she sank against him, sobbing into his shoulder. He wanted to take her back home and strip her of her cold clothes and hard defences and sink her into a warm tub, preferably with him, and make love to her for a week until she admitted the truth—that she was right for him. She was a fool sometimes, but not so much of a fool she couldn't admit to that truth if he made it absolutely clear to her by whatever means he possessed.

Just not in the mud, perhaps.

She finally calmed, wiping her eyes with his cloak and leaving streaks of mud like war paint from temple to chin.

'I'm covered in mud, Benneit Lochmore.'

He smiled and carefully brushed a smear from under her eye and brushed his mouth across hers again.

'Serves you right for bolting, little pixie. I don't blame you for not having faith in my ability to rescue my sorry behind from my own stupidity, but I will become annoyed if you don't have more faith in yourself. And in my love for you. Now up we go. Jamie is likely to be frantic that I have not managed to catch you and Mrs Merry and Beth will have my hide for keeping you out in the rain like this and destroying another dress. I shall count on you to redeem my character on all fronts.'

They squelched up to the carriage and Ewan opened the carriage door, his face split in a grin, but he said nothing as Benneit helped Jo inside. Benneit placed his boot on the step and stopped.

'Ewan. I'm going to impose on you a little further. Ride Lochlear to the village and have a word with Father McManus. I want his politic opinion about how soon I can wed Mrs Langdale in light of my being jilted by the McCrieffs.'

'Knowing McManus, he'll say as soon as humanly possible. He's no fan of the McCrieffs and the villagers themselves are still of two minds about the possibility of a Lochmore marrying a McCrieff. They'd likely rather than English-woman, especially this Englishwoman.'

'I'm glad to know we are of a mind, Ewan. This week, then, if not tomorrow. Have him invoke some local custom or saint that will make this a boon.'

'I'll say you made the offer inside the Standing Stones. That will go down well and you know McManus will spread that word faster than he can down a dram of whisky.'

He swung on to the gelding as Benneit entered the carriage and pulled Jo on to his lap to wrap his cloak about her, wishing he could unwrap her and hold her to him, nothing but Jo. They were wet and muddy and cold and he was so happy he felt foreign to himself.

'You shouldn't do this, Benneit. I do not wish to cause problems.'

'It is far too late for that, *mo ghràdh*. You were a problem from the day I agreed to Lady Theale's demand. You've turned my brain to pudding and my body into a green lad's and made me envious of my own son. McCrieff is well compensated for my freedom and it is not in his interest to cause trouble. We will weather the speculation and the villagers are already predisposed in your favour since Mrs Merry and Beth would go to battle for you and their word is law on Lochmore land. And they're kindly disposed towards me at the moment, thanks to the distillery plans and all that fine gold coming in. Now stop looking for loopholes and do something about warming me. It was a long, wet ride catching up with my runaway Duchess.'

'There is the blanket.' She gestured to the colourful afghan on the seat across from them.

'That wasn't what I meant, pixie, and you know it.' Still, he reached for the blanket, tucking it around her, gently wiping the mud that still clung to her flushed cheeks. 'I remember that day, in the carriage—watching you cuddle in this and wanting to touch you. I knew you were trouble, but I had no idea what was in store for me.'

'And if you had?'

He smiled and traced the sweep of her lips, soft and warm and his. His. The joy was so sharp he couldn't speak for a moment and when he did his voice was rough.

'And if I had, I would not have changed a moment of it. Not even if we could not have been together, not even to escape the pain. I will never disregard what a gift I have been given, to live my life with you, Jo.'

Her eyes widened and warmed, blurring with tears, the sky blue around her pupils very evident now. She pulled his hand under the warmth of the blanket, her fingers tangling with his as she pressed it against her heart, his thumb brushing the weight of her breast.

'Neither will I. I cannot even begin... You don't know how much I love you, Benneit.'

'Tell me, then.'

'I will. Often. You will be begging for silence.'

'I don't think that is what I will be begging for.' She laughed.

'I don't know how I can ever thank Tessa. We must do something wonderful for her, Benneit.'

'We will see she does not suffer from this if we can help it. Once we return.'

'We are going somewhere?'

'You and Jamie deserve a voyage so you can torture me with your dampened skirts again. We won't be gone long. I want to return in time to make love to you in the garden while the wisteria is in bloom. You will like my...*our* bedroom there better than the castle—it has a view over the garden to the sea and the sunsets are even more spectacular than from the castle.'

'Would it be terrible to admit I like The House better than the castle already?'

'We can live there if you like. We can live in a cottage in the village if you like. I'll take a muddy hovel with you over Lochmore without you, Jo.'

'Not muddy. I don't think I can afford to ruin any more dresses, Benneit.'

He slid his hand through the opening in the pelisse and stopped, drawing back abruptly as he realised she was wearing one of Celia's dresses.

'Jo! Good God, woman. I thought we were well rid of these horrors.'

'Mrs Merry didn't want to give a stained dress to Widow McManus, but then we managed to remove most of the stains. I did not wish...'

'You wished to make a grand and wholly unnecessary gesture, you prickly little pixie.'

'It wasn't unnecessary to me... Benneit! What...? You cannot do that here!'

Benneit continued unbuttoning the dress.

'I can and will. This dress is not passing through the castle gate.'

She laughed helplessly as he tugged off one sleeve.

'You are mad, Benneit.'

'Whose fault is that? Raise your delectable posterior so I can—that's better.'

The dress sank on to the carriage floor with a sullen *thunk*. With a deft twist he opened the door of the carriage and with a swipe of his boot the dress was gone. He smiled at Jo who was giggling helplessly, tucking her back against him and pulling the blanket about her.

'I'm freezing.'

'I'll warm you, I promise.' He slid his hand under the blanket, closing it over her breast. With nothing but the soft chemise between them he felt the warmth of her flesh and the hard peak pressing against the heart of his palm, spreading fire through his body.

'You've missed me,' he murmured.

'It's cold,' she countered, but her voice was uneven, the laughter fading.

'No, you missed me.'

Her breath shuddered out of her.

'Yes. Horribly. I need you to love me, Benneit. Please.' Her hand covered his and he bent to touch his mouth to hers, capturing the sweet spring scent of roses. For the first time in his life he felt at peace.

'It will always be my pleasure to please you, *mo chridhe*. Always and for ever.'

* * * * *